A Forbidden Rumspringa

Also by Keira Andrews

Contemporary

Honeymoon for One
Beyond the Sea
Ends of the Earth
Arctic Fire
The Chimera Affair

Holiday
Only One Bed
Merry Cherry Christmas
The Christmas Deal
Santa Daddy
In Case of Emergency
Eight Nights in December
If Only in My Dreams
Where the Lovelight Gleams
Gay Romance Holiday Collection

Sports
Kiss and Cry
Reading the Signs
Cold War
The Next Competitor
Love Match
Synchronicity (free read!)

Gay Amish Romance Series
A Forbidden Rumspringa
A Clean Break
A Way Home
A Very English Christmas

Valor Duology
Valor on the Move
Test of Valor
Complete Valor Duology

Lifeguards of Barking Beach
Flash Rip
Swept Away (free read!)

Historical

Kidnapped by the Pirate
Semper Fi
The Station
Voyageurs (free read!)

Paranormal

Kick at the Darkness
Kick at the Darkness
Fight the Tide

Taste of Midnight (free read!)

Fantasy

Barbarian Duet
Wed to the Barbarian
The Barbarian's Vow

KEIRA ANDREWS

A FORBIDDEN
RUMSPRINGA

A Forbidden Rumspringa
Written and published by Keira Andrews
Cover by Dar Albert

© 2014 by Keira Andrews
Print Edition

Dedication

To Anne-Marie, Becky and Rachel for the amazing beta work and enthusiasm for this book. Isaac and David thank you, and so do I. Also to the ex-Amish who so generously shared their stories and answered my many questions.

Author's Note

The most surprising thing I learned while researching this book was how much variation exists in the Amish world. My settlement of Zebulon is fictional, but is based upon the practices of the Swartzentruber Amish, one of the most conservative subgroups of the Old Order. While there are many similarities, I discovered that even among the Swartzentrubers, each community has its own specific rules. Something that may be true of one Amish settlement might not be true of another.

PART ONE

Chapter One

"*D*AVID LANTZ?" ISAAC realized he was catching flies, and snapped his jaw shut.

With a frown that drew his dark bushy eyebrows together, Father placed a ribbon over his page and closed his worn leather Bible. The wooden kitchen chair creaked as he sat back.

Beside him at the battered table, Mother faltered in her sewing. Her face was shadowed in the flickering light of the kerosene lamp. It was running out of fuel, but Father and Mother were apparently content to squint. In her long navy dress and black apron, Isaac thought Mother would all but disappear in the low light if not for the stark white cap— its pleats precisely half an inch apart—covering her light blonde hair. The untied strings hung over her shoulders.

Isaac shifted from one bare foot to the other, a loose floorboard squeaking beneath him. None of them wore shoes in the house except during church, and in the summer they were often barefoot around the farm as well. He traced a seam on the floor with his big toe.

The aroma of the chicken stew Mother had served for dinner still hung in the air. While minutes ago he had been happily full, now Isaac's stomach churned. He tugged on his collar, sweat prickling the nape of his neck.

"It's only that he's…" Isaac's mind raced, but he failed to find a suitable term in their dialect of German to describe David Lantz. Even if they were permitted to speak English in the house, words failed him. He fell silent and clasped his hands behind him to keep from fidgeting with the small piece of wood and folding knife tucked into his pocket.

His father, Samuel, stared for an uncomfortably long moment before continuing in his usual measured tone, his words slow and considered as if each was being etched in stone. "You want to be a carpenter, and David Lantz is the best in Zebulon."

Guilt roiled in Isaac like acid in his stomach. Father had arranged this job since he knew how Isaac loved woodworking. Father had been generous, and this was how Isaac repaid him? Still, the idea of spending almost every day with David Lantz made him feel surprisingly unwell. "But…" Isaac cast about for a good reason. "He's not even following church yet."

"Ruth, didn't Abram's Sarah say David will begin his instruction this Sunday?"

Mother didn't glance up from her sewing. "Yes."

David Lantz was finally joining the church? While Isaac should have felt joy at the news, his chest was strangely hollow. There had always been something different about David, but that would surely disappear once he was baptized and took a wife. And why should Isaac object? He wished he understood the nonsense that went through his mind sometimes.

As a thud echoed, Mother narrowed her gaze toward the main room. She called out sharply. "Boys. Into bed."

Isaac suspected the footsteps scurrying upstairs also belonged to his little sister Katie. Once all was quiet once more, Mother spoke again, her needle poised over the patch she was sewing over the worn elbow of Ephraim or Joseph or perhaps Nathan's shirt.

"You aren't baptized yet either, my Isaac." She jabbed the needle into the cloth. "We're not sure what you're waiting for. Isn't it time you joined the church? Don't you want to grow a beard and be a man? Find a wife?"

Not really. "I'm barely eighteen! David Lantz is twenty-two already."

Father stroked his long beard. Although his brows were still somehow dark as pitch, his hair and the beard hanging from his chin were mostly gray. "It is not unwise to show patience and have surety before committing to join the church. After all, this is why we're baptized as adults rather than children. So we can make a commitment to God and the community with our whole hearts."

"Yes, Father," Isaac mumbled.

"We know you'll find the path to heaven. Every man and woman must come to their choice in their own time, just as you will. The right choice."

Isaac resisted the urge to snort. *Choice.* The word was meaningless in Zebulon. Of course he would join the church. What else was he to do? At the thought, a current shot through him—a mixture of dread and the dark excitement he kept locked away, using the key only in the smallest, blackest hours of the night. He cleared his throat.

"I just wonder if he's ready to take on an apprentice."

"There's no reason he should not," Father replied. "Unless you wish to stay working with me on the farm after all."

"No, no," Isaac answered with far too much haste. "As long as you can milk the herd without my help."

"We'll manage."

"It's just that…"

"Has David Lantz been unkind to you?" Mother asked, a furrow in her forehead and the sewing abandoned in her lap.

"Not at all. It's only that he's…" *Terrifying.* "I'm only surprised, I suppose. I didn't expect this opportunity."

Mother smiled slyly. "It's good you should get to know him better. He might be your brother before too long."

"Mom!" Flushing, Isaac wished he could be anywhere else.

Mother stared with tight lips, and Father raised a bushy brow as Isaac realized what he'd said. It had been a struggle when they came to Zebulon to stop calling his parents 'Mom and Dad,' but the new *Ordnung* the community followed decreed the words too modern and worldly. "I'm sorry. Anyway, I hardly know Mary Lantz."

Mother *tsked*. "Of course you do. We all know each other in Zebulon. Oh Isaac—still so shy with the girls. Your father was the same way." She chuckled, and her fingers flew, the silver needle glinting as she lowered her head to her task once more.

The black wood-burning stove belched, and Isaac listened to the ticking of the clock Mother wound at the start of each month. The only other item hanging on the white walls was a simple calendar from the feed shop. With enough Amish customers from Zebulon now, the owner had started making a calendar without pictures.

Isaac closed his eyes for a moment, glimpsing his future working shoulder to shoulder with David Lantz while courting Mary, for he'd need a wife after he started following church. His stomach lurched again, and he wasn't sure what to feel. Should he try to dissuade Father?

With a silent sigh, his mind returned to the Bible passage most familiar to him—repeated so often it was practically carved into his bones. They were only permitted to read the Bible in German, but he thought of it in English. His pitiful little rebellion, since of course he would do as he was told.

Children, obey your parents in the Lord, for this is right. Honor thy father and mother; which is the first commandment.

Father returned to his Bible and sipped his mug of tea. "You will begin Monday."

And that was that.

THE DRONE OF the engine was little more than a vibration in the air, underlying the symphony of the cicadas beyond the barn, but Isaac toppled over the milking stool in his haste. Ephraim's head shot up.

"What?"

Isaac was already out of his milking stall and at the open barn door, blotting his forehead with the sleeve of his navy shirt and straightening his flat-topped straw hat. With a swipe of his fingers he made sure the black band around it was neat. He'd undone the three hooks at the neck of his collarless shirt, so he quickly redid them before straightening his galluses and brushing off the seat of his black pants.

"Wait! You got to go last time!" Ephraim joined him at the door, hands on his hips. At sixteen, he was almost as tall as Isaac—possibly even taller and brushing six feet with the unruly mess of sandy curls atop his head.

"I'm older. Finish the milking."

Leaving Ephraim's huffs and muttering behind, Isaac hurried past the chicken pen, the birds clucking and squawking as he kicked up dust. He was so used to having dirty feet after seven years living with Swartzentruber ways that he hardly noticed. He ducked under listless sheets on the clothesline that ran between the washhouse and their home.

Isaac knew his brother had a perfectly valid point about fairness, but they didn't get many visitors. He couldn't resist—especially when Father was on the other side of their land tending to the small crop of soybeans he sold to neighbors.

Holstein cattle grazed on the rolling hills beyond the barn, their cream and black hides stark amid the sea of green. They had seventeen cows, and sold two tons of milk a week to a local organic dairy. The dairy picked up the milk, but their truck never came this late in the day. Isaac's pulse raced as he glimpsed the vehicle approaching.

The late afternoon sun glinted off the silver chrome of a big car the English called an SUV. Isaac wasn't sure what it stood for, but it was a sight to see—high off the ground like a buggy, but sleek and shiny. Formidable. He wondered how it would feel to have that engine thrum beneath him. Hot tightness in his belly warned of the danger of such thoughts, and he focused on the couple clambering down from the vehicle.

The man greeted him, smiling widely as he took off his sunglasses. "Hello! We saw the sign at the end of the drive. Hope we haven't come too late in the day, but my wife would love to see the quilts." He swatted at a horsefly.

"Not too late at all. I'll get my mother." Isaac glanced at the house, knowing she would be glued to the kitchen window. The black curtain fluttered, and Mother appeared in the doorway a few moments later. Isaac called out in German to tell her to bring the quilts.

Isaac turned back to the English couple. "It'll just be a moment."

The redheaded woman was about forty. There were dark sunglasses perched on her head, and her lips were bright red. She wore shorts that didn't even reach her knees, and a sleeveless shirt with buttons down the front.

"What a cute place you've got here!"

"Thank you." Isaac smiled politely. Their simple two-story wooden house was trimmed in dark gray on the ground floor and navy on top. Black curtains hung in all the windows, and the roof was battered tin. It was anything but *cute*, and the dark red barn, washhouse and little ice house all needed new coats of paint. At least the outhouse was hidden from sight in a stand of trees.

Mother dragged a trunk outside, and Isaac hurried over to help. Katie was close behind with another armful of neatly folded quilts she could barely see over. At ten and the only daughter left, she was already an experienced quilter. Around her load, Katie peeked at the visitors.

Isaac returned to them. "You can go on over and take a look."

The man was tapping his phone, and didn't join his wife. He stood a head higher than Isaac, and had very broad shoulders. His light hair was close cropped, and he had a short beard and mustache. Isaac tried to think of something appropriate to say.

Is it rude to talk to someone when they're using their phone? Am I standing too close? Although the man wasn't talking on it, just touching the screen with his thumbs.

"Are you speaking to someone when you do that?" Isaac blurted.

The man jumped as though he'd forgotten Isaac was there. He tapped a few more times and slipped the narrow phone into his jeans pocket. "Sorry, I was just texting my mom. She's looking after the kids for the weekend."

"That's all right. So…that's sending a message? Texting?"

"Oh right—I guess you don't text around here, huh?" He pulled out his phone again. "Do you want me to show you?"

Yes! Isaac glanced toward the house. Mother was smiling politely as the English woman chattered and crouched down to examine the quilts. They were far enough away that Isaac couldn't make out the words, but Mother met his gaze.

She called out in German. "All right?"

Isaac nodded and turned back to the man. "Thank you, but I'd better not."

He shrugged and pocketed his phone again. "Sure."

An awkward silence followed, and Isaac thought maybe he should just leave the man to his texting.

"Is that Dutch your mother's speaking? What do they call it…Pennsylvania Dutch?"

Isaac smiled. "It's actually a German dialect. I'm not sure how it came to be called Dutch."

"Is that right? I'll be damned." The man raised a hand. "Excuse my language."

"It's fine."

The visitor opened the door of his SUV and pulled out a plastic water bottle. "My wife was thrilled to see there's an Amish community here. She loves buying authentic crafts and that kind of stuff."

"That's…good." Most English tourists who came through happened by when Father was home, and Isaac couldn't remember the last time he'd spoken to one. *What do English people talk about?* "Uh, where are you from?"

"Winnipeg—up in Canada?" He extended his hand. "I'm Darren Bell, and my wife is Michelle."

Isaac shook his hand. "Isaac Byler. Nice to meet you."

"How long have you all been here, Isaac? I don't remember there being any Amish folks living down this way the last time I was through. Although that was quite a while ago, I suppose."

"We've lived here about seven years."

"Did you come from Pennsylvania?" Darren took a drink from his bottle, his throat working as he swallowed.

"No, from Ohio. A place called Red Hills."

"Ohio, huh?" Darren leaned an elbow back on his vehicle, his white T-shirt stretching across his muscles. "And why did you move to northern Minnesota? Winters weren't cold enough for you?"

Isaac realized he was staring at Darren's chest and the faint shadow of dark hair beneath the white cotton. He jerked his gaze up to Darren's face, laughing uneasily. "They were definitely cold enough for me. But we wanted to break off and start our own settlement, and the land here is plentiful and a good price." It was true enough.

"What's the population of this place? I'm actually not sure of the name since there doesn't seem to really be a main part of town."

"Zebulon. There are about a hundred and eighty of us."

"Guess you know everyone here, huh? I grew up in a little place in eastern Manitoba, and it's not quite the same living in the city." He laughed. "Not that Winnipeg is a booming metropolis. Still, it's nice to have people around you can depend on."

"It is." Although Isaac often wondered what it would be like to live in a city and be free to do what he wanted without everyone finding out.

"Why did you all want to start a new community?" Darren held up his hands. "I'm sorry—stop me if I'm being too nosy." He glanced at his wife and smiled ruefully. "She could be here a while."

"I don't mind." Isaac could imagine how Father would grumble after the English left if he'd been asked these questions. "Our bishop felt our old settlement had become too modern and worldly. Sixteen families followed him here. Two more came after, and another last year."

"Too modern?" Darren laughed. "Really?"

Isaac chuckled, nudging up his hat to scratch his forehead. "I know it must seem crazy to the English."

"I'm sorry—I don't mean any offense."

"Don't worry." Isaac glanced behind and lowered his voice. "It seemed pretty crazy to me at first. There were already a lot of rules in Ohio, and here we have even more. I don't think an English person would last long in Zebulon."

Darren tilted his head, still smiling easily. "So Michelle and I are what you'd call English, right? Why English and not American? Or Canadian as the case may be."

"I asked once when I was a boy, and Father said it's just our way. He says that a lot."

"I bet." Darren took another swig of water. "So it wasn't strict enough before for your old man and the other people who moved here?"

Isaac stared at a drop of water on Darren's lower lip. "Uh..." He shoved his hands in his pockets and refocused. "Yeah. They thought the Amish where we lived had become too lax. There were rubber-covered rims on buggies instead of steel, and some families even had telephones. Not inside the house, of course—but in little shacks at the end of their driveways. There was indoor plumbing, and..."

Darren waited, his eyebrows raised.

"And young people were running too wild." *Ruining it for all of us.* "Here in Zebulon we follow the ways of the Swartzentruber Amish."

"Swartz...Swartzentruber? What does that mean?"

"It's a name. After they separated from the bigger Amish community in Ohio the bishops were called Swartzentruber. It stuck, I guess."

Darren crossed his tan arms, the plastic bottle dangling from his fingers. "Well, you learn something new every day. I thought all the Amish were the same."

"It's all right, most English people think that. But there are Old Order, New Order, Swartzentruber, Beachy." Isaac smiled. "Of course we all think *our* Ordnung is the right one. Our rules, I mean." He shouldn't be speaking so frankly with a tourist, but something about Darren loosened Isaac's tongue. "And I guess we think you're all the same too."

Darren's teeth gleamed as he smiled. "Fair enough." He called to his wife. "Sweetheart, we shouldn't keep these folks too much longer. It's almost suppertime."

"Just another minute," she answered.

"Don't worry." Isaac reassured him. *She can take as long as she wants if she buys something.*

"All right, where were we?" Darren stroked his beard. "When did all this happen? The Swartzenhubers first going out on their own, I mean."

Isaac was struck with the bizarre thought of what Darren's short beard would feel like against his own cheek. He stared at his dirty feet and didn't correct Darren's mispronunciation. "Oh, a long time ago. A hundred years or so, I reckon. There are Swartzentrubers all over the place now. Some here in Minnesota, down in Fillmore County. We're a little different up here in certain ways. Most settlements are. We all like to do things our own way."

"Do you mind telling me how you're different?"

Isaac hooked his thumbs under his galluses. "One thing is that we wear two of these. Some Swartzentrubers only use one."

"Suspenders? Why not two?"

"They say it's too vain." Isaac shrugged. "But I think they're great for holding up your pants. Bishop Yoder agreed, fortunately." He watched as Darren stroked his chin. "Is that itchy?"

Darren's brow creased. "Is what itchy?"

Isaac fiddled with the brim of his hat before shoving his hands in his pockets. "Having a beard all over your face like that. Not just on the bottom."

"Oh, that." Darren shrugged. "It can get a little hot in the summer, but no, it's not itchy. Amish men don't have full beards?"

"Honey?" The woman's voice rang out. "Which one do you think would go better in Mom's apartment? Come and look."

Darren smiled. "Excuse me—duty calls."

Isaac watched him trot over to where his wife examined the quilts. With their bright colors and intricate patterns, Isaac didn't understand how the quilts weren't too worldly. But they sold for a pretty penny to the English, and he certainly wasn't going to complain.

With everyone's attention on the quilts, Isaac drifted closer to the SUV. With a quick glance to be sure Mother wasn't watching, he stood as near as he dared to catch a glimpse in the mirror on the side. Although he'd grown up with a mirror in the bathroom, in Zebulon Bishop Yoder had declared them to be the devil's plaything—dark instruments that encouraged vanity and pride. Isaac had rarely seen his reflection since he was eleven.

Heart racing, he ducked his head. Beneath the straw hat, his short sandy hair swept over his forehead in the style of most Amish men, but his hair didn't have to cover his ears and he wore no beard since he hadn't been baptized yet. It was so hot in the summers that Isaac kept his hair as short as he dared.

His light yellow-brown eyes had long lashes, and as he peered closer he could see faint freckles brushed across the bridge of his nose and over the tops of his cheeks. He was tanned from the summer sun, and he looked sturdy and strong. Handsome even.

Not as handsome as David Lantz.

Shame flushed him, and he almost tripped over his own feet as he put a respectable distance between himself and the English car. He wasn't sure where the thought had come from. It was wrong to have any pride in his own appearance, and to even notice David's was just...

The word English kids used to call him when he went to town in Red Hills popped into his head. Yes, it was *weird* to think of David that way. In two days he'd start work with him, and here he was having crazy notions.

Isaac gave his head a shake. What was wrong with him? It was such nonsense to be alternately admiring and frightened. David Lantz was joining the church. He was an honorable and good man. Hard working and decent. What was there to fear?

"Isaac!" Mother's voice rang out.

He hurried over to help carry the three quilts Michelle had picked.

With the shadow of winter looming around the corner, it was a good thing to make any extra money they could from tourists now. Isaac wished they could sell the quilts in Warren, but the Ordnung forbade it, even though people were allowed to go to market in many other Amish communities. In Zebulon, Bishop Yoder was determined to keep them away from the unclean world.

Plus it was twenty miles there and back, which would take hours and was a hard journey for Roy, the Saddlebred who pulled the family buggy. Warren wasn't even a big town at all, but Isaac longed to return there. It had been more than three years now since he'd been away from the farms of Zebulon for even a day.

Darren pulled money from his wallet and peeled off the bills, giving them to Isaac. Then he extended his hand again. "It was a real pleasure to meet you, Isaac."

Isaac shook his hand. "Hope we'll see you again sometime."

"I hope so. One more question: why don't Amish men have mustaches?"

Isaac was very aware of Mother hovering some feet behind, but he saw no reason not to answer. "Too militaristic. It goes back a long way—to Germany."

Michelle hooked her hand through her husband's arm. "Isn't that interesting? I'm so glad we stopped. Hey, can I take a picture?" She reached into her purse.

Isaac raised his hand. "No. I'm sorry, we're not allowed to pose for photographs." At Darren's inquisitive expression he added, "They're graven images. It's against the rules. But again, it depends on the settlement. Some Amish will pose." But Father had always told them to say no, and even though he was in the fields, Mother was hovering.

Michelle smiled. "I'm sorry. I didn't realize. So your name's Byler, right? We'll be sure to mention your gorgeous quilts on Trip Advisor."

Isaac had no idea what she meant, but smiled and nodded, waving as they left. It had been a dry summer, and even now into late September the heat lingered. A cloud of dust rose in Darren and Michelle's wake, and when it settled, the SUV was gone. Isaac listened to its faint rumble until there were only the cicadas singing, and Ephraim shouting for him to get back to the barn.

HEAVING A SIGH, Isaac flipped onto his other side, poking Nathan harder than he should with his elbow. Of course Nathan was so thin and gangly these days as he sprouted up that Isaac thought it probably hurt his elbow more than it affected Nathan. His brown hair sticking up, Nathan snorted and muttered, swiping a hand over his pimply face.

Of course he started snoring again within a minute. How Ephraim and Joseph could be fast asleep in their bed with Nathan making so much noise, Isaac had no idea. Nathan had slept quietly for years, but the last few months had been a different tale. It was as if one of the freight trains that rumbled by east of Zebulon had detoured through their bedroom.

Dawn was still hours away. He wished he could light the lamp and finish whittling the horse he was making Joseph for his eighth birthday, but he wanted it to be a surprise. The glow could wake his brothers—even if they were apparently deaf to Nathan's snoring.

Isaac closed his eyes and told himself sternly to ignore the noise. He needed to find peace in the spirit of brotherhood and cast aside his anger. Surely sleep would follow. He breathed deeply and counted out the seconds of his exhale. Beside him, Nathan snorted and rolled over.

For a moment there was only blissful silence.

Followed by a familiar roar that grew to a fevered pitch before receding again. Over and over, until Isaac jerked back the quilt and fled. After closing the door gently behind him, he tip-toed downstairs. He might as well visit the outhouse since he was awake.

Although the days had been hot, Isaac shivered as he ventured behind the house, the ground surprisingly cold beneath his bare feet. With only a crescent moon lighting his way, he paused, debating whether to return for the lantern. But it wasn't as though he hadn't traveled this route a thousand and one times. He hurried into the trees.

Inside the outhouse he gathered up his nightshirt, wincing at the chill of the wooden seat. He shuddered to think of how frigid it would be before long. At least the seat was smooth and polished with so much use. At Noah Miller's new farm, Isaac thought he would get splinters in his rear end. With all the work the community put into raising the Miller's barn, some care could have been spared for the rest of the buildings.

Once he finished his business, Isaac wandered into the trees, in no rush to return to Nathan's cacophony. To make it worse, tomorrow was Sunday—and it was a church day. He knew it was awfully sinful, but Isaac couldn't help but look forward to the Sundays when they didn't have church. He'd heard that Christians in the English world had church every Sunday, so he should be grateful he only had to withstand the services every other week.

Yet the idea of sitting on a hard bench crammed into the Hooley's house while Bishop Yoder and the preachers droned on inspired little gratitude in him. He wasn't sure when it would be his family's turn to host church services at their house again, but he hoped it wasn't for some time.

And of course Sunday night after church was set aside for the singings, and Isaac could already imagine Mary Lantz's eager gaze and sweet smile. She was a nice girl, and would make a fine wife. Yet Isaac felt only a puzzling sense of emptiness when he tried to imagine a future with David Lantz's sister.

At the thought of David, heat arced through him. In the shadows of the leafy trees, at least no one would see him go red right to the tips of his ears. Beginning Monday he would see David Lantz every day. He would spend hours with him—and with those light blue eyes that shone with something Isaac couldn't identify. Something that made him feel guilty just to see it.

Yet Isaac could think of no time over the years when David Lantz had broken the Ordnung. He'd barely known David in Red Hills, and after the terrible thing that drove them to create Zebulon, to Isaac's knowledge David had lived as he should. If he hadn't, the whispers would have certainly reached Isaac's ears. Keeping a secret in Zebulon wasn't easy.

Although it had been odd to them all that David had waited to join the church. Perhaps one of the girls had finally caught his eye at the singings. Isaac swallowed thickly, his throat suddenly dry. Isaac had expected David to court Katie Miller or Rebecca Yoder or Sarah Raber long ago. Yet he'd hardly dated any of them. Surely that would change in the weeks to come.

Isaac leaned back against the trunk of an Ironwood. The bark was rough through his nightshirt, but he didn't mind. Since it was a Saturday he'd had a bath that evening, and he slipped his hand under his collar to rub at his pleasantly tight skin.

The memory of the frolic at the Kauffmans' farm unfolded in his mind. Barn raisings were Isaac's favorite kind of frolic, when the community came together to help with a task. He wasn't keen on slaughtering hogs at the Rabers' or harvesting corn at the Ottos', but barn raisings were fun. At the Kauffmans' that spring day he'd found himself up near the roof of the barn's frame, hammering nails next to David Lantz.

It was cool and cloudy, but sweat prickled down Isaac's spine. He strad-dled a thick joist near David, each of them working silently on the frame, although Isaac gnawed his lip to keep from rambling nonsense. Why he was nervous he had no idea. It was probably the distance to the ground below.

He glanced up beneath the brim of his straw hat. A few feet away on the other side of a post, David's head was bowed as he hammered, his hat covering his thick dark hair and the brim obscuring his face as he bent to his work.

Isaac's gaze roamed. The black material of David's pants stretched over his powerful thighs, and his forearms were muscular where he'd rolled up the sleeves of his gray shirt. Dark hair sprinkled his arms, and Isaac was gripped with the bizarre urge to sweep his hand over David's bare skin. His breath stuttered.

In an instant David's head was up, his light blue eyes fixed on Isaac. He was clean shaven since he wasn't following church yet, and his lips were full, and—

"I was just—" Isaac waved his arm, tearing his gaze away from David's mouth. His stomach dropped as he veered dangerously off balance, still holding the hammer and nails. He yelped, but then David had him, clutching Isaac's shoulder with one hand and his knee with the other. Nerves jumping, Isaac tried to smile. The calluses on David's fingers pressed against the base of his neck.

Isaac managed to croak out a word. "Thanks."

David didn't let go. "Keep the nails in your pocket and pull out one at a time. That way you can drop it if you need to and it's not likely to hit anyone down below."

"Right. Good idea." He nodded vigorously. David still held him and Isaac felt as though his shoulder and knee were ablaze even though it didn't hurt at all. "How did you do that so fast?" He nodded to David's hammer neatly hooked onto the waist of his pants, where it had been in his hand only moments ago.

David's lips lifted into a smile and a dimple appeared in his cheek. "Practice. Sure you're okay?" He rubbed Isaac's knee.

Sticky desire spread through Isaac, and he prayed he wouldn't humiliate himself by tenting his pants. Lord, what was wrong with him? He breathed deeply, tearing his gaze away from those pale eyes as he shifted back on the joist and out of David's grasp. "I'm fine!" He laughed like a braying donkey. After a few long breaths, he glanced back up.

David still watched him, but now there was something new in his gaze—a strange and wonderful shine that made Isaac feel unbearably hot all over. He couldn't look away, and the moment stretched out, silence between them, the sounds of work and men all around fading into the damp spring air.

Isaac licked his dry lips, and David jerked his head down again, his face hidden and his chest rising and falling rapidly. He plucked his hammer from his pants, and didn't say another word as he went back to work.

Isaac realized he was clenching the nails in his left hand so tightly they'd almost cut into his palm. His fingers trembled as he tucked all but one into his pocket.

Isaac shifted uncomfortably against the tree, and his palm stole down to rub against his hardening cock just once through his nightshirt before he tore it away. This was why he tried to avoid David Lantz. There was sin threatening to bloom in Isaac's soul, and he had to tamp it down. Had to extinguish that spark before it caught and blazed out of control.

In the distance, a train whistle pierced the stillness. Although he could barely see anything beyond the trees, Isaac closed his eyes and imagined the endless line of cars barreling along the track, carrying unknown cargo to places far from Zebulon. Perhaps the train would tunnel through mountains and arrive at the ocean's edge, passing towns and even cities on its journey.

As he imagined being atop that carefree train, his body hummed as if he were, as though he could feel the power of the locomotive shuddering through him. Images of the thundering metal and distant lands merged with David Lantz's blue eyes and single dimple. Isaac couldn't fight the desperate, terrifying excitement building in him. He hiked his nightshirt to his waist.

Pulling his foreskin back, Isaac roughly touched his cock, his lips pressed together to silence his moans. Even away from the house amid the trees in the dead of night, he had to be careful. No one could know his secret.

The cool night air whispered across Isaac's bare skin. He shivered, but his excitement grew at the wickedness of being half naked right out in the open, touching himself as he knew he shouldn't. He wasn't far from the outhouse, and if anyone else used it they'd undoubtedly discover him.

But he couldn't stop.

His toes curled in the grass as he flexed his thighs and pumped his hips, bracing his upper back against the tree and arching into the tight grip of his hand. In his mind he was naked in the night air, flying on top of the train, the wind whipping his hair back from his forehead.

David was there, his eyes blazing, seeing right into Isaac's soul. Then it was David's hand touching him, his breath hot on Isaac's face as he leaned in so close, lips soft, and then fierce as he claimed him—

The train's whistle sounded again, closer this time, and Isaac's cry echoed with it as he spilled over his hand, the bliss tearing through him and leaving him quivering and messy. He opened his eyes, jerking his head around to make sure he was still alone.

Chest heaving, he yanked down his nightshirt and scurried back to the outhouse. He tore off a ream of scratchy toilet paper to clean himself as best he could with shaking hands.

When he was back in bed with his brother's snores, Isaac prayed for forgiveness and the dawn.

Chapter Two

T HE LONG WOODEN bench groaned as Isaac took his seat next to Mervin and tucked his black hat underneath. It was already warm with all the extra bodies inside the Hooleys' home, and Isaac wished he could blink away the next three or four hours in an instant. At least there were more children than adults in Zebulon, and they didn't take up as much room.

He supposed it would be wrong to ask the Lord that the service would be on the shorter side today, and said a quick prayer of forgiveness for even thinking it.

As everyone squeezed in, Isaac found himself wondering—not for the first time—why they couldn't just build a church the way the English did. He knew the tradition of hosting church at members' houses had been born from persecution of the earliest Amish in Europe, who had to hide their services. But in America they were free to worship however they pleased. To Isaac it seemed a tradition that served no purpose. Of course he kept that to himself.

At least he'd had the good fortune to be born only weeks apart from his best friend. They always sat together at church, with all the men filing onto their benches in strict order of age from eldest to youngest. Mervin was fairly vibrating with excitement, but when Isaac lifted an eyebrow, Mervin gave a wink that meant *later*. His green eyes sparkled beneath his mop of reddish-blond hair.

In the meantime he gave Isaac a playful shove with his thick shoulder. Mervin Miller was short and stocky, yet surprisingly pale for all the hours he spent in the fields.

He whispered, "When are you going to ask her out?"

Isaac followed Mervin's gaze to where Mary Lantz sat with her friends on one of the women's benches on the other side of the room near the back door the women entered through. His eyes met Mary's, and she jerked away, ducking her head close to her sister beside her to whisper something. Their pinned wheat-colored hair blended together perfectly beneath their black caps. Anna was barely a year younger, and they looked almost like twins.

In Zebulon girls wore black caps and the married women white, although the girls who were finished school wore white caps at home during the week. Never off the farm, and never on Sunday, though. They all wore black bonnets over their caps if they were out in a buggy. Back in Red Hills the women had rarely worn bonnets at all, and their dresses had been lighter and a little shorter.

In Zebulon dresses had to reach the tops of the feet, and Katie had grumbled that morning about the thick black socks she had to wear with her shoes to church even in summer, although she had never known anything different. No elastic or rubber was permitted, and they tied black shoestrings around their calves to keep socks from slouching down. And of course the women and girls had long sleeves on their dresses all year round, even when it was so hot the air shimmered off the road in waves.

Often the Ordnung did not seem to follow any logic Isaac could identify, but of course it was not for him to question. He'd asked Father once why the bands on their hats had to be precisely five-eighths of an inch, and why brims on married men's hats were four inches, while for the bishop and preachers they were four and a half. Naturally the answer was that it was because the Ordnung decreed it. It was their way.

"You should ask her brother to ask her for you. It'll work, I know it," Mervin added.

"Shh," Isaac hissed. David Lantz sat on the bench in front of them, but five men down to the right. Isaac glanced at David's profile, the tip of his nose just visible. Around him the men all wore their hair past their ears, the strands forming little wings where it had curled beneath their hats. But since David wasn't following church yet, he was allowed to keep his hair a little shorter like Isaac did. David stared straight ahead and didn't seem to have heard Mervin's too-loud comment.

"Do you want to hear something?"

Isaac tore his gaze away from David and stared at his scuffed boots. After a summer being barefoot most of the time, his toes felt hot and confined. But come winter he'd have to get used again to boots every day. At least they didn't wear their heavy felt hats inside. He wished they could wear their straw hats in the heat, but in Zebulon it wasn't allowed on church days. "Do I have a choice?"

"Ha ha. I talked to Jacob."

"Eli's Jacob?"

Mervin huffed. "Why would I talk to him? No, New-corn Jacob."

"Oh." Jacob Stoltzfus had recently planted rows of corn on his farm on the outskirts of Zebulon. "What did he have to say?"

Mervin rolled his eyes. "How are you still so dense? I asked him to ask Sadie if she'd go out with me!" He grinned. "She said yes! I'm driving her home after the singing tonight."

"But we're supposed to go to the lake tonight!" At the sharp glance from Josiah Yoder nearby—Hog Josiah he was called, since he raised pigs—Isaac lowered his voice. "You said you were going to show me that trick you do when you jump off the rock."

"We can go to the lake any old time." Mervin glanced at Sadie Stoltzfus across the room and sighed. "She's the prettiest girl in Zebulon. Isaac, don't you want a girl of your own? We're eighteen now. Mark is already joining the church and he's going to marry Josiah's Katie come spring. What are you waiting for?"

Isaac shrugged, since he didn't trust his voice not to waver. It was a fine question, and he wished he knew the answer. Mervin was right—the time to be men was upon them. Mervin had already dated Rebecca

Hooley, but they hadn't been a good match. If Sadie was, soon he'd be courting her.

Isaac glanced at Mary Lantz again. She was pretty enough—more than enough, with her kind smile and big blue eyes that were darker than her brother's. There was nothing wrong with Mary. But Isaac was beginning to think there was something very wrong with him.

He was saved from further reflection by one of the men beginning the service with a hymn. As the congregation joined the slow chant, Zebulon's one bishop, two ministers, and one deacon rose and silently walked up the stairs to the Obrote, a separate room where they could confer. On this day, Isaac guessed the Obrote was the Hooleys' biggest bedroom. The five people who were taking instruction on joining the church followed. David Lantz was last, and he closed the door at the foot of the stairs behind him, his expression blank.

Isaac joined in singing the mournful German song, relieved that it was one of the shorter hymns—only ten minutes. Of course it didn't really matter, as they'd sing as many hymns as necessary while the preachers did their business. The next hymn was nearly twenty minutes, and the applicants returned at the end of it. David retook his seat with a new tightness to his jaw.

They sang on while the church leaders conferred privately. Isaac remembered what his brother Aaron whispered to him when he'd asked what went on in the Obrote.

"It's nothing, really. We sit there piously and they admonish us for our sins. We listen to them blather on about how wonderful the church is, and how we won't regret this choice." He laughed softly. *"At least once I'm baptized I won't have to go in there and pretend to listen."*

The words of the hymn died on Isaac's tongue as his breath caught, the longing to see Aaron again like an anvil dropped on his chest. He stuck his hand in his pocket, feeling the smooth folded handle of the knife. It had been next to his pillow when he woke that awful morning, and Isaac hadn't needed to read the neatly creased piece of paper on Aaron's side of the bed to know his brother was gone.

He closed his eyes against the memories of Mother's shocking sobs—never had he witnessed her come so undone, not before nor since—and Father's silent desperation. It had felt like the end of the world. After a few weeks without word from him or a chance to help him change his mind, the bishop excommunicated Aaron and added him to the *Bann*. He was of course to be shunned. *Meidung*.

Isaac shivered just thinking of it. As much as he dreamed of what waited beyond the borders of Zebulon, to be cast out alone in the world was unimaginable. He'd wanted to hate his brother for leaving like that—for stealing away in the night and not even saying goodbye—but he'd only been overcome with loss and longing.

The preachers rejoined the congregation about fifteen minutes later. Daniel Lapp delivered the short sermon, although at forty minutes, "short" was not what Isaac would have called it. A kind old man, at least Preacher Lapp had a pleasant speaking voice. It was a relief to kneel for prayers. Although the wooden floor was hard on his knees, it gave Isaac's backside a rest.

Jeremiah Stoltzfus read the Scripture as always. A barrel of a man, Deacon Stoltzfus had been a blacksmith before drawing the short straw. He was one of the dozens of Stoltzfuses in Zebulon, and Isaac's least favorite. He read the chapter of Scripture in a flat monotone, his bushy black hair sticking out over his ears, and his beard hanging to the top of his chest.

While the deacon droned on, Isaac thought back to the Sunday several years ago when they'd chosen him. The previous deacon had died of old age, and now every baptized member of the church made their nominations for his replacement. Men with three or more votes were candidates. Isaac had always wondered how Jeremiah Stoltzfus had gotten any nominations at all for the post, let alone three or more.

Bishop Yoder and the preachers had shut themselves away, and returned with a stack of seven songbooks, each tied shut with white string. Seven men in the lot. A few of the younger candidates had visibly trembled. Church that day was at John Otto's farm, and while the house was fairly large and airy, Isaac remembered it being unbearably oppressive. While Mervin usually had a joke or two to whisper during a service, on this day he'd sat like a statue beside Isaac, his pale freckled hands clasped in his lap.

One by one, the candidates chose a songbook and opened it. For the men with no slip of paper inside, they sagged with relief, some weeping their joy. To be a preacher or deacon meant a lifetime of service with no salary, and the end of the man's life as he'd known it. In Isaac's experience, few joined those ranks with happiness. Isaac shuddered at the thought that it could happen to him one day, but all baptized men knew it was a possibility.

Jeremiah Stoltzfus had been second to the last in the lot. When he pulled out the paper from his songbook, he made no sound, his expression impassive. He'd accepted his fate utterly calmly, and Isaac remembered thinking that perhaps Deacon Stoltzfus was a man who would enjoy the power of his new position.

As deacon, he enforced the Ordnung and collected alms for those in need in the community, although he was so glowering and gruff that Isaac suspected people gave generously because they were eager to be away from his beady glare. It was not a pleasant thing to have the deacon at your door for any reason, but if you'd broken one of the Ordnung's regulations, Isaac had heard it was an altogether terrifying experience.

At least Deacon Stoltzfus never deviated from his assigned reading to deliver an impromptu sermon of his own, as Isaac remembered the deacon in Red Hills doing. For that, if nothing else, Isaac could be grateful.

Some of the children were asleep by the time Bishop Yoder delivered the main sermon. Isaac's eyes drooped, and he pinched himself. He hoped the sermon wouldn't be two hours as it had two Sundays ago. In Red Hills there had been four preachers who took turns delivering sermons, but that community was much larger. Bishop Yoder liked to sermonize, so at almost every service, he stood before them and rambled. The preachers never used notes and always spoke German in church.

"For Joseph was a humble man, just as we in Zebulon are humble. We trust in God and follow the Ordnung, caring not what outsiders might think. For we live holy lives in a true community of fellowship with our brothers and sisters. We reject worldly temptations."

A tall, thin man, Bishop Yoder's hair was almost white. His face was as narrow and pinched as his body, but his voice boomed. On and on he droned about the Bible and the rules of the Ordnung. Isaac thought it would never end. Although the small windows in the house were open to the September breeze, precious little air found its way to where Isaac sat in the crush of men.

"And when we came to this prosperous land and called it Zebulon, we dedicated ourselves to the true faith."

Isaac perked up. Bishop Yoder always ended his sermons with a message about how smart and God-fearing they were to have left Red Hills, so at least it was almost over.

"We must never forget the sin and worldliness that drove us here. Remember how narrow the escape was for our children, who here are firmly on the path of righteousness. In Zebulon, holiness holds sway over the wild and ruinous excesses of the past. Our young people recognize the path to salvation and do not need to taste the evils of the unclean English world. They are wise beyond their years, and fill our hearts with thankfulness."

Excesses. In Zebulon—as was the Swartzentruber way—they never uttered the word *rumspringa*, and the younger children had no concept of it. Thoughts of Aaron flickered through Isaac's mind, unbidden.

He'd come home from hunting with the other boys in Red Hills smelling of cigarettes, with moonshine on his breath. How Mother and Father would scold him, shaking their heads and muttering about Aaron's soul. *"At least he's dating Marvin's Rebecca the proper way. He will come to the church soon and leave this foolish time behind."*

Isaac tried to imagine their reaction if he dared be caught now with a worldly cigarette or worse. While none of the parents in Red Hills had ever encouraged the running around, they had grimly tolerated it, punishing the youngies when they went too far, and doing everything they could to convince them to join the church. But in Zebulon? He shuddered to think of the consequences for running wild.

In the silence that followed the Bishop's sermon, Isaac held his breath. Blessedly, they all said a final prayer and escaped.

Outside, the women served lunch, and they ate in shifts at the long tables. When Isaac and Mervin said their silent grace and took their seats next to each other, someone else sat on Isaac's other side. When Isaac looked, he froze. It was David. Isaac stuffed a forkful of cabbage salad into his mouth so he wouldn't have to say anything.

He was painfully aware of how their shoulders and arms brushed, and he kept his knees pinned together under the table to avoid touching David's thigh. He wished he knew what it was about David that put him so off-kilter.

As he shoveled in a spoonful of chicken corn soup, Isaac's attention was drawn to the older man on David's other side, Noah Lapp.

"Your hair is too trimmed, but look at the length of your sideburns. Too worldly."

David swallowed his soup. "Thank you for your guidance." His tone was even.

"Why aren't you letting your beard grow? Your baptism is approaching. Do you not want to be a good Amish man?"

"Of course," David answered. He offered no reason for why he was still shaving.

"Why do you not drive any of the girls home from the singing? You are joining the church. You must find a wife." Noah slurped his soup.

David opened his mouth, but after a moment closed it again, and blew out a long breath. "Yes, you're right. Thank you for your guidance. I promise to do better."

"Good, good." Noah eyed David critically. "You will be at the singing tonight?"

"Of course."

"Your buggy seems a little tall."

"I've had it for four years and no one's complained." David took another sip of soup, his spoon clenched in his hand. "The buckboard's seventeen and a half inches, just as it's prescribed in the Ordnung."

"Hmm. Is it? Perhaps we should measure after lunch."

David smiled, his lips pressed together. "Of course. Thank you for your guidance."

Isaac and Mervin shared a pained glance. This haranguing was routine for anyone joining the church, and they all knew they had to smile mildly and bear it. Any signs of rebellion or resentment could mean a delay in joining—and more scrutiny. The preachers were bad enough, but most in the community joined in, criticizing the smallest things with what Isaac thought was secret glee.

"When are you boys joining the church? It should be soon, shouldn't it?" Noah asked.

Isaac's stomach dropped as he realized Noah was speaking to him and Mervin. He cleared his throat. "Soon."

"Yes. Very soon," Mervin added.

Noah nodded before speaking to David again. "You took so long to join that other youngies might get ideas. We must all help each other find the true path and honor God."

He could sense the tension in David as old Noah Lapp went on and on, with others at the table soon joining in. Through it all, David smiled and nodded, keeping his gaze on his lunch. When Isaac finished eating and stood, David turned to look at him.

"See you tomorrow."

Isaac smiled tentatively, and David smiled back, the dimple in his cheek appearing.

Although he'd just had three cups of water, Isaac's throat was dry, and he refilled his cup from the jug, gulping the cool liquid down before hurrying to catch up with Mervin.

PULSE RACING, ISAAC stared at the metal and plastic contraption in Mervin's hand, his plan to find a good whittling stick forgotten. "Is that a *phone*?"

"It's a Touch." Mervin was busting with obvious pride.

Isaac peered at it closely. "What does that mean?"

Mervin shrugged. "Dunno. But that's what it said in Leroy's note. It's a Touch, and if I put it in the sun in this case, it charges the battery."

Isaac glanced around. They were still alone in the woods near the Hooleys'. They had to be back soon for supper and the singing, but he wished there was some way they could stay hidden away in the long shadows of the trees with the gift from Mervin's cousin in Red Hills.

"What does it do?"

"Here." From his pocket, Mervin pulled out a long white cord with two round knobs dangling down. "Put these in your ears."

Isaac stuck one in, but it popped out.

"No, that's for your other ear. See how it has an L for left and R for right?"

Once Isaac had the little things in his ears properly, he nodded. "Now what?"

"Listen." Mervin tapped the glass front of the rectangle and it burst into life with color and picture.

A moment later, Isaac jumped as music filled his ears. This music was faster like the songs they'd sing tonight, but so much noisier, and of course there were instruments. The beat thumped through his body. A woman sang about applause, and Isaac peered at the screen, his jaw dropping. *Lady Gaga*, it said. She had blonde curls and dark makeup around her eyes, and wore a tight dress that barely covered her chest and was practically see-through.

He wasn't sure what to make of the song, and when it was over, he took the knobs from his ears. "Wow."

Mervin grinned. "Isn't it great? Leroy put a bunch of songs on it, and there are movies too!"

Isaac stared at the device. "How did he get it to you?"

"He mailed it. Wrapped it in plastic bubbles and it fit right into an envelope!"

"What if your parents had opened it?"

"No way," Mervin scoffed. "It's my job to go all the way out to the road to check the mail."

"Do they even know Leroy writes to you sometimes?"

"Of course not. Man, Leroy's so lucky his parents stayed. He gets to do rumspringa, and have a car and everything. He says they nag him about it every day, but at least they don't stop him from going out and seeing the world."

Isaac could barely even imagine the freedom. "But you know why they don't allow it here."

Mervin huffed. "So a few kids went and did something stupid. Now we all have to suffer?"

"But...it's better for us. We shouldn't want to try all these worldly things. They're unclean." He pointed at the contraption. "That's unclean. Leroy shouldn't have sent it."

"Oh, so you don't want to watch a movie?" Mervin's eyebrows disappeared beneath his bangs.

"Well..."

Laughing, Mervin clapped Isaac's shoulder. "Always trying to be such a good boy. Don't worry, I won't tell. Come on, I'll show you—"

"Mervin!" A girl's voice echoed through the trees.

"Damn it," he muttered as he jammed the Touch back into his pocket with the white cord. He sprang to his feet, guilty now as well for cursing.

Isaac followed suit, pulling out his knife and picking up the nearest fallen branch. He and Mervin leaned casually against a tree just in time for Mervin's little sister to appear.

Esther put her hands on her hips. "What are you doing out here?"

"Whittling." Isaac held up the branch.

"We're leaving. It's time for you all to have supper. So hurry up!" With that, she turned on her heel, her long dress flowing around her ankles as she raced off.

By "you all," Isaac knew she meant the young people. He and Mervin hustled back to the Hooleys', and took their seats at the long table inside the house. Mary sat across from him on the girls' side, and Isaac resolutely kept his eyes on his plate. David was a few seats over from him.

The singing began at eight o'clock sharp. Isaac enjoyed these songs much more than the dour chants from church. While they still sang about God and worship, the tunes were lively and fun. Between songs, they chatted with each other, and Mary naturally spoke to him.

"Do you like chicken?"

Isaac nodded. At least it was an easy question. Who didn't like chicken?

"I'm making chicken soup and biscuits for lunch tomorrow. And shoofly pie." She smiled widely and tucked a stray strand of hair behind her ear.

Isaac's gut clenched. Somehow in his worrying about what it would be like to work with David, he'd overlooked the fact that he'd be seeing Mary every single day. He forced a smile. "I'm sure it'll be delicious."

"Your Katie said you love shoofly pie."

"I do. Thank you. I…um…" It was only polite to make conversation and ask Mary something, but his mind was utterly blank.

Fortunately Mark began another song, and Isaac was spared.

By the time they filed outside a couple of hours later, Isaac was walking so quickly he almost didn't hear David call him. He spun back around as David said something to Mary and trotted over. Although David was a couple of inches taller than him, it was no reason for the intimidation buzzing through Isaac's body. He wished he knew why David made him so nervous.

"Hi, David." Isaac laughed nervously—that unfortunate braying sound.

David regarded him seriously. "I think my sister's expecting you to ask to drive her home."

"Oh." That was the first move in dating. Panic bubbled in his chest. "Uh...I don't have my own buggy yet. We can't afford it. I've only got the old spare, and it's not nice enough for her. It's so bumpy and uncomfortable. It's falling apart."

David stared for a long moment before nodding. "All right."

"Tell Mary I'm sorry. It's not that I don't like her. She's a very nice girl. She just deserves something better."

David watched him again in his unnerving way. "I'll tell her you said so. See you in the morning."

"Uh-huh." Isaac felt like he might jump right out of his skin.

David gave Isaac's forearm a squeeze where Isaac had pushed up his sleeve. "Don't worry. I won't bite." Then he was walking away.

After Isaac tightened Silver's black harness and clambered up onto the rickety single-seat buggy, he put the reins to her. She was an old draft horse who couldn't pull the plow anymore, but she could manage this.

The buggy was five feet long and painted black inside and out. There was no cushion on the seat, just as there were no cushions anywhere in their house. In a newer buggy it wasn't so bad, but the springs in this one were long worn out. The black oilcloth roof leaked in any rain beyond a drizzle.

It really wasn't a nice enough buggy to take a girl riding in, but Isaac had a feeling the excuse would only fly for so long. Maybe he should just ask Mary out and be done with it. It wasn't as if there was another girl he liked better, so what was he waiting for?

The steel-rimmed wooden wheels clattered, and Isaac's backside was already sore as he bumped down the drive at Silver's top speed, the feeling of David's hand still hot on his skin.

Chapter Three

I T WAS STILL dark when Isaac and his siblings woke for morning prayers and chores. Joseph, Nathan, and Katie were still in school, and would head off down the drive to the one-room schoolhouse a few miles away when the sun came up. Mother always watched from the kitchen window, one eye on the water heating on the wood-burning stove to wash the breakfast dishes.

In the barn, Ephraim grumbled as Isaac saddled Silver in the light of a kerosene lamp, petting her head and murmuring nothing words. She was more gray than silver, but her mane had a light gloss. He gave her a sugar cube, and she licked his palm.

"It's not fair. Now I have to do all your work as well as my own."

Isaac tried to reassure him, although he'd likely feel the same in Ephraim's shoes. "Father will be doing some of it, and Nathan's in grade eight now. This is his last year at school."

"He won't be finished until almost summertime! That's practically a year away." Ephraim slammed down his stool and bent to milking one of the cows. "It's not fair that you get to go have fun."

"Fun? I'll be working just as hard as you are."

"Yes, but you're always playing around with your carvings. You love working with wood. Meanwhile, I'll be stuck here on this stupid farm."

Although he didn't raise it, Father's voice made them both jump.

"This is our home and livelihood, Ephraim." He stood in the shadows cast by the lamp, and beyond him through the open barn door, the sky was lightening. "This is not a stupid thing."

Ephraim shot to his feet, opening and closing his mouth before hanging his head, his straw hat hiding his red face.

Isaac jumped in. "You know he loves the cattle and working the farm. He didn't mean it, Father. He's just a grouch this morning. Nathan's snoring kept us awake." In truth Nathan had blessedly slept on his stomach most of the night and spared them.

Father stepped into the circle of lamp light, smiling softly. "Ephraim, I understand how it is at your age, but you must wait your turn. You're sixteen—not a youngie yet. Still in your learning years. When you're seventeen you can attend the singings and spread your wings. Isaac is our oldest son, and he must be first to find his way."

Our oldest son. A memory of Aaron filled Isaac's mind. He'd raced across a golden field, almost out of sight, and Isaac's lungs had burned as he ran, stalks of wheat smacking his face as he tried in vain to keep up, his little legs pumping. He could still hear Aaron's voice in the wind. *"Can't catch me!"*

Wishing he could lock his treacherous thoughts away in a canning jar, the lid ever so tight, Isaac banished the memory. Yet he still reached into his pocket to slide his fingers over the familiar handle of the knife. He kicked at hay with his boot.

"Yes, Father," Ephraim said, head still bowed.

"I should get going." Isaac led Silver from her stall to where the old buggy waited.

Father followed and watched him, stroking his beard. "It's high time you had your own. Brand new."

Mary Lantz's hopeful smile flashed in Isaac's mind. "No, no! Not yet. We can't afford it." It was certainly the truth, especially with winter coming. "I don't mind. Really."

Father sighed. "In the spring, then."

Isaac clambered up into the buggy and straightened his hat. It was an odd feeling to be leaving the farm instead of starting his regular work. In all his worrying about working with David he somehow hadn't thought about the fact that he wouldn't be home nearly as much. Exhilaration buzzed through him.

Of course he could always go back to work on the farm if carpentry wasn't for him in the end. If there was one thing that was a guarantee in life, it was that there would always be something to do on the farm.

"Ephraim, I'll help you with the evening chores after dinner."

From the door of the barn, Ephraim mumbled, "Thanks."

Father reached up suddenly to squeeze Isaac's hand, and Isaac froze, holding his breath. He couldn't remember the last time Father had made such a display. Ephraim stood nearby watching with wide eyes.

"Be good, Isaac, and do good work. I pray that you will find your joy in this vocation."

Isaac swallowed thickly, his heart thumping as he grasped the unfamiliar warmth of Father's hand. "Thank you. I think I will. Father..." He struggled for the words.

"Yes?" He waited patiently.

"I must have seemed ungrateful when you told me about this new job. I'm sorry."

"Ah, Isaac." Father smiled. "It is natural to feel some hesitation when we begin a new chapter in life. I confess I would keep you here with me for many more years if I could." He cast a glance at Ephraim nearby. "But do not worry, boys. I will help you find your own way to adulthood. And to the church, of course. My heart's greatest desire is to see all my children happy and healthy in life."

Even Aaron? "I know, Father. We're grateful to you. God blessed us when He chose you and Mother for our parents." It was the truth—one Isaac realized with shame he'd never said aloud. They didn't speak of such things.

"It's not a stupid farm," Ephraim added.

Father was silent before taking a deep breath. "Thank you, my sons. We are all blessed by the Lord."

They murmured their agreement, and Isaac gave Silver a gentle flick. He was past the house when Ephraim's voice rang out.

"Isaac!"

He reigned in Silver and leaned out to see Ephraim still standing in the barn door.

"I'll miss you."

Isaac swallowed hard over a swell of affection. "Me too," he called. "I'll be home before you know it." He urged Silver on, determined not to look back.

IT WAS THREE miles down the paved county road to the Lantz farm. Silver clopped along the shoulder, and Isaac listened for approaching vehicles, glad the sun was up. He was nervous in the dark with only a lantern and some gray reflective tape on the rear of the buggy to alert cars to his presence on the road.

The bright orange safety triangles they'd put on their buggies in Red Hills were too of the world for Swartzentruber Amish, and Isaac knew he should trust in God to keep him safe from harm. Yet in the darkness of Minnesota nights, more than once he'd wished they could give God a helping hand.

Fortunately few cars passed through Zebulon. Bishop Yoder had searched through different states and up into Ontario for the perfect spot to build their new community. In northern Minnesota he'd finally found a place sufficiently removed from the rest of the world.

As he drove along, for some reason Isaac thought of the last time he'd been to McDonald's before everything changed. He could still remember the tang of the Big Mac sauce on his tongue. It had been a treat for Ephraim's birthday, and they'd parked behind the restaurant in a special spot for buggies. They hadn't been the only Amish family munching salty fries that day.

But in Zebulon, they were discouraged from going to restaurants. The Ordnung didn't forbid it, but they tried their best to live off the land and from the animals they kept. Mother still drove three miles in the buggy to the nearest grocery store each Tuesday morning since they'd never survive otherwise. But Isaac hadn't stepped foot in a restaurant since he was a boy back in Ohio.

Little birds flapped their wings in Isaac's stomach as he drove up the Lantz's dirt driveway. Come winter it would be a muddy, icy mess, and Isaac wished they had the gravel drives they'd taken for granted in Red Hills. No money for that in Zebulon. As he approached the house, he saw a figure in the barn door, and his heart beat double time.

"Stop it. There's nothing to be nervous about," he hissed to himself.

There was no sign of Mary or Anna, but Mrs. Lantz appeared by the house and waved. The Lantz house was very similar to the Bylers', with the same tin roof, and dark paint and curtains.

"Hello, Isaac!" She called in German, wiping her hands on her black apron. Her dark dress brushed her bare feet, and her white cap was bright. She had David's dark features, while her late husband had given the girls their blonde hair. "Welcome."

Isaac pulled the brake handle by the seat, and it pushed against the right front wheel as he reined in Silver. "Thank you, ma'am," he answered in German.

Like most people in Zebulon, he slipped back and forth between English and German with ease, although the kids and youngies almost always spoke English to each other. It wasn't an official system—speaking German with the adults and in church, and English the rest of the time—but it worked well.

David's three youngest sisters waved as they skipped past their mother and down the lane to school in their long dark dresses and black caps, metal lunch buckets swinging. It was a couple miles to the schoolhouse, which was in the corner of Eli Miller's land.

Isaac waved back, wondering what it was like for David to live with his mother and five girls, and no other boys at all. As he realized David must have his own room, a wave of jealousy rolled through him. To even have his own bed would be such a luxury.

The thought of a wide bed and David in his nightshirt danced through Isaac's mind, accompanied by a bolt of excitement. Yes, he was jealous indeed, and it was sinful. Isaac gave his head a mental shake. David was his employer now, and it would do no good to be envious.

Familiar moos, whinnies, clucks and crows filled the empty spaces in the early morning air as he approached the barn. David ushered him inside with a smile after Isaac unhitched Silver. Isaac gaped as he took in the interior. There were stalls for the horses, but the rest of the barn had been transformed. Hand tools hung from nails on one of the walls, and a huge worktable dominated the space. Rolls of paper plans and several rulers rested on the wide surface. Piles of rough wood sat stacked against the other walls.

"Make yourself at home, Isaac." David pointed to a side table holding a water jug and cups, along with a loaf of sliced sweet bread so fresh the hint of apples lingered in the air amid the sawdust. "If you're thirsty or hungry, there's no need to ask. Help yourself."

"Thank you." Isaac glanced out at the fields. "Do you not farm at all anymore?"

David unrolled one of the thick pieces of paper. "Not since my father died. I'm afraid I don't have the touch. I can make a much better living as a carpenter. We sold off most of the acres to the Ottos. What's left is a garden, really, and some land for the animals. My mother and sisters tend it well."

"Oh yes. I remember now." He shifted uncomfortably. It had been more than four years since Mr. Lantz had collapsed behind the plow.

Isaac remembered Mervin running breathlessly up the drive with the news, saying that by the time David had made it to the closest English house to call for help, it had been far too late. An emergency was the only instance when they were permitted in Zebulon to ask the English for anything, or to ride in a car.

"You're handy with an ax?" David asked.

"Of course." *Did that sound vain?* "Only because I've helped with the firewood for the stove these past years. I think I'm okay at it. Maybe. I don't know."

David glanced up from the design. "Isaac, it's all right. You don't need to be nervous." He smiled. "I won't bite, remember? Just be yourself. I'm told you're a hard worker, and as long as that's true, we'll get along just fine."

"Right. Okay." Isaac nodded. "I am. A hard worker, I mean. I won't disappoint you."

David picked up a ruler. "I'm sure you won't. There's a felled tree outside. Chop it into big pieces like those others." He nodded toward the stacks of wood against the walls.

Isaac scurried off to do what he was told, eager to prove himself and officially start his life as a carpenter, even if he was only chopping wood. Although he was used to going barefoot in the barn at home, he noticed David wore his boots, and Isaac kept his on as well. The last thing he wanted to do was drop one of the tools on his toes.

By eleven-thirty, his excitement had faded. The tree seemed never ending, and Isaac lifted his hat to swipe his sleeve over his forehead, blinking into the bright sunshine. David had brought him a cup of water midmorning and reminded him to help himself, but Isaac hadn't wanted to seem weak or lazy on his first day. Yet now as Mrs. Lantz called them for lunch, he felt unsteady.

By the kitchen table, he swayed a little as he bowed his head for quiet grace, and felt David's strong hand on his waist. As Isaac recited the Lord's Prayer in his mind, he didn't dare breathe. They all raised their heads in unison and took their seats, David beside him, and the women across the table.

Isaac gulped down three cups of water, Mary refilling his tin cup each time. He smiled apologetically. "I got a little warm out there."

David ribbed him kindly. "Now will you help yourself to the water in the barn like I suggested?"

"Yes," Isaac mumbled sheepishly.

"Maybe you should have a drink of vinegar if you're still feeling faint. It works every time," Mrs. Lantz said, starting to get up.

"No!" Isaac cleared his throat. "Really, I feel much better now. Thank you." He cringed inside at the thought of choking down the vinegar. It was one of his mother's favorite remedies.

"All right. Please be at home here, Isaac." Mrs. Lantz said, passing a plate of biscuits while Anna walked around the table to ladle out bowls of the chicken soup.

There was no reason he shouldn't be at home, as the house was similar to his own in almost every way on the inside as well, from the white walls and stark, uncushioned furniture, to the wood-burning stove in the kitchen corner.

While the three littlest Lantz girls were in school, at seventeen and eighteen, Anna and Mary were home all day to help their mother until they married. Isaac realized he'd never seen them at home in their white caps before, only on weekends or out and about in their black caps. In the white they looked older to him somehow. He supposed they would be married women before too long.

He glanced at Mary as she poured him more water. *Is she going to be my wife?* He felt another wave of dizziness and stared at his bowl.

"It's good for David to have another man about the place." Anna gave her brother a friendly nudge as she stood behind him and filled his bowl. "He hardly has any friends. Too busy working."

"David has friends!" Mrs. Lantz insisted. "No one has said a bad word about our David."

It was true—although the community had certainly whispered about how long it took for David to decide to follow church, Isaac had never really heard anything bad said about him. Yet Anna was right that David didn't seem to have close friends. He'd always kept to himself.

"All those nights he goes off to fish—of course David has friends," Mrs. Lantz added.

Anna said nothing as she sat in her place, suddenly engrossed in fiddling with the strings of her cap.

"It's all right, Mother. You don't need to defend me," David said.

"Still, I think it'll be good to have Isaac here. Don't you think,

Mary?" Anna's smile had altogether too much forced innocence to it.

Cheeks flaming, Mary stared at her bowl and nodded as she took a mouthful.

Isaac desperately tried to think of something to say. "You're so lucky you get your own room, David. I have to share with my brothers and—" He stopped, shame prickling his skin. "I didn't mean to say it was lucky that...I'm sorry."

Mrs. Lantz's smile was strained. "It's all right."

Anna shrugged. "He wouldn't be living here still anyway. He'd have his own farm, or he'd be out in the world."

"*Anna.*" David stared daggers.

She dropped her spoon with a clatter. "What? It's the truth. Why can't we talk about him? It's as if he was excommunicated after he died. We talk about Father, don't we?"

"Father did not dishonor our family, community and the Lord." Mrs. Lantz spoke quietly, her gaze locked on the table. Mary placed her hand on her mother's arm.

"Joshua made a mistake!" Anna insisted. "He wasn't bad."

Isaac glanced from one Lantz to the other, wishing fervently the floorboards would split apart and swallow him whole.

David spoke firmly. "He ran wild, Anna. He had no fear of God in him. It was more than a mistake. Rachel and Martha died as well because of him."

"I know, but..." Anna's eyes filled with tears. "He was a good brother, and I loved him."

Isaac held his breath. He wasn't sure he'd ever heard someone talk openly about *love*. It just wasn't their way.

Blinking rapidly, Anna bowed her head in the silence. "I'm sorry, Mother. I shouldn't have said anything."

Mrs. Lantz kept her voice steady. "I just thank the Lord that something good came out of it. Now we're in Zebulon, and there will be no rumspringa to endanger my children. We've all forgiven Joshua in our hearts. At least he's not part of this sinful world anymore. God decided it was his time."

It was the Amish way to forgive the sins of those that had wronged them, but Isaac wasn't sure he quite believed that forgiveness had reached the Lantz family's hearts.

Mrs. Lantz went on, "And now our David is being baptized at long last. I only wish Father were here to witness it. How happy he would be to see his son join the church and yield to God. For it is the only way."

Isaac peeked at David, who gripped his spoon so tightly his knuckles were white.

After a few more moments of silence, Mrs. Lantz spoke again. "Isaac, we apologize for Anna's outburst. This is not how we welcome guests in our home, I assure you. It will not happen again. Will it, Anna?"

"No," she whispered.

"There's no need to apologize. It was my thoughtlessness that started it." He picked up a warm biscuit and took a bite before smiling awkwardly. "Mary, these are delicious."

"Do you think so?" Her face brightened. "It's a special recipe."

Isaac asked as many questions about lunch as he could think of, and by the time the plates were cleared, the dark cloud had lifted. "Should I get the water from the well for the dishes?" he asked.

Mrs. Lantz waved him off. "Of course not. The girls will do it."

Mary had the bucket in hand already while Anna stacked the dishes by the dry sink. Mary smiled. "But thank you for offering."

Isaac quickly plucked his hat from the peg by the kitchen door and followed David outside, certain he could still feel Mary's eager gaze upon him. He could imagine what Mervin would say, and the kissy noises he'd make. Isaac picked up his pace and walked alongside David, leaving Mary behind.

BY LATE AFTERNOON, Isaac was not only sweating profusely, but covered in fine sawdust. He put his sandpaper down to wipe his mouth on his sleeve, wincing at the grit on his tongue. With all the farm work he'd done his whole life, Isaac's hands were rough, but he could see why David's were particularly callused.

"I'm sorry for what happened at lunch."

Isaac blinked as he raised his head. They hadn't spoken in hours, and David's gaze was still on the length of wood he was carefully measuring for a new church bench for Eli Kauffman.

"But I'm the one who should apologize."

"It wasn't your fault." David made a notch in the wood.

"I was thoughtless." Isaac folded the sandpaper and fiddled with the edges. "Especially since I know what it is to lose a brother."

David's hands stilled, and he caught Isaac's gaze. He said nothing.

"Not that it's the same, exactly," Isaac hastily added. "My Aaron isn't...he was taken by the world."

"He might as well be dead, though." Something mournful passed over David's face, dimming the light in his eyes. "That's how I imagine it to be, at least."

Isaac swallowed thickly. "Yes. He's lost forever unless he returns to the church. I don't think that'll ever happen. He couldn't handle the restrictions of our old church. I can't imagine him accepting our ways here in Zebulon."

"No." David ran his long fingers along the wood. "Where do you think he is?"

Isaac watched the motion of David's hand. "I don't know. He spoke sometimes of the ocean." Isaac didn't add that he also longed to see the vast expanse of the sea. To feel the sand between his toes, and the water rushing over his feet. He squeezed the sandpaper, the heavy grit digging into his skin. "I wonder if he even knows where we are now. Probably not." *I wonder if he thinks about us at all.*

"Do you hear from your sisters in Red Hills?"

Isaac relaxed his grip. "Yes. Bishop Yoder discourages it since their husbands decided against moving here, but it's not forbidden. My mother writes with Abigail and Hannah every month. Your sister Emma is still there as well, isn't she?"

"Yes. She just had her sixth child. A girl. She writes every few weeks." He smiled sharply. "Mother doesn't respond herself, but Mary writes back, and Mother practically dictates every word as she does, hovering over her shoulder."

He waited for David to say more, but after a few moments, David went back to his work. Isaac returned to sanding the rough wood on a new chest of drawers. He was pleasantly surprised to find that he was able to lose himself in the pleasure of the work, even if it was only sanding, and feel comfortable in David's presence.

Some time later, David spoke. "That's enough for today."

Isaac jumped at the sound of David's voice, and realized the sun was setting. "I'll see you again tomorrow?" He felt suddenly uneasy. What if David wasn't happy with his work? He should have tried harder. Maybe if he—

"Of course." The dimple appeared in David's right cheek. "You did very well, Isaac. Don't worry so much."

"Thank you. I'll try." He brushed off his shirt, frowning at the sawdust on his skin.

"You can shower here if you'd like."

Isaac gaped. "*Shower*? But how?"

Eyes alight, David dropped his hat on the worktable and headed for the passageway past the animal stalls. "I'll show you."

Isaac left his own hat behind and followed, his pulse picking up like a horse into a trot. They only usually bathed once a week on Saturday nights, filling a tub in the kitchen and filing in one after the other. Isaac was always glad to get to go before Katie and his younger brothers, so at least the water was fairly clean.

In the very back corner of the barn was another wooden stall, this one narrow, with a door and walls taller than a man stood. With a flourish, David pulled the wooden handle and stepped aside. Isaac peered in.

The floor was made of smooth planks that slanted toward a round hole in the corner. On the wall there was a carved alcove where a bar of yellow soap rested. Above was a large wooden barrel, built into one of the thick beams of the hayloft with pipe jutting out over their heads. A rope hung down.

Isaac stared, mouth open. "But how?"

David tugged him inside the stall and pointed up. "There's another pipe attached to the back of the barrel leading to a drainage system I set up on the roof. The barrel fills up, and even in summer there always seems to be enough. Pull on the rope and it pours out."

Laughing, Isaac turned in a circle, gazing up at the apparatus. There was enough room for the two of them in the stall, although he brushed against David with his arm. "It must freeze in the winter, though?"

"It does, but I have a secret in the hayloft. I rigged a lamp under the barrel. I light it before I shower, and there's warm water flowing into the barrel in no time."

Isaac gaped. "That's genius. You should make one of these for everyone! We all had proper plumbing in Red Hills, and this is the next best thing."

David's expression sobered. "I don't think Bishop Yoder would approve. My mother won't let the girls use it. She doesn't stop me at least. Even though she tells me every chance she gets that it's a threat to my salvation."

Isaac ran his fingers over the length of rope hanging down. "But it doesn't break the Ordnung does it? There's no electricity. And it isn't inside the house."

"It doesn't break the rules explicitly, but Mother thinks it too worldly. And of course if you think so, you don't have to use it." He placed his hand on Isaac's arm. The stall door had swung shut, and they were in shadows. "Just promise you won't tell anyone about it. They wouldn't like it."

"Of course not." Isaac was frozen, his skin flickering where David touched him. "I'd like to use it if you don't mind."

"I thought you might." David dropped his hand and turned. High in the corner by the door, there was a cut-out box with a lamp inside. He turned the knob, and the familiar hiss of kerosene and golden light filled the shower.

David pointed to a series of metal hooks on the wall outside the stall. "Shake out your clothes and hang them here." He nodded at the rope. "No need to pull too hard. The water might be a bit cold unless you want to wait to warm it. It should be fine until October, though."

"It's okay. Thanks."

Isaac waited until David's footsteps retreated to remove his galluses and unhook the three eyes at the collar of his shirt. Despite the day's lingering heat, goose bumps spread over his skin as he shook out his shirt and bent over to unlace his leather boots, stuffing his socks inside.

He unbuttoned the flap at the front of his pants and peeled them off. Isaac knew English men wore shorts underneath, although it seemed a strange idea to him. Making sure his knife was still safely tucked in his pocket, he hung his clothing on a peg next to a towel.

He closed the stall and eyed the barrel above him. Being completely naked in David Lantz's barn made him nervous, even though he'd closed the door. It was silly, since he was used to bathing in the kitchen. Sure, everyone knew to stay away while they took turns in the tub, but it wasn't as though he hadn't been naked around his brothers a million times in their room getting dressed and undressed.

He reached for the rope, running his fingers over the dry braid. His first tug wasn't hard enough, but on the second, a stream of water ran out. He yelped at the cold and let go of the rope, stopping the flow. Isaac lathered his hands with the citronella soap and scrubbed his hair and body quickly. The wet floor was smooth under his feet, and he could imagine how long it had taken David to sand. He'd probably gotten down on his hands and knees to refine the edges once the stall was built.

Isaac's balls tingled, and he bit back a groan as he soaped them. Blood rushed to his groin, and the urge to touch himself was overwhelming. Breath coming fast, he wrapped his palm around his cock, just for a moment. He knew it was wrong, but...

"How's it going?"

Isaac jerked his hand away. David was right outside the door, and Isaac hadn't even heard him approaching. "Fine," he squeaked.

"I brought you a fresh towel. It's hanging out here." David's footsteps retreated once more.

"Thanks!" Isaac called.

The last thing he needed was to disgrace himself in David Lantz's barn, so Isaac tugged hard on the rope. The rush of cool water doused him, and he thought about sitting in church listening to the preachers until his body settled. When he cracked open the door he was alone, and he quickly toweled off and re-dressed.

At the worktable, David was bent over one of his designs again, scratching notes with a pencil. He glanced up. "How was it?"

"Great. Wonderful." Isaac forced a smile. Lord help him, what would David think if he knew what Isaac had been so tempted to do? "Thank you," he added.

"I'll make sure there's a towel for you every day." David dropped his pencil and ran a hand through his dark hair with a yawn. "I should wash up myself."

At the thought of David being naked where Isaac had just stood, he sucked in a breath and made for the door. "See you in the morning!"

Silver waited in a small paddock, happily munching grass. He harnessed her, petting her head and scratching her neck just where she liked it. They plodded down the lane, the old buggy creaking with every rut. Isaac was almost home when he realized he'd forgotten his hat, but the way the breeze caught his wet hair made him think of a train flying on the tracks, and he spurred Silver on faster.

Chapter Four

"**W**ELL?"

Isaac glanced up from his bowl and slurped the bean soup on his spoon. "Well what?"

Mother and Father chuckled, and Ephraim rolled his eyes. Nathan elbowed him. "You've been working with David Lantz for days now, and you've barely said a word about it!"

"Oh." Isaac pulled his spoon back and forth through his soup. He was oddly embarrassed, and thinking of David made his belly flutter. "It's fine. I can't complain."

"Isaac." Father's smile faded. There was soup dribbled onto his chin, and he plucked a paper napkin from the simple wooden holder Isaac had carved for Mother last Christmas. Father wiped his mouth and dabbed at his beard. "Are you not happy?"

"No, no. I am!" Isaac smiled. "Really. It's just a change. Takes some getting used to."

Mother frowned. "Are you feeling well? I'll make you some sage tea before bed."

"I'm fine. Really."

"We know you were hesitant about working with David," Mother said. "Are there problems?"

"No. I promise everything's fine. He's very kind and patient." Isaac felt such a glow when he thought of David. "He really is a remarkable carpenter. I can learn so much. He's teaching me about the different kinds of wood, and which ones work best, depending on what you're making. I've always just used whatever wood was around."

"And you've always been able to do so much with it." Mother beamed. "The spoon you made me when you were a boy is still the best one." She pointed to the pot of soup on the stove, the worn handle of the spoon sticking out. "You have a gift, my Isaac."

He shrugged, secretly pleased. "I still have a lot to learn. But now I can devote the time to it. And Father, David's giving me my pay every Saturday."

Father took a bite of bread. "That will be fine. Leave the envelope in the top drawer of the desk. We'll put a portion aside for you each week."

Blinking, Isaac glanced between his parents. "Really? But until I'm twenty-one you're supposed to get everything."

"Yes, and when you're twenty-one you'll keep your whole salary and start paying for your room and board," Mother replied. "But you'll be getting married soon after that, and if we set aside a little bit every week, you'll have some savings to get you started."

"We know it's not normally how it's done, but our young couples in Zebulon are struggling to get on their feet." Father took a sip of water. "You should already have your own buggy. We will pray to the Lord for a bountiful harvest this year, and that our cows will stay healthy and their milk plentiful. We can't give you as much as we'd like, but we want the best start in life for you, Isaac. For all of you," he added.

Isaac took this in. "I don't know what to say." His mother's words echoed. *"You'll be getting married soon after that..."*

"Thank you would probably work," Nathan suggested.

As everyone laughed, including Father, Isaac joined in, pushing his thoughts aside. "Of course. Thank you."

Mother and Father nodded.

Isaac was afraid he might well up right there at the dinner table. "Thank you," he repeated. "And...how are things here?" He realized with a flush that he hadn't even thought about it, let alone asked. His mind had been consumed with thoughts of David Lantz all week. He supposed it made sense since it was the biggest change in his life in the five years since he'd finished school.

"Just fine, Isaac." Father nodded. "Ephraim's working very hard."

Ephraim shrugged, but a smile tugged at his lips. "Maybe it turns out Isaac just never did much," he teased.

Isaac reached behind Nathan to poke Ephraim's hip. "I taught you everything you know."

"Did you now? And who taught you?" Father chuckled.

Laughing, Isaac stirred his soup. "Aaron." He inhaled sharply a moment later. *Did I just say that out loud?* Judging by the wide eyes staring his way, he had. He swallowed hard. "I didn't mean...I'm sorry." He dared a glance at Father.

Sorrow weighted Father's face, a heaviness that seemed to pull all his features down toward his beard. Silently, he broke off a piece of bread and chewed it.

Anger would have been preferable. Isaac knew he should likely just stop talking, but the words tumbled out. "I didn't mean it. You know it's you who've taught us everything. He..." Isaac didn't say Aaron's name again. "I'm sorry," he repeated. Why had he said it at all? Why was he thinking of Aaron so much lately? Isaac felt as though his brain had been unbalanced in the days he'd been working with David—that everything had been sent off-kilter.

Mother held her spoon so tightly it looked as though it might snap. "Of course your father has taught you well."

"Who's Aaron?" little Joseph asked, brow furrowed.

It was like a physical blow to Isaac's gut, the realization that of course Joseph didn't even know of Aaron's existence. Katie watched them all with big eyes brimming with tears. She'd only been a baby. Had Isaac and Ephraim really never talked about Aaron with them? He wasn't even sure if Nathan knew his name, but judging by the tension in his frame, Isaac thought he did.

"No one," Father answered.

And that was that.

HE WAS ALMOST at the Lantz house the next morning when Silver stumbled. Isaac's heart was in his throat as he hopped down from the old buggy. "You okay, girl?" He stroked her neck, squinting at her hooves. "Darn," he muttered. He tossed his straw hat onto the buggy seat before bending over.

Running his hand down her front left leg, Isaac crouched and lifted Silver's hoof. The shoe was clean off, and she grunted as he inspected the hoof wall. "Shh. I know. I'm sorry." He glanced back at the deep muddy puddle he should have steered around.

"Isaac!" A little voice called out.

He glanced up to find David's youngest sister, Sarah, running out of the house, her long dark dress swirling around her bare feet. She was seven, he thought, and had David's dark hair and blue eyes. She wasn't wearing her cap yet.

She skidded to a stop. "I saw you from the window, and I wanted to say hi." Her smile faded. "Is something wrong with Silver?"

Nodding, Isaac quickly unhitched Silver from the buggy. "She threw a shoe on her front leg. Got caught up in the mud and probably stepped on it with her back foot."

Sarah's eyes widened. "Is that bad?"

Isaac scratched Silver's muzzle. "Usually not, but her hoof is damaged."

In an instant, tears welled in Sarah's eyes. "Are you going to shoot her?"

"What?" Isaac blinked. "No, of course not."

"Really?" Tears spilled down her cheeks.

"Hey, hey." Isaac dropped to his knees and held her arms. "She's going to be just fine." He squeezed her gently. "I promise."

Sarah threw her arms around him, her face buried in his neck as she cried. Even for a girl her age she was tiny. Isaac hugged her, not sure what else to do. He hadn't been held since he was very small, but it had always made him feel so much better. She mumbled something he couldn't make out.

"Hmm? What is it? You can tell me."

She inched back and raised her reddened face. "Wayne Hershberger told me if a horse gets hurt they shoot it because horses can't be fixed."

"That's only if a horse breaks a leg, or it's really, really sick. Silver just needs to see Mr. Schrock to get fixed right up."

Sarah bit her lip. "Are you just saying that to make me feel better?"

He smiled and tapped her nose. "No. I promised, remember?"

"And you're like David, right? Once you make a promise you always keep it?" She wiped her nose with her sleeve. "Mother thinks Mr. Otto next door should give back the land he hasn't paid for yet, but David said he gave his word." She recited the sentence like lines from a book she'd memorized.

Isaac raised an eyebrow. "I have a feeling you weren't supposed to be listening to that conversation."

She bit her lip again. "Probably not. But you promise, right? Silver's all right?"

"I promise."

Sarah nodded. "Okay."

He gently nudged her. "You'd better finish your breakfast."

"Bye!" She flew back to the house. "Hi, David!" she shouted as she went.

Isaac got to his feet and found David standing nearby with a strange expression on his face, half in shadow under the straw brim of his hat as the sun rose.

"Sorry. She was upset. Am I late? The thing is—"

"You're not late." David smiled softly. "Thanks for doing that. Calming her down. You're good with her. Sometimes children just need a hug." He kicked at a rock. "Mother doesn't really do that, especially after we settled in Zebulon."

"Same with my parents. Not that they were ever ones for hugging much. They don't coddle. Too much affirmation leads to vanity, as the bishop says. But sometimes with little ones, it's what they need. Just…reassurance, I guess."

"I think so too." David stared intently.

Isaac shifted from foot to foot, not sure what else to say.

"Your knees are muddy."

"Oh." Isaac wiped at his pants and only succeeded in getting his hands dirty. "I didn't notice. I'm sorry, I can—"

"Don't be sorry."

Isaac turned to Silver, scratching her head. "I have to walk her over to Farrier Samuel's."

When he glanced back, David was still watching him with a gentle expression that sent warmth flowing through Isaac. He cleared his throat. "You know, Samuel Schrock."

David blinked. "Yes. Of course." As if he'd woken up suddenly, he approached Silver and crouched down. "She threw a shoe?"

"The wall of her hoof is cut too, but it doesn't look too bad. Still, I don't want to wait. It's my fault—I wasn't paying attention."

"No, I should have fixed that hole in the spring." David shook his head and patted Silver. "Sorry, girl. You get extra sugar later."

As if she understood him, Silver nuzzled David, and Isaac laughed. "Good thing you're a man of your word, because Silver will collect on that promise."

David chuckled. "What exactly was Sarah saying to you?"

"Just singing your praises." Isaac waved his hand.

"She was listening when I talked to Mother about the land, wasn't she?"

Isaac ran his fingers across his lips, sealing his mouth shut.

David smiled. "All right, we'd better get Silver fixed up. I've got a new rasp handle for Samuel. I'll walk over with you."

"Are you sure? I can take it." Although the idea of a morning walk with David did make him oddly happy. "I don't want to set us back."

"It's fine. Besides, it was my fault Silver lost the shoe in the first place. I'll get the handle." He hurried toward the barn.

As Isaac hauled the buggy off the driveway, he waved to Sarah and her sisters as they went off to school. Mary gave him a wide smile on her way to the washhouse, and familiar guilt washed through him. When David returned, Isaac grabbed his hat, and they ambled down the lane with Silver.

"I can stay late tonight to make up the time," Isaac said.

"Am I such a taskmaster? Isaac, you work hard every day. Stop worrying so much. You're the best apprentice I could have asked for."

Isaac looped Silver's reins over his wrist, trying not to smile. "Thank you."

"You're always on time, you learn fast, and you have the knack for it. Plus, you have another very important quality."

Isaac smiled self-consciously. "What's that?"

"You keep little girls' secrets."

He laughed. "Always."

"But seriously, Isaac." David clasped his shoulder. "It's great working with you."

It was as though he could feel the heat of David's touch through his shirt. Must have been the sun arcing higher in the sky. "I...you too. Thank you for taking me on. I'm learning so much."

As David lowered his hand, his fingers brushed Isaac's arm. "It's nice to have a friend around too." He huffed out a laugh. "Anna's right that I don't have many these days. Anna's right about most things, just so you know."

"Yeah, I've noticed. Does she always say exactly what she's thinking?"

David smirked. "Yep. Nine times out of ten."

"At least you always know where you stand." Isaac gave Silver a scratch. "I guess you don't have much time for friends with all the work you have to do. I can't imagine being the only man at home."

"You get used to it, I guess. Like anything." David looked off at the horizon. "At first you think you'll never be able to go on. That just getting out of bed every morning is impossible. But you do, and after a while it just becomes your life."

"That's what it must be like following church and getting married," Isaac blurted.

David stopped in his tracks, staring at Isaac. His lips parted as if to say something, but then he snapped his jaw shut.

"Not that I don't want to!" Isaac's heart hammered. "It's only that it seems so different from my life now. I can't really imagine what it'll be like. But I'll get used to it. It'll be good. It'll be great." He laughed sharply. "I'm just talking nonsense." He strode forward, leading Silver.

"It's not nonsense."

Isaac stopped and looked back. David gave him a smile.

"It makes perfect sense."

"Oh." Isaac tried to think of something else to say.

David started walking again, and they continued on, taking a dirt road that was a shortcut over to the Schrock farm. They were silent for a few minutes.

"Do you think it's stupid?" David asked.

Isaac's pulse still hummed. "What?"

"Not to take back some of the land from Josiah Otto." David scooped up a stone from the road and tossed it ahead of him. "He paid for half of it up front, but he's been late on the other payments. Mother thinks we should take it back and try to farm it ourselves, or hire some boys to do it. But I gave him my word that the land was his."

Isaac pondered it. "But he hasn't held up part of the arrangement. No one would blame you for being at the end of your patience."

"But I know how hard he's been working—I see him out there every day. He'll pay what he owes as soon as he can. If I go back on our deal now, what would he do? He has a new baby, and four others already. I made a commitment, and I should honor it. Give him some more time, at least. He insisted on paying interest. We wrote it out on a piece of paper."

"Sounds fair enough. We're supposed to help each other, after all."

"And it's not that Mother doesn't want to help them," David added hastily. "It's just that money's tight, and she's worried." He blew out a long breath. "I'm sorry, I shouldn't bother you with this."

"It's not a bother."

"You're a good listener."

Isaac felt oddly pleased. "Well, we're friends, right?" He brushed a fly off his cheek. "That's what friends do."

"Right." David gave him a little smile. "There's—" He pointed. "Dirt."

Isaac swiped at his face. "Did I get it?"

Laughing, David stopped. "Here." His tongue darted out to lick his thumb, and he drew it down Isaac's cheek.

Isaac held his breath. David was standing close now, his eyes on Isaac's face. He brushed the corner of Isaac's mouth with his thumb, and Isaac felt like there were hummingbirds inside him.

Their eyes met, and David jerked away as if he'd been burned. He shoved his hands in his pockets. "Got it."

"Thanks." Isaac's voice cracked, and he cleared his throat as they walked on. After a minute, he said, "David?"

"Uh-huh." David stared straight ahead.

Isaac found himself smiling as he rubbed Silver's neck. "I don't think it's stupid. To help Josiah Otto. Not even a little."

The dimple appeared in David's cheek, his teeth flashing. "Thanks, Isaac." He scooped up another rock from the ground, tossing it to the horizon, his arms swinging.

"But how do they get up and walk away?"

Mervin rolled his eyes. "It's *pretend.*"

"Yes, but if we crashed a buggy we'd end up dead or in an English hospital, let alone if we crashed one of those going that fast." Isaac stared at the screen, unable to take his eyes away as another car flipped over in a screech of rubber and metal that made him wince.

Mervin nudged him. "Shh."

They were shoulder to shoulder under an Ironwood tree that was starting to drop its yellowing leaves as October settled in. Mervin had one of the white knobs in his left ear, and Isaac the other in his right. They'd taken off their heavy black hats so they could keep their heads close together as they peered down avidly at the Touch's screen. Isaac glanced around, making sure they were still alone. His knife and the chunk of wood he'd intended on carving sat abandoned on his lap.

As another car exploded with flames that licked the sky, Isaac shivered. He drew his black coat around him tighter, although he knew it wasn't the cool breeze to blame. "A lot of people die in this movie."

"That's how it is out in the world, I guess."

The sun was hidden behind gray clouds, but Isaac could tell the afternoon was waning. "We should get back. It'll be dark soon, and it won't be long before the singing."

"It's almost over."

As Isaac opened his mouth to remind Mervin that Sadie Stoltzfus awaited, there was a noise behind them. He twisted around to find David standing there in his hat and coat with a strange expression—not anger, but not happiness either. Isaac jumped to his feet, the white knob yanking out of his ear. He was aware of Mervin's frantic motions to hide the Touch, but of course it was far too late.

Mervin's words tripped out. "We weren't—it's just—don't tell. *Please.*"

Isaac shook his head. "He won't." After only two weeks of really getting to know David, he wasn't sure why he was so certain, but he was.

For a moment, David watched him, but then his lips twitched into a tiny smile. "No. I won't tell."

Mervin exhaled loudly. "Thank you." His pale face was bright red. "We didn't mean any harm. We just wanted to see."

"I understand. I have my own curiosity."

"Even now?" Isaac blurted. "I mean…you're joining the church. I thought…" He scooped up his knife and folded it back into his pocket. "I thought you wouldn't anymore."

David shrugged. "I think it's human to be curious, no matter how old we are." He nodded at the ground. "Don't forget your hats."

As they walked through the trees with Isaac in the middle, Mervin began chattering. "Are you going to drive a girl home tonight, David?"

"Perhaps." David pulled off a low-hanging leaf and rolled it between his long fingers.

With his eyes locked on David's hand, Isaac stumbled over an exposed root, and David reached out to steady him. Isaac's smile was tremulous. *What is wrong with me?*

"Sadie's father will only let me drive her home once a month. I have to wait two more weeks! I wish we could just go steady now. We can write letters, at least." Mervin kicked the dirt. "But it's not fair. Once a month? She said her father likes me, but her uncle doesn't think it's proper to rush things."

Isaac grimaced. "At least Deacon Stoltzfus is only her uncle. Can you imagine having him as your father-in-law?"

"He wasn't so bad before. He used to smile, at least. But after…" Mervin glanced at David. "Sorry."

David shrugged. "Don't be. It's not like we all don't know what happened. I can't blame Deacon Stoltzfus for mourning his daughter. Martha deserved better. So did Rachel." He crushed the leaf in his hand, scattering the debris.

"So did Joshua," Isaac said softly.

David met his gaze with raised eyebrows. "I imagine you're the only person aside from the family who really thinks that."

Isaac shook his head. "Maybe just the first one to say it."

David stopped, gazing intently. "Either way, thank you."

A strange thrill zipped through him, and Isaac smiled. "It's just the truth. Joshua made mistakes, but he never meant to hurt anyone. Not that I really knew him, but he was your brother, and you're… Well, I can't imagine he intended any of it."

"He didn't." David opened his mouth and closed it again. "He was curious about everything. It was so stupid what he did."

"He didn't know what would happen. It was an accident."

"Accident? I'm sorry, but doing those drugs wasn't an accident," Mervin said. "Drinking is one thing, but doing that powder? That was way over the line. And Martha and Rachel would never have taken drugs if it wasn't for him," Mervin said. He crossed his arms. "They would never have died like that."

Isaac gritted his teeth. "Joshua drowned too. Who can say how it happened?"

"If not for him they wouldn't have been messed up in the first place, and—"

"You don't know that!" Isaac said sharply. Every criticism of Joshua felt like an attack on David, who'd never done a thing to deserve it. It just wasn't fair.

Mervin's voice rose. "Are you kidding? My sisters knew Rachel and Martha. They were good girls. No way they would have done that crystal whatever stuff if Joshua Lantz hadn't talked them into it. And we all wouldn't have had to leave Red Hills."

"He's right," David said quietly.

Isaac blinked at him. "But…"

"It's all right, Isaac. I appreciate it."

Mervin kicked at a stone. "I'm sorry, David. None of it's your fault. And of course we forgive Joshua."

Of course. Sometimes forgiveness felt like nothing more than empty words. Isaac wanted to say a lot more, but he shoved his hands in his pockets.

David started walking again. "What were you saying about Sadie? Tell us more."

Mervin shrugged. "Just that she's the one. I should never have wasted my time on anyone else."

Isaac blinked. "The one? Really?"

"Of course!" Mervin sighed dreamily, all tension apparently forgotten for the moment. "She's got the prettiest eyes, and her skin looks so soft. I just want to touch her all over."

David chuckled. "All over, huh?"

"After we're married, of course!" Mervin insisted. "Well, maybe a bit before that if she lets me. But I'm definitely going to marry her. I'm aiming for spring or summer."

Isaac couldn't believe his ears. "So soon? You'll only be nineteen."

"What's the sense in waiting?"

"It's just...most boys wait a year or two longer." Isaac nodded at Mervin's pocket. "There'll be no more of that once you follow church."

Mervin scowled. "You think I don't know that?"

They continued on in silence.

Finally Mervin spoke again, his tone forcefully light. "David, I think John's Grace would be well pleased if you asked to drive her home after the singing tonight."

"Would she?" David asked flatly.

"Of course! You can't be that blind. She's wanted you to ask forever. You haven't dated any of the girls in ages! We all thought you and Isaac Yoder's Fannie would have children by now. Why'd you let her go? Although Jacob Raber certainly thanks you, I'm sure."

Isaac elbowed Mervin. "He had to take care of his mother and sisters, remember?"

Mervin took a sharp breath. "Of course. I'm sorry."

"It's all right." David snapped off another leaf and rolled it, the dry edges flaking over his fingers. "I didn't think it was fair to make Fannie wait. She and Jacob seem very happy."

"Do you think your mother will marry again soon?" Mervin asked. "You can't stay home forever. Or you could just build another house beyond the barn for you and your wife."

Isaac really wished Mervin would change the subject. Acid bubbled in his belly, and he quickened his pace. He was obviously hungry for supper.

"Mother was deeply grieved. I'm not sure if she'll marry again. Anyway, I'm content at home for the time being." The leaf he was rolling snapped, and David crumbled it in his fist.

They neared the house where they'd suffered through church service that morning, and Isaac sighed to himself as Mary smiled in their direction. It had been two weeks now that he saw her for lunch every day, and while his opinion of her hadn't changed—she was good and kind—nor had his feelings of ambivalence.

Mervin brightened. "There's Sadie! See you later." He walked so quickly he might as well have run.

At least now Isaac felt largely at ease in David's company. He spied Grace darting glances at David and whispering with her friends.

"Do you want to go talk to Grace?" Isaac asked, since he felt he should.

David looked at him evenly. "No. Do you want to talk to my sister?"

Isaac wasn't sure what the right answer was, so he told the truth. "Not really." He hastily added, "Not that there's anything wrong with her."

"I know. It's okay." David glanced around before peering at Isaac closely and lowering his voice. "Thanks for what you said. About my brother."

Isaac shrugged, flushing under David's attention. "It was just...it wasn't a big deal."

"It was to me. I haven't been able to talk much about it. You saw what happened with my mother when Joshua came up. It's been years, but it still feels like something forbidden."

"I know what you mean. I don't even know what really happened."

David sighed. "Apparently they went down to the river to have a party. It seemed they decided to go swimming."

"I heard..." Isaac hesitated. "I heard your brother was naked when they found him. And that the girls were only in their underthings."

With a clenched jaw, David nodded. "It was shameful."

"If it had been my brother—" He broke off, his breath shallow at the thought of Aaron being dragged from the river, bloated and pale. "No one deserves that. No matter what."

David swallowed thickly. "Sometimes I feel guilty when I remember the good things about him. But I'm resentful too. I don't blame Mervin. And I think about Rachel and Martha, and how I'd feel if I had a daughter and something like that happened. Or if it was one of my sisters. I'd probably hate Joshua too."

Isaac scoffed. "But no one hates him. We're not allowed to be angry. All is forgiven, remember?"

David's lips quirked into a rueful smile. "I thought I was the only one who didn't quite believe that."

"No. Not the only one." Isaac's pulse fluttered. "You can talk to me about whatever you want. I may not know what to say, but I can listen."

"Thanks, Isaac. You know you can say anything to me, right?" David glanced around. "Anything you want, even if you think you shouldn't say it. I won't tell."

Isaac and Mervin had always kept each other's childish secrets, but with David it felt different somehow. It sent tingles over his skin. He nodded. "Okay."

Beneath the brim of his black hat, David's pale blue eyes gleamed. "Hey, do you want to go fishing next week?"

"Sure." Isaac's palms tingled. "When?"

"Saturday night."

"All right."

The supper bell rang, and before Isaac could say anything else, David was walking away. Isaac followed, wishing Saturday wasn't almost a whole week away.

Chapter Five

"B UT THERE'S NO church tomorrow."

Father swallowed his mouthful and wiped yolk from his lip with his napkin. "That doesn't mean you can stay abed all morning. How late do you want to be out?"

Isaac shrugged. "Not too late. We're just going fishing after we finish work."

"Won't you be tired tonight? You should come home and read. Your father is always so rested after a quiet evening," Mother said.

Beside Isaac, Ephraim spoke up. "Fishing isn't hard work. Maybe I could go with them, and—"

"No." Father's tone brooked no argument. "Just last night you went hunting with some of the boys, and you worked this morning as if the fields were full of molasses."

As Ephraim grumbled, relief flooded Isaac. Not that he begrudged his brother a night of fishing, but it wouldn't be the same with the three of them. He wasn't sure why. "There's no work tomorrow. Only the animals to care for, and I promise I'll tend them properly."

"You'll miss your bath tonight," Mother noted.

He'd kept the shower in David's barn a secret, as he'd promised. "I'll wash when I get home."

Isaac's siblings all looked to their father, awaiting his verdict. Father glanced at Mother before slowly nodding.

It was settled, and Isaac bit back the urge to whoop. As he hurried from the kitchen after breakfast, Mother called out from the sink.

"Bring me home a few nice fish, Isaac! I'll make a stew."

"I will!"

"That's my good boy."

It was a work day like any other, and when Isaac arrived at the Lantz's, David greeted him with a brief smile before going back to his design with a pencil in hand. Isaac was strangely disappointed, although he wasn't sure what he'd expected David to say. They were only going fishing, after all. Still, Isaac was excited.

He picked up his task of measuring and sawing beams for Elijah Raber's new *dawdy haus*. Elijah had taken over running the farm, and now his parents would live out their days in their own little home attached to the main house by a shared kitchen.

As he worked, Isaac wondered if one day before too long he'd build a dawdy haus for his own parents. More likely it would fall to one of the younger boys, and Isaac would have moved to his own land by then. He'd have a wife and children. Yet when he tried to envision that future, his mind remained frustratingly blank.

Isaac always measured twice—and sometimes three times—before putting the saw to the wood. He tried to lose himself in his task, but today the hours dragged by, with lunch being particularly painful. He excused himself as soon as he could, feeling Mary's gaze on him as he walked to the outhouse. He didn't want to be rude, but he was desperate for the time to fly so he could head out alone with David.

It's only fishing by the lake. Why should it be so special?

By the time Isaac showered, he was ready to jump straight out of his skin. He washed himself quickly, taking care not to linger on his privates. He was glad that the water was so cold. When he came back down the passageway to the work area, David was waiting, his hair still damp from his own shower earlier. David popped the last piece of a biscuit in his mouth. Mrs. Lantz had insisted on a late-afternoon snack, and Isaac's stomach was pleasantly full.

"Ready?" David asked. He nodded to where their hats hung on the wall. "You can get your hat on the way back. No need for it out in the woods with the sun going down. Don't worry, no one will see us."

Heart tripping, Isaac nodded and followed outside. Yet David didn't go toward his buggy, but instead to the fence where a tall bridled horse was tied. When Isaac hesitated, David glanced back.

"There's a shortcut across the fields and through the woods." He patted the horse's neck. "Kaffi likes riders. He's odd for a draft horse."

The name must have come from the dark coffee color of the horse's hair. "You're sure he can take us both?"

"Absolutely." David climbed onto the fence and swung his leg over the horse. "Come on, it's easy. We won't go too fast."

"Don't we need fishing poles?"

"I have a hidey hole in an old log by the lake. I keep them there. Hop on."

Isaac had ridden occasionally with a saddle before, but not for ages, and never bareback. The fence didn't waver as he clambered up, but he paused, eyeing the horse's broad back.

David gave him a smile. "It's all right. Just grab me and climb on."

Holding his breath, Isaac grasped David's shoulder to steady himself as he reached his leg over. Kaffi sidestepped as he settled on, and Isaac dug his fingers into David's hip with his left hand. He squeezed his thighs around the horse, anticipation zipping through him.

With a click of David's tongue and prodding of his heels, Kaffi sauntered into the field, following the narrow path between the gardens. Isaac concentrated on breathing steadily and keeping his balance. He should let go of David now that he was getting a feel for it, but Isaac hung on anyway. The pressure on his privates, with only his pants between them and the muscles of the horse's back, sent faint shivers up his spine.

Isaac could tell when they passed onto the land the Ottos now cultivated, the partly harvested crops growing higher and more plentiful. They didn't see any workers, but the sun was already beyond the horizon. He breathed in the familiar smell of the fields, earth and grass—and manure, faded now at the harvest, but always there.

David had clearly followed this route through the woods many times, and he didn't hesitate once they were in the trees. He went steadily east, angling this way and that, Kaffi sure-footed amid the roots and grassy scrub on the ground even as twilight gave way to darkness.

As the moon rose, its ghostly light filtering through the thinning autumn leaves, David brought Kaffi to a stop. The horse bent his head to munch on a low bush, and for a moment the rustling was the only sound. David looked over his shoulder at Isaac with eyes so serious that Isaac held his breath.

"What would you think if we didn't go fishing tonight?"

"Huh?" Isaac realized he was still hanging on although they weren't moving. He dropped his hands from David's waist, making fists to keep from fidgeting.

David watched him steadily. "The truth is, I don't want to go fishing at all."

They sat so close that David's breath tickled Isaac's face. "What do you want to do?" Isaac whispered.

David's gaze flicked a few inches down. "I want..."

Heart galloping, Isaac licked his dry lips.

Suddenly David spun back around, vibrating with tension. Kaffi sidestepped, snorting before going back to the shrubs.

Isaac could hardly breathe as he stared at the back of David's head, wishing he could peek inside. "David?"

He didn't turn, and his voice was low. "Can I trust you?"

Isaac swallowed hard. "Yes." He had the crazy urge to reach up and touch the skin of David's neck, to feel the fine wisps of dark hair there.

"I hardly know you, but I feel like I can. I mean, I've known you since you were born, but...not really."

He wished he could see David's expression to make some sense of this strange conversation. Tentatively, Isaac flattened his hand on David's back. Through the broadcloth, he felt rigid muscles beneath his palm. He swallowed hard. "You can trust me."

"If I take you somewhere, do you promise not to tell? Not anyone?"

"I promise." Unable to resist, he stroked David's back the way he would a skittish horse.

With a shudder, David put his heels to Kaffi, urging him on faster than before. Isaac wrapped his arms around David's waist and squeezed with his thighs, blood rushing in his ears as they cantered into a field under the silver of the moon. His hips pressed right against David's backside now.

Shivering, Isaac glimpsed what he could of David's face, wondering what thoughts warred in David's mind, and where he was leading them with such urgency. He should ask, but instead Isaac simply held on.

A white farmhouse, windows glowing yellow, sat by a small barn and outbuilding. An English pickup truck was parked outside, and as they rode up, a light blazed to life. Isaac gasped. "We're trespassing. They know we're here!"

Yet David only chuckled as he pulled Kaffi to a stop. "It's a motion detector. Don't worry, we're welcome here. Hop down."

Isaac realized he was still clutching David about the middle, and quickly let go to slide from the horse's back, David following. As David tied Kaffi loosely to a fencepost, Isaac peered around anxiously. "Who lives here?"

"A friend. It's all right, Isaac." David smiled and walked toward the outbuilding with the shining light. "Come on."

With no choice, Isaac trotted after him. Inside, he stood at the threshold as David flicked a switch—as if it were *nothing*—and light flooded the workroom. Blinking in the harsh electricity, Isaac stared. "It's…"

"My other workshop." David bounced a little on his toes, gaze eager as he looked between Isaac and the square room.

It was a smaller version of the workshop in the Lantz barn, but here there were tools with cords hanging from them, a small white refrigerator humming in the corner, and of course covered light bulbs overhead. Isaac stepped inside, not sure where to look first. In the pencil sketches tacked to a board on the wall, he recognized David's hand. He opened and closed his mouth like one of the fish they were supposed to be catching. "I…"

"Hi ho!" A woman's voice rang out.

Isaac wheeled around, and she stopped short just inside the door.

"Oh! Hello there." She glanced at David. "I'm sorry. I didn't know you had company."

David's smile was shaky. "June, this is Isaac. Isaac, this is my friend June."

June took a few steps and stuck out her hand. "Great to meet you, Isaac."

For a moment, Isaac could only stare. Then he shook her hand the way he would a man's. June apparently didn't seem to think it strange at all. She smiled, her green eyes crinkling at the corners in her round face. She looked to be in her sixties.

Light hair hung down to her shoulders, part of it held back with some kind of plastic clip. She wore jeans and a soft plaid shirt beneath an open jacket, and brightly colored sneakers on her feet. After letting go of Isaac's hand, she opened her arms to David. Isaac watched, stunned, as David hugged the English woman, pressing against her tightly as if it were an everyday occurrence.

There was something familiar about June, and it took a few moments before Isaac remembered where he'd seen her before. Mr. Lantz's funeral hadn't been as big as some Isaac remembered from his youth, but David's older sister and a passel of cousins had made the trip from Ohio. Bishop Yoder had welcomed them despite the bitter feelings that had arisen from the split in their former community, surely hoping they'd find Zebulon a better place to come and live. But they'd returned home in the end.

The service had been in the barn. There was only one non-Amish person there—the English woman whose house was the closest to the Lantz farm with a telephone. A memory of her sitting at the back—dressed in black and looking almost like a plain woman but for the lack of cap—flashed through Isaac's mind. He could barely recognize her now with her easy smile and flowing hair as she spoke to David.

"Good news—I have a buyer for the dining table. And there's better news—they want you to make a matching hutch."

David grinned. "I'll start on the design tomorrow."

"But tomorrow's Sunday," Isaac blurted. In the silence that followed, he added lamely, "We're not supposed to work on Sunday."

David held up his hands before letting them fall to his sides with a shrug. "There are a lot of things we're not supposed to do."

June smiled kindly. "A day of rest always did seem like a good idea to me."

Isaac's head spun, and he tried to think of something to say to this woman. "What do you farm here?"

"Oh, nothing in a long time. My husband had a passion for it, but I sold off most of the land when he passed. I like the solitude, but my thumbs are entirely black."

Isaac couldn't help but look down at her hands, which seemed perfectly normal.

She laughed. "It's a saying. Green thumbs mean you have the touch with plants. I was much more suited to office work—I was the county clerk in Warren. Now blissfully retired aside from the venture with David." She glanced at a silver watch on her wrist. "You boys had better get going if you're going to make the movie."

Terror and a thrill coiled in Isaac's belly. "Movie?"

Glancing between Isaac and David, June backed toward the door. "I'll leave some money for you in the truck if you decide to go. Time for this old broad to get back to her *Downton Abbey* marathon. It was nice to meet you, Isaac. Hope I'll see you again."

Isaac forced a smile. "Nice to meet you, ma'am. I...um, thank you for having me."

In the silence, Isaac could hear the crunch of gravel as June returned to the house. His breathing sounded harsh to his own ears.

"I'm sorry if I upset you." David sighed heavily. "We don't have to go if you don't want to. I thought... After I saw you and Mervin last week, I thought you'd enjoy it. Seeing a movie for real, on the big screen. I shouldn't have assumed. And I shouldn't have burdened you with my secrets."

"I'm not..." Isaac scrubbed a hand through his hair. "I don't know how to feel. I don't know what to say. About any of this."

A round clock ticked on the wall above the refrigerator, and David glanced to it. "If we want to see the movie, we have to leave soon. It starts at nine." He looked back at Isaac. "Or I can take you home. I won't be upset. I shouldn't have surprised you with everything all at once."

But excitement pulsed through Isaac, smothering the fear. "Where would we go to see a movie?"

The dimple appeared in David's cheek. "There's a drive-in outside Warren. Takes no time at all with the truck." He opened a chest of drawers in the corner and pulled out a stack of clothing. "These might be a bit big on you, but should fit well enough. This way we blend in." He selected a pair of dark jeans and a green T-shirt, holding them out.

Isaac reached for them before he could stop himself. He stood in the middle of the workshop, holding the English clothing as he might a snake. *Am I really doing this?*

He thought of what Mother and Father would say if they found out—the awful sorrow and disappointment he'd see on their faces—and opened his mouth to tell David to take him back to Zebulon instead. But when he looked up from the denim and cotton in his hands, the words lodged painfully in his throat.

Under the bright electric bulbs, Isaac could see every ripple in David's muscles as he peeled his shirt over his head. Dark hair sprinkled his chest, and his reddish nipples stood up in the chill of the night air. His stomach was flat, and as he unbuttoned the flap on his pants and tugged, Isaac could see more hair brushing his belly, leading down to—

David looked up, and their gaze locked. Isaac was sure the electricity in the room was somehow leeching into him, sparks zipping over his skin, his groin tightening dangerously. With a ragged breath, he spun around. He yanked off his jacket and shirt, quickly tugging the soft cotton over his head.

He didn't dare look back as he unbuttoned the flap on his pants and dragged them off. He struggled to get the jeans on over his black boots, but now that he was bare bottomed, he couldn't take the time to unlace them.

The pants were a little loose, and after he pulled them up, Isaac stared down at the zipper. The jeans and T-shirt were bad enough, let alone that he was in this secret English workshop, even if he hadn't used any of the electricity or modern things himself. His hands hovered in the air by his waist as he contemplated the silver teeth.

"Careful with the zip. English men wear underwear. You don't want to get anything caught." David's voice was close.

With a deep breath, Isaac turned. David smiled softly. He wore jeans as well, and a white T-shirt. He shrugged on a bright blue cotton jacket with a hood and zipped—*zipped!*—it up. Across the chest, it read *Vikings*, with the V shaped like a bull's horns.

"Do you want me to do it for you?" David asked.

Isaac could only jerk his head in a nod. He held his breath as David reached down and ever so gently zipped the fly of Isaac's English jeans. He did up the button at the top, his knuckles brushing against Isaac's trembling belly. They were standing so close that Isaac could see the flecks of gray in David's eyes, and—

"All set." David turned away and pawed through the pile of clothing. "Here, there's no zipper on this sweatshirt. Just pull it over your head."

He handed Isaac a thick gray bundle of a soft material Isaac had never felt. Like cotton, but not quite. Isaac held it up. It was embroidered with a dark red letter *M*, bordered in yellow. He stuck his arms into it and tugged it down. The sleeves hung an inch past his wrists, but it was nice and warm.

"What is this?" He rubbed his hand over his chest. Not that he should enjoy wearing worldly clothing, he reminded himself sternly.

"Fleece. Look…are you sure you want to do this?" David waited by the door. He was wearing sneakers now, but at least they were black.

Yes. No. Yes.

Isaac nodded and strode outside. The familiar stars dotted the sky, and Isaac gazed up at them, breathing deeply and getting his bearings. *I can do this. It's only one night. It won't hurt anyone.*

When David got into the truck, Isaac muttered a quick prayer and opened the door on the other side, climbing up before he could change his mind. The long seat was almost like a buggy's, but made of leather and impossibly soft. He'd ridden on a bus to Zebulon, but if he'd ever been in a car as a boy, he didn't remember it.

At least I'm not driving. Guilt flooded him, for what of David's soul? They were sinning, and for what?

But David was unconcerned. He pulled down a flap above him and the key tumbled out. There were also folded bills of money, which he tucked into the pocket of his jeans. He slid the key into a metal slot, and looked at Isaac.

"Ready?"

Isaac's throat was bone dry. "Yes," he croaked.

With a wink, David twisted his hand, and the engine roared to life. Isaac could feel its power all around him—and *in* him, a tremor at his core. If he'd been with Mervin, he'd have been terrified. But with David, Isaac knew he was safe. He wasn't sure why, but he wasn't afraid.

As they rumbled down the lane on sinful rubber tires, headlights splitting the night, the world was suddenly within his grasp.

Chapter Six

"HOW DID YOU learn to drive?" Isaac gripped the door handle, watching the fields zip by.

"June. I don't have my license, but it's not far to the drive-in, so she doesn't mind. She taught me the basics, and I'm careful to always go the speed limit."

Isaac was glad of it, since they were going plenty fast enough. He wiped his sweaty palms on his jeans. The fabric felt stiff against his privates, and he shifted on the seat. "Did you know her before? Before your father…"

"No."

"I'm sorry. I shouldn't…"

David's gaze stayed on the road, a yellow line leading their way. "Even though I'd ridden Kaffi across the fields like we did today, I couldn't seem to catch my breath, and she sat me down on the porch steps and put my head between my knees. I knew it was too late already. When I got to him in the field, it was…he was gone." A breath shuddered through him.

Isaac waited silently.

"But I had to try. June called the ambulance and drove me back. I didn't even think about the fact that I'd left Kaffi behind. When I went back the next day, she gave me lemonade and we talked. That's how it began, I guess. I know it must seem strange to you."

"No!" Isaac insisted. "Well, a little."

As they neared the railroad tracks, a thrill shot up Isaac's spine. How wonderful it would be to see the red flashing lights, and watch the freight cars lumber by. He peered both ways as they bumped over the tracks, but there was only darkness.

Lights flared ahead of them, and then disappeared as the road curved. Isaac watched as the approaching car came back into sight, mesmerized by how different it felt being out on the road at night in a truck rather than a dangerously dark buggy. He could actually enjoy this drive.

"What is *it*, exactly? You build furniture and she gives you money? Like for the movie tonight?" With a sinking sensation, he added, "But I don't have any money. How will I get in?"

David laughed. "Don't be silly. I'm paying for you. Don't worry, it's not much. Anyway, with June we split everything half and half. She buys the raw materials and the tools, and does the selling and shipping. Most of my half she deposits into my bank account, but she keeps cash for me as well."

"How does she put money in your account? Don't you have to be there?" Isaac's father had one at the bank in Warren, but Isaac had never been inside.

"It's all online now. That's what they call it when it's on the computer. June has one upstairs. We have a website too. She puts up pictures of my furniture, and people from all over can buy things without ever leaving their house. At first I thought there was no way—the pieces were so heavy no one would pay to have them shipped. But I've discovered there are people out there with a lot more money than we could even dream of."

"Buying things without leaving the house?" Isaac shook his head. "Without ever touching something or seeing it for themselves?"

"I know, it seems weird, but that's how it works a lot of the time now in the English world. People want convenience."

Isaac frowned. "Seems wrong. Sinful, somehow."

"Maybe." David slowed at a stop sign and turned down Highway 1.

"But I can't support my family only selling to people in Zebulon. The English pay triple or more what I can charge our neighbors. The Ordnung tells us men should stay on their farms, but most of us here are barely scratching by."

"I know, but..."

"You remember how different it was in Red Hills? Men could work in factories and do other jobs. Bishop Yoder hardly even wants us to sell to the English. There are other Swartzentrubers who do, but we have to hope for stray tourists. Doesn't God want us to prosper in this land? Why is it okay for us to sell to the English if they come to us, but we can't go to them?"

Isaac couldn't argue. "But once you join the church, you'll have to stop all this. Right?"

David's fingers tightened on the steering wheel. "I suppose so."

Ahead a bright sign came into sight. A huge red arrow pointed to a field where a sea of cars and trucks were parked. "Sky-Vu," Isaac read. He blinked through the windshield at the enormous screen on the other side of the field where huge images flickered. It looked like one of the verboten comic books Aaron used to read with him late at night, their heads together, keeping the lamp low.

They drove up to a windowed booth adorned with yellow lights and a red sign that said *Budweiser*. Beneath it on a white board, black block letters spelled out the admission prices and a message:

WHERE FRIENDS MEET FRIENDS.

When David pulled up and rolled down the window with a press of a button, the white-haired man in the booth grinned.

"Hi there, David. Glad you could make it for the last show of the season." He ducked his head a bit and eyed Isaac. "I see you brought a pal. I'll give you our customer appreciation rate since the first flick is almost over. It'll be eight dollars total." He ripped off a piece of paper.

"Thanks, Mike. This is Isaac." David handed over a bill and put the paper on the dashboard.

"Howdy, Isaac. Hope we'll see you again in the spring." He passed two bills back to David.

"Thank you," Isaac replied.

David found a place to park amid all the other vehicles. He turned the key, and the engine went dead with a rattle. Neither of them said anything for a few moments. Isaac stared up at the screen and monkeys dancing with what looked like joyful polar bears. "I don't hear anything," he blurted.

With a smile, David turned the key one notch and pressed a button. The radio dial lit up, and music filled the truck. As David turned the knob, there was static and bursts of music until the number *94.1* appeared. David twisted another knob, and there were voices. After a moment Isaac realized it was the monkeys on the screen debating whether or not to share something with the bears. He found himself smiling. "Wow."

"Cool, huh? You stay here and watch. I'll get us some snacks."

"No!" The thought of being alone in the truck in his English clothes watching a movie made Isaac queasy. "I'll come with you."

As they walked toward a small rectangular brick building with an illuminated sign that proclaimed it the Snack Bar, Isaac's cheeks burned. Most people were in their cars watching the movie, but he felt certain everyone was staring. That they *knew*. He kept his eyes on the ground.

Inside it smelled deliciously like grease and popcorn, and a youngie girl with her long blonde hair pulled back through a baseball cap grinned.

"Hey, David! Who's this?"

"Jessica, this is Isaac."

Isaac nodded. "How do you do?"

She grinned again. "I do just fine, thank you. What can I get you? David, you want the usual?"

"Of course." David pointed out the menu board to Isaac. "Shorty's Valley Famous BBQ Sandwich. The sauce is amazing. Or you can get a hot dog—or a chilli cheese dog. Or nachos. Jessica, we'll get a large popcorn with extra butter too." He glanced at Isaac. "Pepsi or 7-Up?"

"Pepsi." Isaac's mouth watered. "I haven't had one since I went to Warren the last time."

"Been a while, then?" David perused the chocolate bars in a glass display case in the counter.

"Three years."

"I'd say you're due."

At least eating and drinking English food wasn't explicitly a violation of the Ordnung. They just didn't get much of a chance in Zebulon. "Should I get a hot dog or nachos?"

"Both." David nodded to Jessica, who took tongs and plucked a hot dog from inside a machine that rolled the meat around.

By the time they made their way back to the truck, they had so much food Isaac could barely hold his share. The first movie seemed to have finished, and words scrolled up the screen.

"The people here are nice," Isaac noted. "Do they...do they know where we're from?" He mentally kicked himself for mentioning in front of Jessica that he hadn't had Pepsi in years.

David settled in behind the wheel. "I'm sure they do, but they've never said anything about it."

"You don't think it's dangerous? What if they told someone?"

David snorted. "Who would they tell? It's not like Bishop Yoder's going to come to the movies."

"I suppose not." Isaac pushed up the sleeves of his sweatshirt and eyed the food resting on the dashboard and the seat between them. "I'm not sure where to start."

David unwrapped his sandwich and took a huge bite. "Anywhere," he mumbled.

Laughter bubbled up in Isaac's chest, and before he knew what he was doing, he dragged his finger across David's chin, swiping away the red sauce that dripped there. He brought his finger to his mouth and flicked his tongue out to taste. "Wow. That really is good." He slowly sucked his finger clean, savoring the smoky-sweet flavor. Then he licked his lips.

Staring at Isaac, David swallowed his mouthful with an audible gulp. "Uh-huh." He didn't take another bite, and silence stretched out.

A loud noise made them both jump. The sound rolled in a rhythm, and Isaac stared at the radio. As more instruments joined in, up on the screen a yellow statue spelled out *20th Century Fox*. Isaac and David smiled at each other, chuckling. Isaac picked up his hot dog and settled in, ignoring the voice in his head that screamed of these wicked, worldly deeds.

Two hours later, Isaac rubbed his eyes. His belly was full, and he felt as though he'd hardly blinked. The movie on Mervin's Touch was one thing, but seeing explosions and practically naked women bigger than life on a huge screen was another.

"Did you like it?" David asked. Other cars were pulling away toward the exit across the field, but he didn't turn the key.

"I don't know. I..." Isaac exhaled. "That's a lie. I did like it. It just seems like I shouldn't! All those people dying, even if they were bad. But it was exciting to watch." His fingers were sticky with butter and cheese, and he wiped them with a paper napkin, finishing off his Pepsi with a loud slurp.

"I liked it too." Eyes alight, David whispered, "Your secret's safe with me."

Isaac's skin prickled, and he felt too warm. "I guess we should get back."

With a sigh, David nodded and joined the line of cars inching toward the road. "Sorry—it takes a while to get out of here when it's busy."

"It's okay," Isaac said, finding that even though it was getting late, he really didn't mind at all.

JUNE'S FARMHOUSE WAS dark when they drove up, but the light over the workshop faithfully turned on as David parked the truck near it. Isaac had no idea how it worked, but it was a handy thing, this motion detector. *Lanterns do just fine. Don't go getting carried away after one night in the world.*

Inside, Isaac changed back into his clothes with his gaze resolutely on the floor. After a deep breath, he pulled down the zipper on his borrowed jeans himself. He hopped back into his pants, buttoning the flap over his fly with fast fingers. He didn't bother with the three hooks at the top of his shirt, and shrugged on his jacket over it. He could see David moving in the corner of his eye, but didn't dare look until he was sure David was dressed.

"Oh, before I forget…" David said, his voice muffled.

Isaac turned to find David bent over and peering into the little refrigerator. His black pants stretched tightly over his backside, and Isaac willed himself to look away as a deep ache set his cock and balls tingling. It must have been an after effect of the movie, or perhaps the huge amount of Pepsi he'd drunk. He just had to relieve himself, that was all.

David pulled out a clear bag holding whole fish. He wrapped them in a cloth before dropping them in a black sack and handing it to Isaac. "For your mother. I'll tell mine they weren't biting tonight."

Isaac took the sack, his fingers brushing David's. He steadied his breath. "I need…is there an outhouse here?"

"There's a bathroom in there." David pointed to a door at the rear of the workshop. "But you can go outside if you'd rather."

"I'd better. I think I've done enough sinning for tonight." Now that they were returning home, the earlier euphoria was giving way to reality.

David turned away. "Sure. I'll meet you by the fence."

After he did his business by a tree, Isaac waited where Kaffi was loosely tied, head bowed and munching away. He stroked the horse's flanks. When David arrived, his shoulders were tense, and he didn't look at Isaac as he untethered Kaffi. Behind them, the light on the workshop went out, and they were in darkness but for the moon. Isaac blinked as his eyes adjusted.

"I'm sorry if you regret going tonight." David's words were bitten out.

"David, I don't. At least, I don't think I do." Isaac's heart skipped. "Are you angry with me?"

Head down, David laughed, but it was razor sharp. "No, Isaac. Only with myself."

"Why?" Isaac touched the sleeve of David's coat. "I wanted to come. I'm glad you trusted me."

When he looked up, David's eyes shone with unshed tears. "I was selfish to bring you here. Please forgive me."

"What?" Isaac dropped the sack of fish and stepped closer, rubbing David's arm. He hated to see him upset. "There's nothing to forgive. You said yourself Mervin and I were watching a movie just last week. We're all curious. We're all tempted. The tighter they try to lock us away from the world, the more we wonder. They try to prevent rumspringa, but they can't stop it. Most of the time I feel like I'm drowning in sinful thoughts. A zipper and a movie aren't so bad, really."

A tear slipped down David's cheek, and he took Isaac's head in his hands. "Isaac, if you knew what I really wanted—" He broke off.

Was it possible? David was touching him in a way he never had. Did he mean what Isaac thought he meant? His heart thumped, and the dark desire that secretly hummed through him day and night rose to a crescendo like the music at the start of the movie. "I want it too," Isaac whispered. Oh God, he did. He wanted it. He wanted *this*.

David took a shuddering breath, swiping his thumb across Isaac's bottom lip. Before he could think better of it, Isaac sucked the calloused pad of David's thumb into his mouth. David moaned low in his throat, and a warm puff of air feathered across Isaac's face.

He wasn't exactly sure how it came to be that David's thumb was replaced by David's lips, pressing gently. The world tilted, Isaac's head so light it might float away. He was certain he had to be back in his bed, with his brother's snoring about to wake him from this wonderful dream at any moment.

Because he couldn't possibly be leaning into the solid warmth of David Lantz, feeling David's arms steal around him, their bodies in a tight embrace as they explored each other. He'd never kissed anyone before, and it wasn't possible that he was kissing another boy—a *man*—the scrape of David's late-day stubble exhilarating against his skin.

Isaac couldn't be parting his lips and kissing David more deeply, tasting meat and salt and something sweeter than molasses in the next breath. It was impossible that his hands were roaming over David's back, touching the firm, trembling muscles, wishing there was nothing in between them—that they could rut together flesh on flesh like the animals in the barn.

Impossible! Isaac groaned, his body flowing with something that had to be electricity.

Then he woke, David's warmth ripped away from him with a gasp. Isaac blinked, waiting for the familiar dark shapes of his bedroom to materialize. But there was no chest of drawers or dark clothing hung from pegs on the wall. He was still standing by the fence at June's farm, his breath shallow, and his mouth wet.

David stumbled back. "No. I've done enough. I can't do this to you too." He lurched up the fence and onto Kaffi. "We have to go home. Come on."

Isaac stared up at him, his mind spinning hopelessly. "Wait." He shook his head. "David…"

But David wouldn't look at him. "Isaac, get on. Please." After a moment, he added, "*Please.*"

Once Isaac was on the horse's back, David urged Kaffi onward almost into a gallop, and Isaac bit back a cry as he clutched David's waist. They thundered across June's field into the woods, and as they tore around a group of oaks, Isaac lost his balance, terror twisting through him.

David yanked on the reins, but it was too late. Isaac let go so he wouldn't take David with him as he tumbled to the grass and fallen leaves. The air slammed from his lungs, and he opened his mouth with a silent cry, blinking at the branches arching overhead. A moment later, David's face was above him, eyes bright, lips parted.

"Isaac!" Kneeling beside him, he cupped Isaac's cheek. "I'm sorry. I'm sorry! Are you hurt?"

It took a few moments for Isaac to drag in a breath, and he shook his head. A couple of bruises would likely be the extent of it.

"Are you sure?" David ran his hands over Isaac's limbs, pushing and prodding. "Did you hit your head? I'm so sorry."

"No," Isaac croaked. He took a long, deep breath. "I'm all right. I swear."

"Thank you, Lord." David leaned over him and pressed a kiss to Isaac's forehead. "If you were hurt, I don't know what I'd—" He inhaled sharply. "And it was because of me." He shook his head. "Can you forgive me?"

"Of course." Isaac reached up and brushed back David's hair.

His face was creased with misery. "You should run far away from me, Isaac. I'll drag you down. Lead you to temptation."

Isaac considered his choice—the first he'd truly had in as long as he could remember. It was easy, really. With another deep breath, he tightened his fingers in David's hair and pulled his head down. "I'm already there," he whispered.

This time he didn't hesitate to open his mouth, seeking David's tongue with his own as they came together on the forest floor. He had no idea what to do, but some kind of instinct spurred him on, and he urged David on top of him, spreading his legs and moaning as David rubbed against him. They kissed deeply, gasping for air and exploring every corner of each other's mouths.

The ground was cold with impending frost, but Isaac was alight, consumed with fire from the inside out. "Please, David. I need...I need..." He arched his hips, his cock hard as a rock in his pants. It felt so good, and he was desperate for something he couldn't name.

"Are you sure?" David held himself up on his arms.

He'd traveled the devil's path all night, and he couldn't stop now. Didn't want to stop. Isaac gripped David's rear and yanked him down, grinding up against him. "Yes. *Yes.*"

Groaning, David tugged up Isaac's shirt and stole his hand beneath it, sending tremors through Isaac's belly. The feel of David's long fingers caressing his bare chest and nipples had Isaac bucking up wildly. Everything was taste and sound and sensation, and they panted together in a frenzy.

David kissed Isaac messily as he rubbed against him. "Oh help me. I've wanted this for so long. Wanted to touch you and hear you cry out for me. I can't believe this is real."

"David," Isaac moaned, working his hands beneath David's shirt to grip his sides and feel the muscles flexing there.

"Let me hear you, Isaac."

His cries and calls echoed through the rustling leaves as Isaac gave himself over to the growing fervor within him, the pure bliss licking out through his body like flames spreading through a hayloft. David buried his face in Isaac's neck, his lips soft and wet as he thrust against him.

Isaac wondered what it would be like without their pants on and nothing between them. Gasping, he tangled his hands in David's hair, breathing his name as he reached the edge. When he tipped over the side, it was like falling from Kaffi's back all over again. Yet this time he didn't come down, instead launching above the treetops as if he could touch the stars.

He floated back into himself and held David close, not caring that he'd made a mess of his pants. He could feel David's hard shaft through the material, and he wrapped a leg around David's hip to encourage him. Straining, after another minute David shook and exclaimed something Isaac couldn't understand. He petted David's hair as they caught their breath, tangled together.

This can't be true.

David kissed his neck as he moved up to Isaac's face, pressing pecks to his cheeks, forehead, nose and chin, and to the corners of his eyes. His lips were gentle, and Isaac had never felt so cared for. So special.

"My little *eechel*."

The endearment was nonsense—little acorn—but Isaac's heart swelled. David kissed him again, this time finding his mouth tenderly. Nearby, Kaffi ambled, rustling the foliage as he munched contentedly.

Isaac waited for the horror of what they'd done to reach him—to grip his soul in mortal terror. Yet as they kissed and breathed each other in, sticky and sated with the oaks standing sentinel, Isaac felt only a peace and wholeness he hadn't realized he'd been missing.

That it was a sin, he had no doubt. But it was the sweetest he'd ever known.

Chapter Seven

"JUST WHERE DO you think you're going?"

Heart sinking, Isaac froze by the front door, straw hat poised over his head. He glanced back at Mother in her rocking chair in the main room, Father reading a prayer book in his rocker next to her. Father turned the page, but Mother raised an eyebrow.

"Isaac, you look like you did when I used to catch you sneaking an extra piece of streusel. Don't wander far—we're going visiting at the Lapps' shortly."

"But I promised Mervin and Mark we'd go to the lake." The lie flowed easily.

"Surely that water's far too cold now. You should take your other hat too. Time to put the summer hats away. Don't you think?" she asked Father.

"Mmm," he affirmed, eyes still on his page.

"All right, I'll get my other hat." Isaac's pulse raced. "So can I go?"

Mother eyed him sharply. "What's at the lake? You can't be swimming. More fishing? Didn't you have enough of it last night? Not that you actually caught anything. Seems to be a waste of time."

He'd completely forgotten the sack of fish by June's fence after David kissed him. It was incredible to even think the words—*David kissed me.* The memory of what they'd done should have shamed him, but hungry desire sparked instead. *The sweet wet of David's mouth, his breath hot, rutting together, and—*

Isaac dropped his gaze to the floor and forced his mind blank. "We were just going to play around."

Father cleared his throat. "The Lapps are expecting us all."

He sighed. "Yes, Father." He knew that when Father used that tone, his pronouncements were as carved in stone as the commandments.

Squeezed in the back of the family buggy with his brothers and Katie before long, Isaac winced. His back was sore from where he'd tumbled to the ground, and the bumping of the buggy didn't help. He fiddled with the knife in his pocket and remembered the night before, careful not to let his mind stray too close to what had happened on the forest floor. He was liable to tent his pants.

After he and David—a current pulsed through him just at the thought of David's name—had become too cold in the night air and straightened themselves, they'd remounted Kaffi.

He'd rested his cheek against the stiffness of David's jacket. His arms wound around David's waist, and he'd held on tighter than before, closing his eyes to the dark forest and sure he could drift off right there. The gentle rocking as Kaffi walked home made him like a baby in a cradle. Just to hold David close was bliss.

"Don't fall asleep now," David had teased.

"Mmm." Isaac had opened his eyes.

Reaching back, David had stroked Isaac's thigh. Wonderful warmth flowed from David's hand all through him. They'd continued on in comfortable silence, and still Isaac had waited for the proper disgust for what they'd done to find him. It remained mysteriously absent.

When David's darkened house came into sight, Isaac had roused himself enough to sit up straight and keep a respectable few inches between them on Kaffi's back. In the stable, David had turned the lantern on low, and Isaac led Silver from her stall, dreading the buggy ride home on the dark road. David had fiddled with a curry comb, and they'd stared at each other.

Now it would happen, Isaac had thought. The guilt and accusations. The blame for the sins they'd committed.

But they'd only moved into each other's arms as if they had a hundred times before. Isaac held David close, Silver's reins looped over his wrist. "Thank you," he'd whispered.

David took a deep breath. "I don't want to wake up from this." He'd pulled back and pressed their lips together. "Get away tomorrow if you can. They'll all be visiting. I'll make an excuse. Mother won't question me."

"I'll try." The very notion that there would be a tomorrow for them had made him so happy.

David had drawn his fingertips down Isaac's cheek. "This will be our own little rumspringa. They never have to know."

A tendril of fear unfurled in Isaac as he'd remembered what they were risking, but he'd pushed it away.

"Isaac!"

He blinked back to attention, jostling against Nathan as the buggy lurched over a dip in the road. His siblings watched him. "Huh?" he asked.

"What's up with you today?" Ephraim regarded him suspiciously.

"Nothing!" Isaac willed himself not to blush.

"So?" Katie said, watching him expectantly. "What about David?"

"David?" He felt hot under his felt hat and wished he'd worn the straw even if the wind was whipping today.

She rolled her eyes. "Do you like him?"

"Why would I?" Isaac's heart was like rain beating on the tin roof.

"Is he really good to work for? You're away so much now we hardly talk to you." Ephraim leaned in and lowered his voice. "We just want to know what it's like being off the farm."

"It's...good." Isaac didn't trust himself to say anything else at the moment.

"One day I'm going to be the teacher," Katie pronounced.

Nathan laughed. "No way. You have to help Mother at home until you get married."

Her eyebrows drew together. "It's not fair I'm the only girl left."

Giving her cheek a pat, Isaac smiled at Katie. He kept his voice to a whisper. "You'd be a good teacher."

She beamed with her crooked smile.

There were cakes and pies and happy greetings at the Lapps', but Isaac quickly stole away to the paddock beyond the barn. Clouds hung heavy, and soon enough he'd see his breath in the air. He glanced back and realized Father and Joseph followed. It seemed he wouldn't have any peace this day. If he couldn't be with David, then he wanted to be alone so he could remember every moment they'd shared.

Mr. Lapp greeted him by the fence, watching two horses circle each other. Isaac could see right away it was a stallion and a mare. He could also see the stallion's engorged cock. It shouldn't have sent a shiver deep within him, but his blood stirred. Now that he'd experienced that kind of sin with David, he itched for it.

Father frowned. "Isn't it late in the season for mating?"

Mr. Lapp nodded. "That it is, but we need another foal. We'll try, at least."

Father and Joseph took up places by the fence. They all watched in silence, and Father stroked his graying beard. He wore his thick jacket, and it stretched over his belly. Mother would have to make him another soon. With each year Father seemed to grow outward despite the hours of work he did.

Amid a flurry of whinnies and grunts, the stallion mounted the mare. Isaac's breath came shallowly, and he was surely touched by the devil given the thoughts polluting his mind. It was dangerous, and he wished he could escape to some privacy and relieve the growing pressure.

What would it be like to have David behind him, taking control of him—possessing him? Throat dry, he dug his fingers into the weathered wood of the fence. As surely as the mare was in heat, so was Isaac.

He could imagine himself on his hands and knees, offering himself up. He'd cry out and tremble, and take every inch of David. He remembered the heavy thickness of David's cock through their pants, and imagined the heat of it inside him like a poker, branding him and—

"Is that sodomy?" Joseph asked.

Isaac almost swallowed his tongue, and coughed roughly. Mr. Lapp slapped him on the back unhelpfully.

At eight, Joseph's face was still round with baby fat, and his hat almost seemed too big for him. He peered up at Father from beneath the brim. "Eli Hooley said sodomy's a sin. I didn't know what it was, and he said it's what horses do."

Awkward silence stretched out before Father finally spoke, his words measured and sure. "Horses are free of sin. This is their natural way. It is as God intended."

Joseph watched the stallion finish and stagger off the mare's back. "But for people it's a sin?"

"Yes."

Isaac's mind knew the truth of it, but in his soul he couldn't deny his desire. Bishop Yoder had rarely touched upon the abomination of men lying with men. It seemed to be taken as a given that it was blasphemous, and not something the preachers felt needed repeating. It was the modern, unclean ways of the English with their technology and pride that the preachers railed against.

Father and Joseph drifted away with Mr. Lapp, but Isaac was rooted to his spot by the fence. How could he daydream about entering into an abomination so willingly? With such anticipation and *joy* in him? He should take joy in his family, and the Lord. In his work, and one day in his wife and children.

His stomach soured. For years he'd wondered at his lack of interest in Mary or any other girl. If he'd known this seed of sin was growing in him, waiting to bloom, perhaps he could have cut it down. Salted the earth so it would never grow again.

Had he known deep down? He wasn't sure. But knowing and admitting were sometimes as far apart as Zebulon and New York City.

"Isaac! Come and eat something," Mrs. Lapp called.

"I'll be right there!" He forced his hands to unclench from the fence. The grooves of the wood had made red marks on his palms.

Last night David had been eager to see him again, tender with his kisses and goodbye. But what if in the gray light of this Sunday, he'd realized they were being crazy? That it was far too dangerous.

Putting one foot after the other, Isaac rejoined the others. The next morning could not come soon enough, and until it did, he could only wonder.

DREAD WAS HIS companion as Isaac urged Silver faster along the road. The sun wasn't up and he would be early, but he had to know. Rain pelted the buggy, spraying him from the front and dripping through the roof, rolling off his heavy hat. He shivered and called to Silver to go faster, flicking the reins over her back.

Lanterns glowed from the Lantz house in the gloom, and Mary opened the door to wave as he arrived. Isaac jerked his hand in reply, continuing on to the stable. It was too miserable for Silver to stay outside, and he quickly unharnessed her and pushed the barn door open. In lamplight, David already stood by his worktable, pencil in hand. He wore no hat, and stared at Isaac uncertainly.

Silver neighed, shaking herself, and Isaac tore his eyes away from David to bring her to a stall. As he settled her and gave her an apple core from a bucket to munch on, he heard the barn door closing, the rain now muffled. When Isaac turned, David was back by the table. He leaned over a large sheet of paper.

"You should hang up your hat and coat to dry." His tone was flat.

Isaac was all thumbs, awkward and unsteady as he dropped his coat on the dusty floor. He shook it out and hung it beside his hat, hay and dirt still stuck to it. He was afraid to look at David, and the air felt like molasses. *I should have known he'd come to his senses.* Isaac swiped at his coat, hands trembling.

"Isaac... I'm sorry."

In that moment, Isaac could have dropped to his knees and wept like a child. He couldn't force any words past his too-thick tongue. He sucked in a breath, staring at the hay scattered by his boots.

"I should never have taken you to June's or the drive-in. And I should never have..." David choked off. "I've never been able to talk to anyone the way I can with you. I feel like you understand me. But I let myself get carried away. I pray for forgiveness."

"From who?" Isaac curled his fingers into fists, struck with the urge to break something. He spun around. "From God? Or from me?"

David bowed his head. "From you both."

"Well, I don't. I won't ever *forgive* you. Not for something I wanted. Something I'll hold in my heart, even if you would pray it away."

David's head shot up, his eyes wide. "But I thought...when you didn't come yesterday..."

"My parents wouldn't let me. We visited with the Lapps, and I had to go. I wanted to come here more than anything."

"Truly?" David whispered. He was around the table before Isaac could blink. Tentatively, he reached for Isaac's hand. "You aren't sorry?"

Isaac exhaled shakily and squeezed David's fingers. "I know I should be. But I'm not."

They clutched each other, mouths open and tongues pressing to-gether. Isaac stumbled back against the wall and held David to him, groaning softly. He was soaring, and he thought of the distant trains, and how fast he and David had flown over the roads in June's truck. It was as if he had a roaring engine within him now.

The barn door jumped open with a creak and a gust of wind, rain slanting in. David stumbled away, wiping his mouth, chest heaving. They both stared at the opening, but no one walked through. The wind howled, and the door jumped again. Isaac exhaled and thumped his head back against the wall.

With a shaky smile, David closed the door, sliding across the heavy wooden bolt.

"Won't they wonder if they come out to bring food?" Isaac ran a hand through his hair. His bangs were damp, and he brushed them away.

David was already tugging Isaac's hand and leading him into an empty stall off the passageway. "If they come out in this weather, I'll tell them the door wouldn't stay closed. It's the truth."

Of course David wouldn't be telling his mother or sisters the other truth—that he was dropping to his knees in the clumps of hay and unfastening the buttons on Isaac's pants. It smelled like dirt and sweat and animals, and Isaac was hard already. He breathed deeply as he leaned back against the wooden slats, watching with lips parted, his body humming. "What are you...?"

David lowered the flap on Isaac's fly and glanced up with gleaming eyes. Then he unfastened the galluses and tugged Isaac's pants down to his knees. Reverently, he traced his fingertips along Isaac's length. It was the first time anyone had touched Isaac there, and he bit his lip, trembling at the sparks of sensation.

Leaning in, David licked his lips. "Do you want me to stop?"

Isaac was completely exposed, and goose bumps spread over his thighs as his cock twitched, David's hot breath ghosting across it. A memory of Mervin, Mark, and the other boys talking about a dirty magazine one of them had bought in Warren sprang to Isaac's mind. They'd crowed about the things the women had done with their mouths.

Isaac swallowed hard, blood rushing to his cock. "Don't stop." He caressed David's dark hair. "Please."

His eyes still locked with Isaac's, David leaned even closer. Then he wrapped his lips around the head of the shaft and sucked. Isaac's knees almost buckled, and he slapped his hand over his mouth at the incredible pleasure shooting through him. He thrust his hips helplessly.

Lips curving into a brief smile, David's eyes sparkled as he licked up and down, and all around.

"Oh my. It feels so good." Isaac pressed his lips together. He finally understood why fornication was such a popular sin.

A string of spit hung between Isaac's cock and David's mouth as David pulled off. "Tell me. I want to hear it." He traced the throbbing vein that ran along the underside of Isaac's shaft with his tongue. "Do you like this?" he whispered.

Isaac nodded so hard he was in danger of giving himself a concussion as he knocked his head back against the wall.

"Tell me." David explored Isaac's heavy balls, his fingers stealing back to rub at the sensitive skin behind them.

Gasping, Isaac flattened a palm on the wooden slats behind him. He could barely talk. "It feels so good. Your mouth—your tongue. Hot and wet. So much better than my own hand."

David sucked him hard, slurping as his lips stretched around Isaac's cock. It was so dirty and wrong, and Isaac never wanted it to end. To touch someone with your mouth that way should be disgusting, but he couldn't wait to taste David.

When David pulled off, he slid down Isaac's foreskin and licked the pearly drops from the head. Isaac's lungs stuttered. He peered through the slats of the stall to make sure they were still alone, even though the door was bolted. But he couldn't keep his eyes from returning to David, and David's red, glistening mouth.

David's breath puffed over Isaac's straining, sensitive cock. "Do you touch yourself often?"

"Sometimes. I hardly ever get to be alone."

"What do you think about?" David ran his fingertips over Isaac's shaking thighs.

"Trains. Going far away. Rattling over the rails so, so fast."

Smiling, David pressed a kiss to Isaac's hip. "I'm going to take you on a train. We're going to hide away, and when the train is going so fast you can hardly stand it, I'm going to kiss you, and touch you all over. I'm going to make you come so hard."

Isaac remembered the first time he'd heard the term—*come*. One of the other boys had said it when they were looking at the secret magazine, and Isaac had wondered what it really meant.

But with David he'd discovered the meaning. It was to come utterly undone, to be pulled inside-out with pleasure so hot he was surprised it didn't burn his flesh. The words croaked from his lips. "Will you mount me like a stallion?"

Shuddering, David clutched Isaac's hips and took him into his mouth again, going deeper now, his head moving back and forth as he sucked hard. The rush overtook Isaac, and he couldn't stop his cry as he shook and spilled, head tipped back and stars behind his eyes.

His knees gave way, and he slid down. The hay was scratchy on his backside on the cold floor, and his pants were around his ankles. He reached for David, who wiped a thick string of Isaac's seed from his mouth as he sat back on his heels. David's fly bulged, and Isaac tore open the buttons.

"You don't have to…" David could barely get the words out.

Isaac tugged him closer. "I want to make you come too."

David groaned, his eyes fluttering shut. His cock throbbed in Isaac's hand, and Isaac stroked him, reveling in the feeling of it. He bent over to get his lips around it, the need to taste overpowering. He wasn't sure if he was doing it right, but he had to try. The angle was awkward, and his exposed rear was freezing, but all that mattered was the feel of David in his mouth, the musky scent of him filling Isaac's nose.

He sucked and choked, taking in as much as he could, desperate to have David inside him. David whimpered softly, stroking Isaac's head. The sensation of David's cock filling his mouth felt so right. Groaning, he took in as much as he could before gagging and pulling off. Eyes watering, he plunged back down until the nest of rough dark hair at the base of David's cock tickled his nose.

"Easy, easy." David rubbed Isaac's back.

But he didn't want to go easy. He sucked harder, and reached behind to rub the place David had, and roll David's balls in his hand.

"Isaac!" David tried to push him away.

Resolutely, Isaac kept sucking, sputtering as the first salty drops filled his mouth. It dripped out as he kept sucking and licking, and he swallowed as much as he could, not stopping until David cupped his cheek and urged him up for a messy kiss. It tasted of them both, and renewed desire curled through him.

Panting, they broke apart and rested their foreheads together. "I was so afraid you'd turn me away today." The words rushed out of Isaac breathlessly. "That you'd be the one who was sorry."

David drew him up so Isaac straddled his lap. He buried his face in Isaac's neck and gripped him tightly. "No matter what happens, Eechel, I'll never be sorry."

Wrapping his arms around David and breathing him in, Isaac shoved away the thoughts of what might well happen, and simply held on.

Chapter Eight

"ENJOYING THIS INDIAN Summer? So late in the season too—it's practically November."

Isaac looked up as Mrs. Lantz walked into the barn with a fresh jug of water. He put down his saw and wiped his brow, his black hat hanging by the door. David wasn't wearing his either, and Isaac had joked earlier that they should work shirtless. Of course that had led to lustful glances and stumbling recklessly into one of the stalls.

"I am, ma'am. Supposed to be getting awfully cold soon according to Abram Raber. Says he feels it coming in the knee his horse stepped on all those years ago."

"Abram's knee is never wrong." Mrs. Lantz wiped her damp hands on her black apron with a smile. "David, I've left lunch for you boys in the kitchen. I'm going to see to Emma Lapp. Her brother rode over early this morning to tell me it's her time."

"I thought I heard a buggy," David said, eyes still on his planing.

"Her time for what?" Isaac asked.

Anna appeared in the doorway, rolling her eyes. "She's having a baby, dummy."

Anna wore a black cap over her wheat-colored hair, which meant she was going out with her mother. Isaac's heartbeat picked up. Was Mary going as well?

"Haven't you noticed how fat she's gotten?"

David and Isaac glanced at each other and shrugged. Isaac said,

"Honestly, I didn't even know my mother was expecting Nathan until he showed up in his cradle one morning."

"It's so strange how no one talks about it, especially in front of the little ones." Anna shook her head. "Why is it such a secret? We all find out eventually."

"*Anna.*" Mrs. Lantz smiled tightly at Isaac.

"But isn't it all how God created it?" she asked.

Mary appeared behind her, the sunlight framing her head above her black cap. "How God created what?"

"Nothing!" Mrs. Lantz waved her daughters out of the barn. "We're off now, David. We'll return by the time the girls are back from school."

"You're all going?" David asked.

Anticipation uncoiled in Isaac's belly, his groin tightening as he gripped the saw. He and David would be alone. For two weeks they'd stolen every moment they could, but with the harvest, Isaac had spent every spare waking hour helping Father or their neighbors.

Anna rolled her eyes again. "Apparently Mary and I have things to learn."

Mrs. Lantz clapped her hands together. "That's enough."

"Yes, Mother." Anna dropped her head and scurried from the barn.

Mary waved to Isaac. "Have a good day."

Once they were gone, Isaac tried to catch David's eye, but David was bent to his work again. Isaac's excitement faded. Perhaps David was satisfied with their furtive moments in the dark corners of the barn, pleasuring each other in a rush with hands and mouths. He flushed as he thought about how close they'd come to discovery the day before.

"David?" Mary called out uncertainly.

On his knees, Isaac froze, his mouth full with David's thick cock. He met David's wide eyes. They were in a horse stall back near the shower, and distantly Isaac could hear Mary's light footsteps.

"I'll be right there!" David responded, his voice strung with tension. His fingers were tight in Isaac's hair. "Hold on!"

"We need your help," she called. "The laundry wringer's stuck." A pause.

"David?"

David cleared his throat. "Yes! Go back to the washhouse. I'll only be a minute."

"All right." Her footsteps receded.

Saliva dribbling from his mouth, Isaac needed to swallow, and he started sucking again. He knew he should stop, but he fondled David's balls, and a moment later was swallowing his salty release as David shook with little gasps. Once Isaac had licked him clean, he tucked David back into his pants and buttoned his fly. David hauled him to his feet and kissed him deeply.

"You later," David whispered.

Shuddering at the memory, Isaac went to the side table and poured himself a cup of water. It was refreshingly cool, and he closed his eyes. He needed to get control of himself. He was like a dog in heat. When he glanced up, David was still intent on his work. *Which is as it should be!* Isaac picked up his saw again. He was being stupid.

Yet being near David and keeping their distance made him ache. One of the things he'd grown to crave was the easy affection David showed him, and that he was able to show back. He couldn't remember ever seeing his parents so much as brush their shoulders together or touch hands. Forget kissing or hugging.

He'd wondered from time to time if it was different when his parents and other married adults were alone. Because being in the same room with David and not being able to run his palm over David's back, or press a kiss to his neck, or feel the warmth of his breath, made Isaac ache. But David seemed glued to his work. *Which is as it should be.*

After a few minutes, David went to the barn door and disappeared outside. Isaac sawed through another beam with even more force. Then David was back, grinning.

"They're gone."

Grasping for him, David backed Isaac away from the sawhorse, kissing him frantically. "Finally alone," he muttered between kisses, his tongue surging into Isaac's mouth. "I need you." His hands roamed.

Sighing at David's touch, Isaac had to laugh at his foolish misgivings. "I thought maybe you were tired of me already."

Brow furrowed, David leaned back and held Isaac's face in his hands. "Not even a little bit, Eechel. I want you so much. I think about it day and night. It's torture having you near, but not near enough."

Moaning, Isaac yanked David closer, tugging at his shirt. He traced his fingers over David's lips. "I want to kiss you all the time."

"Me too." David licked into Isaac's mouth. "Kissing has never been like this."

Going stiff, Isaac jerked away. "Who else have you kissed?"

David chuckled. "Jealous? Only two girls. Naomi Miller once, and Fannie a few times. It never felt like this. Like kissing you."

"And you haven't...not with any other boys?" For some reason, Isaac hoped the answer was no.

David shook his head. "I never dared. I never thought..." He pressed their foreheads together, his breath warm. "Never thought I'd meet someone like me. Not just *like* me, but...you're so much more than I ever dreamed. I want to kiss you forever."

Before he could stop himself, Isaac whispered in David's ear, his hand tight on David's hip. "I want to taste your cock again. And more."

His pale eyes darkening, David's nostrils flared. "Oh Isaac. You have no idea the things I want to do to you."

Isaac captured David's hand. One by one, he sucked David's fingers and kissed the callused pads. "I love your hands. I love the things you can do with them. To wood. To me."

David surged closer, pressing Isaac back against the edge of the table. He cupped Isaac's cheek. "Do you want...we could..." He swallowed thickly.

Isaac pressed a kiss to David's rough palm. The verboten English word felt dangerous on his tongue. "Fuck me."

They kissed deeply, hands roaming everywhere. Their galluses were stubborn, and Isaac was sure he would actually ignite into flames before they could get their clothes off, and he could feel David completely naked against him.

He licked the sweat from David's neck, salt and sawdust mingling together. "I need to feel you."

Panting, David stepped back. "Yes. I…" He shoved hair off his forehead. "Stay there. Let me just…"

Almost running, David closed the barn door and slid across the long beam. Then he rooted around near the horse stalls and returned to the table with a dark blanket and a small tin. He spread the blanket over the table while Isaac watched, his body vibrating as his mind whirled with hope and fear. David stood before him again, and the table edge jutted against Isaac's lower back.

"This is sodomy," Isaac blurted.

Lips parted, David nodded.

"Will it make us unforgivable?"

David ran his hands up Isaac's sides, his breathing slowing. He made sure Isaac met his gaze. "We don't have to do anything else if you don't want to."

Isaac took a deep breath. "But I do. I want it so much."

"So do I." David kissed him softly. "Touching you feels right. It feels…beautiful. It makes me so happy, Isaac. If it's a sin, then I'll gladly call myself a sinner."

Isaac stroked David's back, his eyes closed. "Sinners both," he whispered. He kissed David slowly, their tongues coming together.

With infinite care, David undid Isaac's galluses, and the hooks and eyes fastening the top of his dark shirt. He pressed his lips to the hollow of Isaac's throat, and then urged Isaac to lift his arms. With his shirt tossed aside, a shiver danced over his bare skin as David stared with wonder, tracing his fingers over the sandy hair sprinkled on Isaac's chest.

"Up." He pulled on Isaac's hips.

Isaac boosted himself onto the table and spread his legs as David stepped between them. David circled one nipple with his tongue, and then the other. Gasping, Isaac was eager to touch David, but David caught hold of his wrists, holding them down.

Bit by bit, as though he was discovering something wonderful, David explored Isaac's body. He kissed the moles that dotted Isaac's shoulders, dragging his tongue between them. He caressed the hair on Isaac's arms, and ran his fingertips up and down Isaac's spine while his eyes drank him in. He sucked on Isaac's nipples until Isaac was sure he would spend in his pants, his hard cock pressing against his fly.

Never had Isaac felt more worthy. He knew it was proud and vain, but David made him feel like such a thing of beauty. It was as though David could see straight to his heart—to the very soul of him. He ran his hands over David's head, holding him close where David kissed Isaac's belly, his faint stubble scratching the pale skin there.

"Please, David."

Nodding, David went to work on the buttons pinning the flap over Isaac's bulging fly. Isaac lifted his hips so David could peel down his pants, and he watched David's dark head at his feet. When his boots and socks were gone, and Isaac was utterly naked, he had to squeeze the base of his shaft and breathe deeply. There was something about David still being fully dressed, wearing his plain clothes and looking so *Amish* that made Isaac throb.

But he needed to see David's body, and he tugged at his clothes, trying to help and likely hindering until David stood naked between Isaac's thighs, their cocks bumping together. "Aren't your feet cold?" Isaac blurted.

He smiled. "Indian Summer."

Isaac drew him closer, wrapping his legs around David's hips and touching him everywhere he could reach. David was a bit broader than Isaac, and Isaac loved the strong, sinewy feeling of his lean muscles. Loved that he could actually touch David like this. The reminder that he *shouldn't* touch David or anyone like this returned, and he pushed it aside.

"It feels so good." Isaac teased the hair on David's chest and dragged his hands over his round backside as David bucked his hips against him.

"I want to be inside you," David muttered.

Moaning, Isaac jerked his head in a nod. "Please. I don't know how.

Do we...should I turn over?"

David pressed their lips together. "I shall take great pleasure in bending you over the worktable in the future, but today I want to see your face."

"But...how?" Isaac's mind was blank. Everything he knew about sex he'd learned from watching the farm animals or from the glimpses of that tattered magazine with his friends years ago. Those pictures had featured women and men, and he didn't know how it worked with only men.

"I have a confession." David smiled wickedly. "One night after the drive-in, I stopped at a gas station and bought a dirty magazine. It showed all kinds of things. Had stories that described...everything." He pressed gently on Isaac's shoulders and eased him onto his back, pulling his hips to the edge of the table. He caressed Isaac's cheeks. "Your ass is so beautiful."

Another verboten word, and it only made Isaac's blood hotter. He looked at the rafters and the edge of the hayloft above, seeing the barn from a new angle. Then David leaned over him, filling Isaac's vision and kissing him.

"Like this?" Isaac asked.

"That's it." David lifted Isaac's legs and pressed a kiss to each knee before he parted them wide.

Splayed and utterly wanton, Isaac's cock leaked, flushed and straining against his belly. He should have felt ashamed or at least embarrassed, but he didn't. He felt powerful. Wanted. *Alive.*

"This should help." David opened the tin of saddle grease and dipped his fingers inside.

Isaac's breath came fast as he watched David press a slick fingertip to his hole. "I don't know if it'll fit."

Leaning over on his other hand, David kissed him gently. "It'll fit. I promise. I'll go slow."

He kissed Isaac lightly as he teased with his finger, prodding and retreating with just the tip until he was stretching Isaac open with a whole finger inside. Isaac grunted, not sure if it was pleasure or pain radiating out. He wouldn't have thought it was possible, but as he relaxed the muscles inside, bit by bit he took another finger.

"Look at you opening up for me. You're amazing, Isaac." David licked his lips. "You're so good."

Isaac squeezed around David's fingers, bearing down and taking him deeper.

David groaned. "You'll be the death of me, Isaac Byler."

Inch by inch, David stretched him patiently until Isaac thought he would explode. "Enough. You now." Isaac lifted his hips. "*Please.*"

"I don't want to hurt you." David moved his fingers inside Isaac.

"I don't care if you do. You won't—please, David."

With care, David removed his fingers and slathered more grease over his rigid cock. He dragged Isaac's hips past the side of the table and leaned over him, spreading his legs even wider. Isaac's knees bent toward his own shoulders, and he concentrated on breathing. *This is actually happening.* Kaffi and another horse snorted and stamped in their stalls, and Isaac imagined it was the pounding of his heart.

"That's it," David murmured, pressing the head of his cock against Isaac's hole and gripping his hips. "Good. So good, my Isaac."

The fire threatening to consume him converged on his ass, the burning bringing tears to Isaac's eyes as David pushed inside. David's thick cock felt impossibly huge, and Isaac cried out. It was too much—he couldn't do it.

"Isaac?" David froze, his muscles trembling, fingers digging into Isaac's hips.

He gulped, willing his body to relax. "Don't stop. Just do it." Isaac was suddenly frantic, the need to have David filling him was like the need for air deep in the lake with the surface far above. "Do it." He grabbed at David's waist.

With a thrust of his hips, David surged in deeper. Sweat dampened his hair as he froze again. "Okay?"

The burning was too much. Isaac couldn't stretch any further—he was going to break. His cock softened, and panic flapped in his chest. He closed his eyes, forcing his lungs to expand. He wasn't going to stop now—he wanted more, searching for the place where the need in him would be filled. He'd come this far, and he wanted all of it.

Panting, Isaac pulled his knees up higher. "Fuck me, David."

Grunting, his eyes impossibly dark, David did as he asked.

He pushed in, going all the way now, reaching deep inside Isaac. It hurt so much, but Isaac took every thrust with joy. David was *inside him.* He hadn't known he could feel like this. Like he'd been born for it. Like he finally understood what living was.

Their skin was slick, slapping together as they jerked and muttered, reaching, reaching, reaching. There was no turning back, and the burn faded as Isaac let go. David rubbed against something inside him that made Isaac's thighs quake as he cried out.

"That's it, Isaac." David leaned over and kissed him, their teeth clashing. He hit the spot again. And again.

And again.

Isaac became aware that the cries echoing through the barn were his own, and he watched a stray bird flap around the beams of the ceiling. He was bent almost in half, his body buzzing as if it flowed with electricity. He rocked with David's thrusts, and his cock leaked. He reached for it in a daze.

But David knocked his hand away. His hips didn't falter as he stroked Isaac's shaft. Isaac stared into his eyes until David hit that secret place deep inside him, and Isaac tipped his head back, mouth open as he spurted. A long strand hit the bottom of his chin, and the pleasure crashed over him again and again until he could only shake and jerk with fading pulses.

David was still huge and hard within him, and Isaac squeezed around him. He opened his eyes. "Don't stop."

To think that David was so excited by *him*—that David was *inside him*—still seemed like a dream. He watched as David thrust unsteadily, trembling and panting now. He was so close to the edge, his face and chest flushed, sweat gleaming on his skin.

"Fill me up," Isaac whispered.

With a gasp, David closed his eyes, jerking as he came. Isaac could feel it hot and wet deep inside him, and he reached out, caressing David's hair and shoulders as David shuddered through his release. David bent over him, his hands gentle under Isaac's ass as he caressed him. He pressed his face to Isaac's neck, still inside him.

"My Isaac," he murmured, pressing kisses to Isaac's damp skin. "You were better than I could have imagined." He licked a stripe under Isaac's chin, cleaning him.

"Your cock feels much bigger than it looks." Isaac was in a daze, and he felt that if David wasn't holding him down, he would float up into the rafters.

David's laughter tickled Isaac's throat. "I'm not sure if that's a compliment or not."

"It is, my David. I've never felt so good. Thank you."

David's smile faded as he straightened up, and gently removed himself from Isaac's ass. He frowned. "Are you sure I didn't hurt you?" He ghosted his fingers over Isaac's slick hole.

"I imagine I'll wish we had cushions on our chairs tonight. But don't look like that. It was what I wanted. You're what I want."

Eyes still on Isaac's hole, David asked, "Can you feel it inside you?" He lifted his fingers, sticky with his own seed where it dripped from Isaac's ass.

"Yes, I can feel it. Can still feel you."

"I want you to come inside me next time." David raised his head, his eyes bright as he climbed onto the table.

They shifted and shimmied until they were both laid flat out, and David rolled on top of Isaac and kissed him with a quiet desperation. "I want you to fuck me, and then we'll both be so deep inside each other, no one will ever be able to tear us apart."

"Yes, my David." Isaac whispered.

Yes, yes, yes.

"Did you hurt yourself, Isaac?"

He glanced up from his porridge to find Mother watching him closely. "No, I'm fine."

"You winced when you sat down," Katie added.

Now with all the eyes of his family on him, Isaac tried to act normal and laugh it off. His foot jiggled. "It's nothing. I just fell on my rear end. But it was my fault. I dropped some nails and slipped on them, which was stupid."

He was close to rambling, so he scooped up another spoonful of porridge. Cinnamon and brown sugar filled his mouth, and he chewed slowly. His explanation seemed to satisfy everyone, and Nathan chattered about school.

The tenderness was a potent reminder of what he and David had shared the day before. It was as though he could still feel David deep within him, and his body hummed at the thought. He couldn't wait until they could sneak off to do it again. To do *everything*.

They'd kissed and touched, entwined on the worktable until their cocks were hard once more. David had rolled over onto his stomach for him, offering himself up so prettily, holding his cheeks open so Isaac could get inside. He thought he would release just at the sight, let alone the sweet heat as he inched inside and covered David's body with his own.

It had felt like nothing else Isaac had experienced. It was similar to the wet suction of David's mouth, but the knowledge that he was inside the core of David's body had made it even more special. The feel of David's hole grasping around him had sent shivers from Isaac's balls to the top of his head.

When he imagined now how they must have looked—sprawled out on the table, locked together and naked, sweating and grunting like animals—Isaac had to shift uncomfortably on the wooden bench. A voice inside reminded him how gravely he'd sinned, but Isaac couldn't seem to care. If he was going to hell, it would be worth it.

"Isaac?"

He blinked. "Hmm?" All eyes were on him again. "Sorry, my mind's somewhere else today."

"We were just wondering how you're getting on with Mary. You see her every day now." Father's tone was deceptively mild.

"Mary? Uh, fine. She's a very nice girl." Isaac felt his cheeks burn.

"Ohhh, he likes her," Joseph teased.

If you only knew. "I like her fine. That's all."

"You should drive her home from the singing on Sunday night." Mother smiled. "I'm sure you'd both like that."

Isaac shrugged. "Maybe."

Mother sighed. "Honestly, I don't know what you're waiting for! Some other boy will snatch her up if you're not careful. Don't make her wait too long. We all know she has her heart set on you."

Isaac put down his spoon, the porridge suddenly tasting like paste. "I don't think that's true."

Everyone—even Father—scoffed amiably.

Pushing around his porridge with his spoon as Mother blessedly changed the subject to Martha Yoder's new recipe for apple-berry pie, Isaac tried not to think of Mary and her hopeful smile. Before long he'd have to drive some girl home from church to at least keep up appearances. He didn't want to lead Mary on, though. Not when he was sinning with her brother, and never wanted to stop.

But I will have to stop.

Isaac reached into his pocket and clutched his knife. He carried it with him every day from habit, but hadn't whittled anything in weeks. It was as though his waking hours were so consumed with David that he had no room for anything else. Even when David was teaching him about carpentry, half the time Isaac stared at his mouth and hands, barely concentrating on what David was saying.

He didn't know what was wrong with him. Even sitting at the breakfast table with his family, he was consumed with need. What would he do when he and David ended it?

He thought of Aaron out in the unclean world. Over and over they had learned that a plain life was the only way to heaven. The preachers never said it outright, but it was the foundation of the Ordnung and the church's teachings. The world was a web of temptation that would trap them, leading them from God's path and drowning them in sin. Yet when he imagined being with David, Isaac's mind flew high and free, so close to heaven he could feel its splendor on his skin.

He grabbed his cup of water and choked it down. Isaac knew that to stay in Zebulon with his family he'd have to join the church. Get married. Have children. David was already joining the church. He'd be a member by the end of January at the latest. They hardly had any time at all. It wouldn't be enough. It would never be enough.

"Isaac?" Mother pressed the back of her hand to his head. "You look positively feverish."

With a scrape, he shoved back his side of the bench and sprang up from the kitchen table. "Don't worry. I'm fine. I need to get going. See you tonight!"

As promised, the weather had turned suddenly cool again, and frost covered the pasture like a fine web. The sun was barely up, but Isaac sped down the road in the buggy, hoping he wouldn't meet any other traffic. He needed to talk to David. They needed to talk about what would happen. How long could they keep going with their secret coupling before they were caught? If only it didn't have to be secret.

His mind spun back to yesterday's lunch. They'd cleaned themselves thoroughly when they were finally sated, and went to the house to eat the lunch Mrs. Lantz had left. Sitting at the kitchen table, they'd eaten in easy silence, smiling at each other and talking of nothing important.

Isaac could almost imagine it was their house, and that they'd have lunch like that every day with no one to see if they happened to steal a kiss between bites or rub their knees together under the table. He knew it was a future they could never have. How would they reconcile what they'd shared with living proper plain lives?

But when he arrived at the Lantz's and hurried to the barn, David smiled that secret smile, his eyes alight. All of Isaac's questions withered away. He didn't want to talk about it now—there would be plenty of time for that later.

With a glance behind, he kissed David. Yes, it could wait.

Chapter Nine

"WHY DO I have to be *Nava Hocca*?" Mervin grumbled. "It's going to be so *boring*."

Isaac unharnessed Silver and gave her a pat. "You know it's an honor to be one of the witnesses."

Mervin straightened his black hat, squinting up at the early morning sun peeking through the clouds. "Yes, but we have to be with them *all day*. I told Ruth I'd make a much better table waiter for her wedding. That way I'd only have to stay for an hour of the ceremony before I got to set up for lunch."

Isaac waved to some of the Lapps as they drove up in their buggy. His family had already dispersed, Father talking intently with some other men, the boys off in clumps with their friends, and Katie and Mother with the women inside. "I bet your mother and sisters have been cleaning all week."

"Try since the minute Ruth and Atlee were published, and the deacon announced their engagement last Sunday. My aunts too. Not just cleaning, but cooking enough to feed Zebulon three times over, I reckon. Mother's determined to make sure no one's whispering about the food, at least."

Isaac frowned. "There does seem to be a lot of whispering. Your sister and Atlee haven't even been going steady that long, have they?"

"Haven't you heard? You must be the only one who hasn't." Mervin leaned in and raised his pale reddish eyebrows. "The thing is, they can't wait."

"Why not?"

With a tilt of his head, Mervin gave Isaac a meaningful look. "Why do you think?"

"Oh! You mean they…Ruth's…" Isaac wasn't sure why he was so surprised, considering the things he'd been doing. At least he and David couldn't get pregnant. "What did Bishop Yoder say?"

"Well, you can imagine. But they asked for forgiveness, and they're doing their penance. The bishop said he might have them shunned for a month, but I guess he decided it was better to get them married sooner rather than later." Mervin shrugged. "There's nothing else to be done now. I think Mother's put all her shock and disappointment into cleaning. We could eat off the floor in the barn, never mind the house. She's barely slept in days."

Isaac nodded to the makeshift tent built on the side of the house covering the long tables, themselves draped with white cloths to protect the place settings. "It looks nice." He grinned. "And her fried chicken is the best in Zebulon."

"Hi, Isaac!" Mary called.

Isaac turned and gave her a wave, his gaze automatically going to David behind her. He watched David help his mother down from the buggy while his other sisters piled out. When Mary followed his gaze, Isaac wheeled back around.

"So." Mervin grinned. "Are you going to ask her to the table tonight for the feast and singing?"

"Uh…I dunno." *No.*

Mervin huffed. "Isaac, what are you waiting for?"

"Nothing! I just hadn't thought about it. Things have been so busy."

"David's really working you hard, huh?"

Isaac ducked his head and swiped at invisible lint on his broadcloth pants, trying to block out the fragments of memory that took over his mind. "I guess."

He was on all fours on the floor in the workshop at June's, a cushion under his knees and electric light bright all around. So exposed. A thrill shot up his spine. "Are you sure she won't come out here again?"

"The house is dark. She's asleep." David spread Isaac's ass open, pressing his cock to Isaac's hole. "Do you want to stop?"

Moaning helplessly, he shook his head. "Don't stop. I want…"

David leaned over him, pushing inside, exhales hot on Isaac's neck. "Tell me what you want."

"I want you to fuck me forever." Bold English words.

Thrusting in deep, David gasped. "Yes, my Isaac. Yes."

Mervin laughed. "I swear, Isaac, it's like you don't want to get a girlfriend at all."

Isaac's laugh was too loud. "Of course I do. Are you asking Sadie?"

"You bet!" His face brightened. "Weddings don't count as dates, so we get an extra one."

"Mervin!" His mother called sharply. "It's almost eight. Time to go to John's."

He sighed. "Guess I'll see you later." He turned toward his older brother's house, which stood some few hundred yards away.

There was so much cooking and work for the women to prepare the two large meals of the day that it would be too much to also hold the ceremony in Mervin's parents' house. Fortunately John and his wife lived close at hand.

"Think it's too late to volunteer as a table waiter?" Isaac called as Mervin left.

Mervin laughed. "Sorry, no getting out of the service early for you either." He loped away.

Isaac's gaze immediately returned to where David unhitched Nessie, the horse that pulled his family's buggy. Their eyes met, and David nodded, a smile playing on his lips. Isaac nodded back, trying not to smile and failing miserably. Only a few hours to go if they were lucky. He turned, and his heart skipped a beat.

Deacon Stoltzfus stared at him from outside the house, and it was as though his gaze seared right through Isaac, seeing his darkest secrets. Isaac dropped his head, pretending he hadn't noticed as he hurried to the front door. He didn't glance up as he passed the deacon, but he could still feel fire on his skin long after the ceremony began.

LUCK WAS NOT on their side.

The initial service went four hours as the preachers expounded on Adam and Eve and the Great Flood, slowly making their way through the end of the Old Testament as was the custom for wedding sermons.

By the time Bishop Yoder asked Atlee and Ruth to stand before him if they still felt as they had earlier that morning, Isaac was barely awake. Mervin and the three other attendants—in Zebulon it was two boys and two girls—stood as witnesses as Ruth and Atlee said their vows. Ruth wore a crisply ironed dark blue dress, while Atlee was in his church best.

Bishop Yoder brought Ruth and Atlee's hands together and declared them man and wife. Isaac thought of how the English exchange rings. Too vain for the Amish, but he didn't see why they couldn't wear plain bands. Of course their commitment to each other and God was what really mattered, he reminded himself. A commitment he and David would never be allowed.

Ruth and Atlee silently returned to their seats a married couple, and Isaac hoped desperately the service would end so he could bring feeling back to his rear end, which had gone numb on the hard wooden bench. His lower back twinged from sitting up straight for so many hours.

It was a Thursday, the typical eleven days after what they called being published—the engagement announcement by the deacon. While it was nice to have an unexpected day off from work, the service was interminable. Isaac needed to stretch.

And he needed to be alone with David.

He said a quick prayer of thanks as Bishop Yoder ended the service, and tried to slip through the crowd as they made their way back to the main house for lunch. Isaac caught sight of David ahead, also walking quickly. If they both made it for the first seating, the sooner they could slip away.

After quiet grace, Isaac managed to sit across from David at one of the long men's tables, and kept his eyes on his plate for fear that everyone would see there wasn't something right between them. The table was dotted with bowls of fruit and vases of celery stalks. One of the bowls sat in front of Isaac, and he plucked out an apple and rolled it from one hand to the other.

Mervin's younger brother was one of the table waiters, and he poured water into Isaac's cup, one of Mervin's sisters following with a huge bowl of salad. Each dish was brought around and loaded onto their plates. The fried chicken really was the best Isaac had ever had, and he couldn't resist licking his fingers after cleaning off a thigh bone.

Beneath the table, David pressed his foot hard against Isaac's. Isaac glanced up to find David's eyes dark with lust. With a small smile, Isaac rubbed his calf against David's, wondering how far up between his legs he dared go.

"Isaac!"

He yanked his foot back, dropping his fork with a clatter. All eyes at the table were on him, and he realized Mary was standing behind him. She held a heaping platter of stuffing, and dropped her hand to his shoulder.

"I didn't mean to startle you. Do you want some?" She motioned to the platter.

He nodded jerkily, glancing at David, who was suddenly very interested in his lunch. "Thank you."

"Of course." Mary smiled. "You're coming to the feast tonight, right?"

Naturally he was—everyone would be there. "Uh-huh." He picked up his cup and gulped. "Thanks for the stuffing." He smiled up at her.

She smiled faintly back. "You're welcome." She glanced at David, who was still engrossed in his chicken. "Well, see you later then."

As Mary continued down the table, spooning stuffing with her lips trembling, Isaac hated himself. His appetite gone, he pushed his mashed potatoes around, not looking anywhere near David.

"Isaac," Mark hissed from a few seats down. A frown creased his brow beneath his dark blond hair. "Why didn't you ask Mary to sit with you at dinner?" He looked to David. "You don't mind, do you?"

For a moment, Isaac and David's eyes met, and Isaac's heart clenched at the sorrow he saw.

David dropped his gaze. "I don't know. Mary's still young."

The men around them murmured, and old Jacob Glick—Beanie, he was usually called, although Isaac wasn't sure why since he didn't grow beans—cleared his throat.

"Isn't your Mary eighteen now? Quite old enough to date." He gave Isaac an assessing look. "Isaac's a hard worker, isn't he?"

"Yes." David shoved a forkful of salad into his mouth.

Beanie stroked his beard in the same way Isaac's father did. "He would make a good brother for you. You need another man in the family."

Isaac actually bit his tongue. He wanted to scream that he would never be David's brother.

"Isaac, when are you joining the church? Isn't it time?" Jacob asked.

He could sense the gaze of every man in earshot. Eyes on his plate, Isaac mumbled, "Soon."

Mark shrugged. "I really don't know what you're waiting for, Isaac."

Their lunch companions blessedly began discussing the recent harvest and how Zebulon would fare for winter. Isaac tuned them out. He was sorely tempted to stretch out his leg again and nudge David below the table, but kept his feet tucked under his bench as he spooned bite after bite of the generous slice of iced apple cake placed in front of him. He barely tasted it.

Mervin appeared and scooped up a dollop of icing from Isaac's plate. He sucked his finger with a groan. "I'm starving, but Mother says everyone else has to eat first."

"Tell us, did your sister step over the broom?" Beanie asked.

Eyes alight, Mervin grinned. "She did! I can't believe it. Guess she was too excited to remember."

"Poor Atlee, married to a wife too lazy to pick up a broom!" Mark guffawed.

It was one of the oldest wedding tricks, to place a broom on the floor just inside the door for when the newlyweds return to the house. Isaac could hardly believe Ruth hadn't noticed it there or tried to come in the back door the way he remembered his sister Abigail doing at her wedding.

As Isaac thought back, he realized with a jolt that he couldn't remember what Abigail looked like. She was just an idea, really. An approximation of the sister he'd barely known before she married and moved out. Yet Aaron's face was etched indelibly into his memory still—pale hair and the gentle cleft in his chin. Isaac said a quick prayer that he'd never forget his brother.

Mervin was called away, and Isaac got up a minute later, making sure not to even glance David's way. There were many men waiting for their turn to eat, including Ephraim, who grabbed Isaac's elbow as Isaac hurried by.

"Are you going to the barn?" Ephraim asked.

"Uh-huh. Of course," Isaac lied.

"I don't want to go sing with the men. Why do we have to sing anyway? I hate singing."

"You're plenty keen to go to the singings on Sundays."

Ephraim huffed. "Well, yeah. There are girls there."

Isaac smirked. "Would you rather go help with the dishes once lunch is done? The men need something to do. It's tradition."

"It's a stupid tradition," Ephraim grumbled.

Isaac agreed, and he had no intention of going near the barn. He drew his coat in tight against a knife of cold wind as he slipped away beyond the house. It wasn't far over a rolling hill to the trees, and when

Isaac glanced back, he couldn't see anyone watching.

It didn't take long to get there, and he navigated the tangle of roots and scrub easily, the path still familiar even though it had been a few years. He knew he was close when he saw the next pasture appear through the thinning trees. He made his way to the edge of the forest and looked up with a smile. The old ladder creaked, but he clambered up easily.

It was more of a tree loft than a house, with no roof other than gnarled branches and a canopy of green in the warmer months. On his knees, Isaac brushed away the dead leaves, damp must filling his nose. The pale wood was rotting in places, and wouldn't last many more winters. Mervin's younger siblings had apparently outgrown the tree house now, and the varnish had worn away. There were three short walls, with the fourth open to the view of the pasture.

But even better than that—a view of the tracks that slashed across the countryside.

Isaac took off his hat even though the wind that ruffled his hair was cold. He tucked his knees up and imagined how strong the wind would be on the back of a train. How many miles did the metal stretch? Up into Canada for certain, and perhaps as far as Mexico. So far beyond Zebulon's borders. Past Ohio, which seemed so distant now, as if there were mountains and oceans between them instead of corn and wheat.

Tearing himself away, Isaac stood up and peered over the back of the tree house, squinting through the branches. He hoped David wouldn't get lost. Perhaps he'd been caught trying to slip away, and was forced to join the other men in song. *Maybe he doesn't want to see me right now.*

Isaac pulled out his pocketknife and tossed it from hand to hand, eyeing the walls of the tree house. Reaching out, he traced his fingertips over the faded letters carved into one of the boards.

Property of Mervin Miller and Isaac Byler—NO TRESPASSING ALLOWED

Closing his eyes, Isaac could hear the cicadas buzzing and feel the sweat that had dripped into his eyes as he nailed in the final board. Mervin's face had been flushed, his reddish hair gone almost totally blond that summer—their first in Zebulon. When the train had approached, they'd stopped everything and watched it rumble by.

Shivering, Isaac got to his feet. After a few minutes of pacing, the boards creaking beneath him, he heard twigs snapping and leaves crunching. "Hello?" *Please be David. Please be David.* Not that it seemed likely anyone else would venture this far afield from the wedding festivities. He remembered Deacon Stoltzfus watching him, and shuddered.

"It's only me," David called.

Isaac realized his voice had wavered, and he took a few long breaths as David climbed the ladder. When David reached the top, he tossed his hat to the corner where Isaac's sat. He ran his palm over one of the walls.

"You built this."

"Mervin helped. It was a long time ago."

David smiled softly. "I can tell it's your work."

"How?" Isaac wanted to reach out across the few feet between them and hold David close, but he wasn't sure if he should.

"The evenness of the boards. The way the corners fit so neatly." He caressed the top of the nearest wall. "I can just tell. You built it with love."

Love. The word echoed in Isaac's mind, his belly flip-flopping.

David blew out a long breath and met Isaac's gaze. "Mary's upset."

"I'm sorry." Isaac's shoulders slumped. "Was I wrong? Should I have asked her to dinner? I don't want her to think that there's something…that she and I could ever…" He shook his head. "I don't want to hurt her." The knowledge that he would one day have to marry a woman, whether it was Mary or someone else, constricted his chest.

"I know. I don't want her to be hurt." David ran a hand through his hair. "I know we should stop this. We'll only hurt all the people we love."

Isaac couldn't breathe. He faced the brown pasture. *No. No, no, no.*

Then David was right behind him, arms wrapping around Isaac so tightly. "But I can't stop. I can't be without you, my Isaac."

Inhaling sharply, Isaac spun and buried his face in David's neck, murmuring against his skin. "We can't stop. Not yet. We will when we have to—but not yet."

"Not yet," David agreed.

For a long while, they clung to each other. The dry leaves blew around their feet, and they were utterly, wonderfully alone. Isaac kissed David's throat and tugged on his hand, pulling him down to the floor of the tree house so they could face the open meadow. They sat on the edge, feet dangling, fingers entwined.

"I could sit here for hours, even after Mervin got bored and went home." Isaac watched the dying grass of the meadow wave in the wind. "I knew if I waited long enough, another train would come."

"Have you ever taken one?"

"No. We took a bus from Ohio. Have you?"

David shook his head. "I suppose people can't ride the trains we get up here anyway. All freight cars."

"I read a book once about a boy who rode the rails, hopping up onto the cars when the trains slowed. He had a dog, and they went on all sorts of adventures." Isaac smiled ruefully. "Father took it away. Said it wasn't the kind of book good Amish boys read. I don't even know where I got it. Aaron, probably. The first time I saw a train here, I could almost imagine I spotted that boy and his dog on their way somewhere wonderful."

David stroked the back of Isaac's hand idly with his thumb as he stared into the distance. "My mother found a book in my room yesterday when she was cleaning. I suppose I didn't hide it. I was surprised she said a word at all. Since Father died, she hasn't argued with me about anything. It was actually nice to be scolded."

"I can't imagine having my own room." Isaac sighed wistfully. "My own bed. It must be wonderful."

"Mmm." David looked over with a gleam. "I wish you could share it with me. At night I close my eyes and imagine you there with me, safe and warm under the quilt. Oh the things we'd do in that bed."

Isaac tingled, pressing his thigh against David's. "I want to be in a proper bed with you so much. It would be such a treat. Not just…being together. But just to sleep with you. Be close to you."

David brushed his lips against Isaac's. They were soft, and slightly chapped at the edges, and Isaac licked across them. As they kissed lightly, the leaden knowledge that they'd never share a bed as a husband and wife could blotted out everything else in Isaac's mind.

"What?" Their hands were still joined, and David squeezed as he pulled back.

There was no sense in discussing the inescapable truth. Isaac felt unbearably heavy at the thought—especially here in the tree house, a place of dreams. He put on an exaggerated frown. "You don't snore, do you? Because I've put up with Nathan's nightly thunder for as long as I can, and I'm afraid I can't take more of it."

"I don't think I do. Joshua never mentioned it. But perhaps *you* snore." It was David's turn to frown, although his eyes danced. "That would be very disruptive."

"But you'd put up with it for me." Isaac let go of David's hand and tickled him lightly. "Say you would."

"Yes, yes." David squirmed and batted Isaac's hand away. "I'd put up with anything to be with you."

In the flap of a bird's wings the sadness returned, and Isaac was desperate to think of anything else but their impossible future. "Which book?"

"Huh?"

Isaac swung his feet, watching his black boots appear and disappear. "The book your mother found in your room."

"Oh. It was written by President Obama. She said I shouldn't read such worldly things. That politics and Washington were no concern of ours." He sighed. "That's true enough. We don't vote after all. Honestly I didn't really understand a lot of it. We barely learned more in school than how to be obedient."

"I can't even remember the last time I read an actual book. All we have are religious stories, or the Bible itself, of course. We don't even get *Family Life* anymore. Somehow an Amish magazine about Christian living and proper ways to discipline your children is too modern."

David snorted. "Yes, too modern for my mother too. She loved it when we lived in Red Hills, but if Bishop Yoder doesn't like something, she wouldn't dare."

"Where did you get the book? The one by the president."

"June. She always gives me books she thinks I'll like after she's read them. I can give you some if you're interested. I just don't want you to get into trouble." He shook his head. "God forbid we *learn* something. That's the last thing Zebulon wants. The last thing any Amish community wants. Or else we'd actually be able to go to high school."

Isaac pondered it. "But there's so much work to do on the farms. If we went to high school, who would do it?"

David picked up a fallen twig and tossed it over the side. "I know, that's part of it. But the bigger reason they don't want us to go to high school is because they know the more we learn, the more we'll question. The more we question and explore, the more children they'll lose to the world."

"I've never thought about it that way. I guess I've never thought about it much at all." He shrugged. "It's just the way it's always been. Is that strange? That I never questioned leaving school after eighth grade?"

"No. But it's not too late to question now. It's never too late. I feel like all I have are questions these days."

"Like what?" Isaac asked, shivering where David absently stroked his thigh with long fingers.

David's pale eyes were intense. "If the modern world is so evil, why did God create it? If God made the Earth and people in a week, didn't he plan all of this too? If we go back to when Jesus was born, the world was completely different. It grew and changed in so many ways. But for us, it's like everything stopped in the eighteen hundreds. *Why?* What changed that made all the inventions and advancements after that sinful and wrong? Why are we stuck in the past, Isaac?"

"I don't know."

Licking his lips, David sat up straighter, his voice louder. "And every community has its own Ordnung. We think we're better Amish than the Old Order, who look down on us for being too primitive. Then we all look down on Mennonites, let alone the English. But didn't God create us equally?"

"I don't know," Isaac repeated. He felt hopelessly out of his depth. Why hadn't he ever thought about this?

David sighed. "I'm sorry. I don't mean to yell at you. It's just that the more I consider it, the less it all makes sense. At least in Red Hills we were prosperous. We were never rich, but men could work in the factories if they didn't want to farm. We did so much more business with the English. In Zebulon some families are practically starving. If I didn't sell extra furniture with June, I don't know how I'd feed my mother and sisters. But they say if we stay working at home we can make as much money as we can make, and that's all we need. It's up to God." He rubbed his face. "But sometimes it feels like it'll never be enough, no matter how hard I try. I know that's wrong to say, but…"

"I know what you mean. In Ohio we had a lot more money. We had a generator and refrigerators in the barn for the milk. Father hired his own truck to deliver to the English. We used to pay a driver all the time to go to town. In Zebulon we hardly ever have any folks visiting from out of town. Not even for a wedding like today. In Red Hills we were Amish, but the world seemed a lot bigger."

A vein throbbed by David's temple. "Bishop Yoder's convinced everyone that if a family doesn't live in Zebulon, they're a bad influence. Not proper Amish. Not the best kind of Amish." He huffed out a laugh. "Pride and vanity are so sinful, yet somehow it's okay to think ourselves better Amish than other communities."

Isaac stared at the metal tracks in the distance, his mind a jumble. "I never thought about it that way—that modern things are God's creation too. There's so much out there I don't even know about. Do you think..." He hesitated.

"What?" David took Isaac's hand and squeezed gently.

He took a deep breath. "Do you think your brother would have left the way mine did?"

David's small smile was sorrowful. "I don't know. Maybe. Joshua was a lot of talk. He was running wild, but I never thought anything would come of it. Not really. I thought he'd sow his oats and settle in like most do. Join the church and marry. Do what we're all supposed to do. I thought once he was baptized that would be the end of it."

"It isn't always. Aaron followed church. I remember how strange it was, to see him with a beard. It didn't get very long before he was gone. Isn't it weird that I barely remember how he looked near the end? When I think of him, it's with a clean face, when he was so quick to smile. After he joined the church, it was like...everything that had been light about him was heavy."

David's grip on Isaac's hand was fierce. "I keep praying that I'll find the answer. That once I'm baptized, God will give me peace. That everything will fit together the way it's supposed to, and I'll see clearly."

Isaac tugged his hand free as foolish hurt struck low in his gut. He whispered, "We fit together, don't we?"

"Yes!" David wrapped an arm around Isaac, kissing him hard. "We do. I know this is supposed to be wrong, but it doesn't feel wrong. Does it?" He cupped Isaac's cheek.

Shaking his head, Isaac leaned into David's touch, those calloused fingers somehow so soft on his face. "It feels so right, David. I think about what it would be like to live with you instead of a wife. To share a bed every night, and work side by side each day. I know it's a terrible sin, but the thought of it makes my heart so glad." He sucked in a breath, trying in vain to stop tears from forming. "I want to be with you forever."

Swallowing thickly, David brushed back Isaac's hair, despair written in the creases on his face. "I don't know what to do. I'm trapped here—I can't leave my family alone. Yet when I'm with you, I feel...*hope*. Peace. The peace I want so badly. I've wanted it for so long, Isaac."

They came together in a tangle amid the dirt and stray leaves on the tree house floor as they crawled back from the edge. David clung to him, desperation in his kisses. Isaac wanted him as always, the craving like a hole inside him that could never be filled. But they only kissed, holding onto each other tightly until they trembled, gasping for breath.

Heads close, their eyes met. Isaac plucked a dead leaf from David's hair and brushed their lips together. Their breath mingled. "I don't know what to do, my David. I pray the Lord will show us the way."

"I pray too." David pressed kisses to Isaac's face.

Burrowing close, Isaac rested his cheek to David's chest. The wind rustled the straggling leaves left on the tree above, and he closed his eyes, listening to the thump of David's heart as it slowed. After a time, he became aware of a low rumble. His eyes popped open and he bolted up. "A train!"

A smile played on David's lips. "Yes." He caressed Isaac's hair and sat beside him. "I wish I could take a picture of your face right now."

Chuckling, Isaac ducked his head. "It's childish, I know. To be so excited by something like that."

"Not childish." David tipped up Isaac's chin with his finger. "Beautiful." He kissed him as his hand made quick work on the flap of Isaac's pants. "Watch your train."

Isaac did, peering into the distance for the first glimpse of that thundering metal as David's mouth found his cock. Leaning back on one hand for fear he would collapse otherwise, Isaac held David's head with the other, weaving his fingers into David's thick, soft hair as sweet pleasure filled him.

Isaac's moans filled the air, and a winter bird squawked nearby—one of the few that didn't escape south, trapped in Zebulon too. As the engine chugged into sight, Isaac arched his hips, crying out. With the wet suction of David's mouth sending forbidden electricity through him, Isaac watched the rusty red freight cars trundle along on their unknowable journey. The train's whistle pierced the afternoon, and he gasped, his balls tightening before he came in a rush.

David swallowed each drop, drawing Isaac's release from deep within as the train rolled on endlessly.

Chapter Ten

"Do you think there are other Amish who are…" Isaac paused, trying to think of how to put it. Just thinking the word *sodomites* made him queasy.

David glanced up from the table leg he was finishing. "Gay?"

Frowning, Isaac gave the nail he was driving into a plank another whack with a hammer. "What do you mean?"

"It's what the English call it."

Isaac took off his gloves for a moment, blowing on his hands and rubbing them together. December had slinked in wet and gray, with a cold that burrowed deeply in the drafty barn. "Why?"

"I don't know." David smiled. "When I started going to the movies last year, one of the first ones I saw was about a bunch of couples who were having babies. They all took a class together and became friends. There were two men, and that's what they called it."

Gay. Isaac rolled the word around in his mind. "Sounds kind of nice."

David's eyes lit up, and he came around the worktable to Isaac's side. "That's the great thing—it wasn't an insult. It wasn't negative. Everyone else in the movie was friends with them, and no one cared that they were together. No one thought it was bad."

"Is that what it's like in the world?" Isaac's stomach somersaulted. Was it possible?

"In some places. No one in the movie minded. They acted like it was just…normal."

"But wait, you said they were all having babies."

"The gay couple had what they call a surrogate. English women who will have a baby for someone else."

Isaac's mind spun. "But…she just gave them the baby?"

"Uh-huh. They paid her. English people do it all the time, I guess. It wasn't out of the ordinary to anyone in the movie."

"It doesn't seem right to me." Isaac picked up a nail from the table and rolled it between his fingers. "What do you think?"

"I don't know. In the movie, the woman giving up her baby said it made her happy to help a new family begin. At the end, the men were so happy too. They never thought they could be fathers."

Isaac had assumed his entire life that he'd be one, even though he'd never given it much thought at all. While he could never imagine a future with Mary or another wife, for a moment his mind was filled with pictures of him and David in ten years, children around them, their playful shrieks like music in the air. "If we were English, we could…"

"What?" David asked, standing up straighter.

"Nothing." Isaac rubbed his face, banishing the ridiculous thought. "But if being…" He tried out the word. "If being *gay* is a sin, then God wouldn't want us raising children."

"No, I suppose not." David leaned back against the table. "Although sometimes I wonder about it all." He picked up one of his discarded gloves and fiddled with it. "Seems to me that what constitutes sin changes a lot depending on who you're talking to. Maybe it's all just words on a page. The Ordnung changes from town to town, after all."

"But the Bible says it's wrong." The nail dug into Isaac's palm as he squeezed it.

David sighed. "I know. When I try to make sense of things, I always end up there. But isn't the Bible only more words?"

"Holy words, though!" Isaac sputtered. "We know everything in the Bible is true."

"Do we? It was written by men, wasn't it? If it's all true, then why don't men sell their daughters into slavery anymore? It's in the Bible. So is being able to buy slaves as long as they're foreigners."

Isaac blinked. "I never thought about it."

"Neither did I. But lately I feel like…I don't know." He traced a groove in the table with his finger. "I have so many questions." He snorted. "I wonder if I should ask the preachers the next time we go to the Obrote."

The reminder that David would soon be baptized made Isaac's gut tighten. "But you believe in God, don't you?" It was something he would never have conceived to ask in the past. To think that someone might not believe seemed impossible. Yet now, as the questions stacked up, he wasn't as sure.

"I do. Of course I do. Sometimes I'm just not sure I believe in men. But once I follow church…" He swallowed hard. "Once I give my vow, I'm sure it will all make sense."

"You don't sound sure."

"I will be. It's the way it has to be." David's smile had sharp edges. "We're Amish. We have to believe."

"What else did you see in the movie?"

David's face brightened. "The gay couple was like all the others. Even when they held hands and kissed each other. The other people didn't even look twice."

"They *kissed?* You saw them?" Despite the temperature, Isaac was suddenly warm from the inside.

David nodded vigorously. "They were even in bed together without their shirts on," he whispered. "I couldn't believe what I was seeing."

"They showed that in the *movie?*" Isaac thought of the Sky-Vu's enormous screen. "In front of all those people?"

"And no one seemed bothered at all! I could see into some of the other cars around me, and they were just watching like it was nothing. Meanwhile I was…" David flushed.

"What?" Isaac edged closer, dropping the nail on the table. Only a few inches separated them. "Did you like it?"

David licked his lips, his gaze flickering to Isaac's mouth. "Yes. I'd seen men and women kissing, and more—you wouldn't believe some of the things they show in movies. There was one where they were practically naked. It was shocking to see, and exciting, but when I saw two men together..." He smiled faintly. "First I wanted to cry. I couldn't breathe. It was the first time I knew that there really were people like me out there. I'd thought there must be, but to see it like that..."

Isaac's heart skipped. "I can't imagine. It must have been amazing."

"It was!" He grasped Isaac's hand. "To know I wasn't alone. And then to see them actually kissing." He shivered.

Isaac bit his lip. "Did it make you hard?" He flushed as the bold words left his mouth.

Eyes dark, David nodded. "It was like...something snapped into place. The way a perfect drawer closes just right. I thought I would crawl right out of my skin. My jeans were so tight it was painful."

Isaac's spine tingled. "What did you do?" His gaze flicked down, and he gathered his courage. "Did you touch yourself?" He leaned in so his lips were at David's ear. "Did you make yourself come right there?" Maybe if they were quick, they could go into one of the stalls, and—

"Daaavid! Isaaaac!"

They jerked apart as Anna's singsong voice rang out distantly. Isaac grabbed the closest nail and hammered it into the wood as David dashed back to his table leg.

When Anna clomped into the barn with a bang on the partially open door, she smiled and went straight for the side table. "We thought you might want some more coffee to warm you up. I made zucchini bread to go along with it."

David cleared his throat. "Thanks, Anna."

Isaac kept his gaze on his work. "Thank you."

"Sure," Anna said. "Having a good day?"

When Isaac looked up, she was watching him with a little smile. "Um...uh-huh."

"Glad to hear it." Then she swept out of the barn, her heavy cape billowing behind her.

Exhaling loudly, Isaac unclenched the hammer handle. "I guess that's enough talk for today. We should just...work."

"Yes. Work." David lowered his head and snatched up his measuring tape.

Isaac lined up another nail, wishing he could silence the questions tumbling through his mind. Yet with each swing of his hammer, a new word echoed.

Gay.

"THEY'RE GONE." DAVID hauled the barn door shut behind him, snow swirling by his boots.

Isaac had barely done a lick of work since Mrs. Lantz had mentioned at lunch that there was another baby being born, this time at one of the Hooley farms. Isaac couldn't remember which one, but it didn't matter. What mattered was that he and David would have the farm to themselves for the first time in more than a month.

He opened his arms for David. "Come warm me up."

David's mouth was hot, and the slick slide of his tongue sent a fever through Isaac's veins. Smiling between kisses, they shrugged out of their coats, tossing them on the worktable. Isaac sucked on David's neck, loving how David shuddered when he found just the right spot.

"It's been too long, my Isaac." David moaned softly. "I've missed you."

"Me too."

"Mmm." David licked Isaac's neck. "I told you to come to June's with me more often."

Chuckling, Isaac squeezed his hand into the front of David's pants and stroked him. "If I went with you every time you'd never get any furniture finished, and my parents would ask too many questions."

Each day—acid gnawing on his stomach and his nails bitten to the quick—Isaac had waited for everyone to see right through him. Yet as the weeks passed, his family and the people of Zebulon went about their business, and Isaac's secret life miraculously remained his own.

"I want you, Isaac." David groaned, arching into Isaac's touch.

"How?" he asked, barely more than a breath.

"Shower." David tugged Isaac's hand out of his pants and pulled him along. "I want you wet."

Isaac dug in his heels. "It's too cold!" He laughed as David reached out to tickle his stomach and get him moving again. "You're crazy."

"I lit the lantern in the loft to heat the water a little while ago." By the shower stall, David pressed him up against the wall. It was dark in that corner of the barn, hidden from the world. "I've dreamed about this. Having you here. Properly, I mean." He pressed a kiss to Isaac's throat, then unhooked his shirt, punctuating each word with another kiss. "Naked. Wet. Begging."

Isaac let himself moan as loud as he wanted. "Yes. *Yes.*" He tore at David's clothes.

The floor was freezing, and they hopped around once they were naked. Isaac shoved at David playfully. "Hurry, hurry. Make it warm."

And oh, as the water flowed down, it wasn't just warm, but wonderfully hot. They stood beneath the barrel's pipe in each other's arms, and Isaac thought he could be happy just staying like that, kissing and soaping each other in the steam that rose around them. Now that the initial reservoir was gone, as more water melted above it streamed over them, sometimes a mere trickle. In that moment, how he envied anyone with indoor plumbing. *When I have a real shower again I'll stay in it for hours.*

Isaac jolted, breaking their kiss. His pulse ran wild.

Frowning, David caressed his cheek. "What is it?"

"Nothing." Isaac shook his head as if he could dislodge the traitorous thought. Despite everything he and David were doing, they wouldn't leave Zebulon and their families. Isaac could never really leave. *Could I?* He kissed David hard, thrusting his tongue deeply.

With firm hands, David spun Isaac to face the side of the wooden stall. "Spread your arms and lean," he commanded, stroking Isaac's spine. "Yes. Like that." His fingers dipped into the cleft of Isaac's ass. "I want to kiss you all over," he whispered, lips hot against Isaac's neck. "Taste you everywhere."

A thrill sang through Isaac, and before his brain could cut through the haze of lust to understand what was happening, David's breath was much lower, whispering over his skin. His lips brushed the mole on the small of Isaac's back. Then he moved down.

Isaac craned his neck for a glimpse of David on his knees behind him, shock and euphoria combining at what he thought David might dare to do. *He wasn't going to...was he?* With infinite tenderness, David spread Isaac's cheeks and kissed his hole, which quivered at the brush of lips. Gasping, Isaac could hardly believe it.

Then all tenderness was lost, and David licked and teased Isaac's ass, spitting into it, his tongue following, pushing inside. The sparks that ricocheted through Isaac's body stiffened his cock and had him trembling. It was so wrong—and he never wanted it to stop.

"David," he gasped. "Oh God." A voice flickered through his head, reminding him not to take the Lord's name in vain, but he couldn't stop. "God, that feels... I'm going to come so hard, David."

He whimpered, closing his eyes as the world narrowed down completely to the sensation of David's tongue licking and fucking him. Isaac's cock leaked, and he hadn't even touched it. He hung his head, arms spread wide as he moaned. Amid the dampness of the shower stall, the usual smells of the barn mingled—hay and sawdust, and horses and the earth.

Isaac felt like beneath it all—the veneer of church and family, community and the Ordnung—he was little more than an animal himself, rutting and sucking and being truly alive in his body with no regard for right or wrong.

As he came undone, his cries surely had to be heard for miles. Panting, Isaac watched as he spurted over the wet wood while David never let up, still working his ass until Isaac had to beg for mercy. Then David was standing behind him, breath harsh as he nudged Isaac's legs closed and pushed between his thighs, grunting. David's hips jerked haphazardly, his fingers dipping into Isaac's hips.

"Isaac," he muttered.

Isaac squeezed his legs around David's shaft, and that was all it took for David to come. It dripped down Isaac's thighs, and David was heavy against his back. He clumsily petted Isaac's wet hair, and Isaac shifted around in his arms so they could kiss again.

He could taste what must have been himself on David's tongue. Perhaps it should have disgusted him, but it only made him feel closer to David, who nuzzled Isaac's cheeks softly.

"I love that you have freckles even in the winter," he murmured. "You're so beautiful."

"Am I really?" Isaac knew it was wrong to care about how he looked and feel such pride and pleasure in David's words, but his heart soared.

"Oh yes." David traced the contours of Isaac's face with his fingertips. "Your eyes are like nothing I've seen before. The color of amber—like something shiny and beautiful, but solid all the same. I wish you could see what I see, Eechel." He kissed Isaac softly.

Blushing, Isaac ducked his head. "Your eyes are like the ocean. Or maybe not. I don't know, paler I guess? But they're what I imagine the ocean could be like." He glanced up. "I love looking at you. When was the last time you saw yourself?"

A smile flitted across David's mouth. "The other day. There's a mirror in the toilet in my workshop at June's. You can look too. You don't have to be afraid."

He hadn't even dared to use the indoor toilet yet the few more times he'd accompanied David to June's. "Next time." It shouldn't have sent a thrill up his spine, but it did. Another of the Ordnung's rules to be broken.

They kissed again, but they were both shivering. David glanced up at the trickle of water. "Guess we should get dry and do some work. Hiring an apprentice was supposed to make me work faster, but I'm falling behind on everything." He slapped Isaac's hip playfully. "You're a terrible influence, Isaac Byler. Corrupting me like this."

Laughing, Isaac tickled David's ribs. "Oh yes, I know. However will you forgive me?"

They were still laughing and giving each other little kisses when they made their way back to the main area of the barn. Isaac patted David's backside. "Next time I get to—"

He inhaled sharply, frozen in his tracks as he blinked at Mervin by the worktable. Pale face flaming, his mouth a straight line, Mervin dropped his gaze to the floor.

"I heard noises, and I thought...I thought something was wrong."

Isaac could see David in his peripheral vision, equally stunned, his eyes wide. He didn't even seem to be breathing. "But the door was locked," Isaac blurted. Of course it wasn't now, standing partly open, snow drifting inside.

"It wasn't." Mervin's voice was gruff.

As if being loosed from a spool of thread, the last however many minutes flowed through Isaac's mind. David closing the door—but not sliding across the long bolt, already kissing Isaac and tugging him to the shower. Not that it mattered now, since Mervin was standing in front of them, arms stiff at his sides. "I..." Isaac tried to think of a single thing to say to his best friend.

There was an envelope on the worktable, and Mervin picked it up before slapping it back down. "For my sister's crib. Father sent me to pick it up."

David jerked his head in a nod.

The finished crib stood nearby, unvarnished wood sturdy and neat, all utilitarian straight lines, where David's secret creations for the English were often curved and smooth. Mervin picked up one end of it, but even with his stocky strength, he couldn't carry it properly. Isaac rushed to the other side and lifted it.

Mervin met his gaze, his expression full of hurt and confusion. With a grunt, he looked away and backed up, carrying the crib outside while Isaac followed with his end. He glanced back at David, who swallowed hard, his lips parted as he breathed shallowly. The terror in his eyes made Isaac want to run to him and hold him close.

Outside, Mervin shuffled backwards through the snow impossibly fast, and Isaac struggled to keep up, his arms aching as he hefted the awkward shape of the crib. They loaded it onto the back of Mervin's buggy on its side, and Mervin threw a blanket over it. He had one foot up to climb into the seat when Isaac reached out.

Snatching his arm away, Mervin stumbled back. "Don't."

"Please. Just listen to me." Isaac's throat was painfully dry. He licked his lips. "Please."

Arms wide, Mervin waited. "All right. I'm listening. What could you possibly say?"

An excellent question. "I…I know how it must look…me and David."

"It looks like sin," Mervin spat, his face thunderous. "It sounded disgusting. I can't believe that was you in there."

The shame roiled his stomach. "I know it's hard to understand."

"Hard? *Hard?* It's impossible, Isaac!" Tears shone in Mervin's eyes. "You're my best friend! I thought I knew you. Sure, it's been different lately. We've had so much more responsibility, and we haven't hung out the way we did at school. But I never thought…" His face twisted. "How could you do that? It's against everything! God, and the Bible, and…nature!"

All Isaac could do now was tell the truth. "It's natural to me. I know that sounds crazy, but it is. I never understood what you and Mark and the others saw in girls. I'm not like you."

"Obviously." Mervin swiped at his eyes furiously. "It's the worst kind of sin, Isaac. You *know* that!" He glanced at the barn and lowered his voice, eyes imploring. "Did he make you do it? He's older, and he's your boss. Did he pressure you? There's always been something off about him—just like his brother! He talked you into it, didn't he?"

For a terribly black moment, Isaac could see the possibility of getting off the hook. The possibility of not losing his best friend.

Mervin went on in a rush. "It's not your fault, Isaac. If you tell Bishop Yoder—"

"No! Stop." Isaac shook his head, the selfish moment of temptation burning his cheeks. "You heard me in there. Did it sound like he was making me? Everything we've done has been both of us. I know you think it's bad, but...we're just different, Mervin. God made us different."

"*God?* You dare say God had anything to do with *that?*" He jabbed his finger toward the barn. "That's the devil's work. It makes me sick, Isaac. You don't know what you're saying."

Tears pricking his eyes, Isaac kept his head high. "I know I love him." As he said the words for the first time, his heart thumped. He did. He loved David with all his heart. "And I know love isn't a sin." It couldn't be. Could it?

Mervin grimaced. "If that's really what you believe..." He sniffled and swiped at his eyes. "If that's what you believe then I pity you. I'll pray for you, Isaac. That's all I can do." He turned to the buggy.

"Wait!"

Mervin didn't look back, but stopped, his shoulders hunched.

"Please, Mervin. Don't tell. Not anyone. It would break my parents' hearts. David's mother. She's lost so much already. Our sisters, and my brothers. I'm begging you. Don't tell."

For a moment that stretched out painfully in the damp December air, Mervin didn't move. Then he nodded and climbed onto the buggy. Isaac watched him speed away with wheels clattering, driving his horse hard. When he was gone, Isaac forced his feet to move back to the barn. Inside, David stood just where Isaac had left him.

"He promised not to tell." Isaac's voice was flat, and he felt like there was a thick fog around him. Any moment he'd wake up safe in his bed with his annoying brother snoring beside him and hogging the quilt.

David's body sagged, and he leaned against the table. "We have to be more careful. We can't..." He scrubbed a hand over his damp hair. "Do you think he'll keep his promise?"

"He always has before. He's always been loyal. A good friend." Isaac blinked back tears. It would never be the same again. "We have to stop, don't we?"

Eyes closed, David nodded. A tremor rolled through him, and then he straightened up and grabbed his hammer. "Let's get started on the drawers for Rebecca Lapp's new dresser," he gritted out.

Fear and sorrow battled in Isaac. He told himself he'd always known they'd have to stop. *But not yet! Not today!* He wanted to scream and cry. *It's not fair. It's not fair!* The urge to go to David and kiss him one more time overwhelmed him. Isaac wavered on his feet. Just one last taste to savor—what would it hurt? No one had to know...

He watched David pound a nail into wood. With a deep breath, Isaac went to the stack of lumber and heaved up a slab of oak. They'd let themselves get carried away for long enough. He picked up his measuring tape, the numbers blurring as he blinked away tears with a deep breath.

They'd always known this day was coming.

Part Two

Chapter Eleven

I SAAC WAS GLAD for his hat brim shielding his face as he heaved the big door half shut and stomped the slushy mud off his boots at the front of the barn. He struggled to keep his tone even and his expression neutral as he looked up. "Good morning."

Standing across the worktable, grim faced with dark circles below his eyes, David nodded. "Morning."

Isaac brushed the snow from his hat and coat and hung them up. Breathing deeply, he faced David, but any words he might have said seemed stuck inside. He kept the broad table between them, clenching his hands against the urge to reach for David. He didn't realize how much they'd touched each other while they worked—a pat here, a caress there. Secret smiles and promises.

"All night I expected the deacon to show up. For the townsfolk to come and pronounce my sins." A ghost of a humorless smile flitted over David's face. "I suppose they still might appear any minute."

"Me too. I kept waiting for the ax to fall." Isaac shuddered. "I prayed most of the night that Mervin will keep his promise. I know I shouldn't pray to God to help keep our sin a secret, but…"

"But what else are we to do now?"

Isaac rubbed his bleary eyes. "We were careless, David."

"*I* was careless." He shook his head. "How could I not lock the door? I hate myself."

Isaac reached his hand out instinctively, and then let it fall. "No,

David. It was both of us. Mervin would have heard me anyway. When we're together, I have no shame, and we've been reckless too many times. We both know we shouldn't...we *can't*. This isn't..." The ache in his chest made it hard to breathe.

"Every morning I've woken up terrified that you'll have come to your senses. That I'll lose you." David swallowed thickly. "But I never really had you. We...if we're discovered, we'll lose everything."

Isaac nodded miserably. "I can't bear to think of it. What people would think. My parents—it would break their hearts. As long as we stay here...as long as we stay Amish, we can't be together."

The truth hung heavy in the air between them.

"Would you ever really leave?" David whispered.

He thought of Aaron, and never seeing his family again, and the hollowness was all consuming. "I don't know if I can."

"I can't...I couldn't leave my family alone." David squeezed his eyes shut. "But I'm so desperate to feel you again, Isaac. To be close to you. It hasn't even been a day, and it's already hell."

David opened his eyes and began pacing, clutching a hammer in his hand. "Every time we go to church, and I listen to Bishop Yoder in the Obrote, telling us what a wise decision it is to be baptized, I want to run. I try to convince myself that he's right—that these feelings I have for you are some childish rebellion. A rumspringa."

Wincing, Isaac waited for him to say more.

"But aren't I a man?" He gestured wildly with the hammer. "I've felt like I was different for as long as I can remember. I used to pray morning and night that the Lord would take these demons from me. But when I'm with you, it doesn't feel evil. Does it?"

Isaac shook his head. "It feels good. Not just...not just touching you, and being touched. It feels good everywhere."

David smiled softly. "When your father asked if I might take you on as an apprentice, I knew I should say no."

"You didn't want me here?" Isaac couldn't help the foolish hurt that flickered through him.

"But I did, Isaac." David stared beseechingly and went to close the distance between them before stopping in his tracks. He gazed at the hammer in his hand as if he wasn't sure how it got there, and placed it on the table carefully. "I did. I wanted you here far too much. Ever since that day at the frolic. Do you remember?"

"The barn raising at the Kauffmans'?"

He nodded. "It was the first we'd ever really spoken. When Mary started going to the singings, she liked you right away. Whenever we were at church or a frolic, I'd watch you. At first it was to get a measure of you. To make sure my sister hadn't set her sights on the wrong boy." He took a deep breath and looked away.

"It's all right," Isaac said.

"Is it?" David asked, his eyes shining. "What kind of brother am I? After a time, I kept watching you because I couldn't look away. You'd grown into a man—that was obvious. And there was something about you I had to see. Something that drew me back every time."

Isaac was afraid to ask. "What was it? Could you...could you tell? That I was...different?"

"I don't know." David's brow furrowed. "I don't think so. But you were beautiful. Your smile. Your eyes. The way you laughed when Mervin told a dumb joke. I barely knew you, but I wanted you all the same." He ran a hand through his hair. "I never thought it was possible, even for a second. Not until the barn raising. Up on that beam, when you lost your balance—my heart just about stopped. At first I grabbed you to keep you safe."

"I knew you wouldn't let me fall." It was as if Isaac could feel the heat of David's grip even now.

"I couldn't resist holding on for just a moment. And when you looked at me..." David rounded the table, stopping a foot away, his eyes going dark. "Then I knew. I felt something with you—saw something— I never had. It made me want to shout for joy and kiss you senseless. For the first time, I thought maybe I wasn't alone here in Zebulon after all."

They moved into each other's arms, and Isaac wished he knew how something so wrong could feel so natural.

David's voice was muffled in Isaac's neck. "I knew I should say no when your father asked. I'd convinced myself it had all been in my head. But I was weak."

"I'm glad." Isaac held on even tighter. "I'm so glad."

"Then I got to know you for real." David lifted his head and brushed his knuckles over Isaac's cheek. "I thought I wanted you before. I had no idea what desire really was."

"Are you sorry?"

David smiled sadly. "I should be. But no."

"I'll never regret it." Isaac took David's face in his hands and kissed him. "Not any of it. We'll find a way. There has to be a way. We can—"

They both heard the approaching voices in the same moment, Anna talking loudly. They leapt apart so quickly that Isaac tripped over his own feet and thudded onto his backside just as Mary and Anna swept into the barn, stamping snow from their boots and shaking their heads, white caps pinned in place.

"Oh!" Mary smiled uneasily, glancing from Isaac to her brother. "Isaac, are you all right?"

Forcing laughter, Isaac heaved himself up and brushed off his trousers. "Just hopelessly clumsy, I'm afraid." He glanced at David, who laughed and devoted great interest to the half-finished dresser drawer on the table.

"You didn't hurt yourself, did you?" Mary asked.

"For goodness sake he's fine. Aren't you, Isaac?" Anna plopped a tray covered with a white dish towel onto the side table. "Sugar cookies."

"Thank you," David said.

"Mary burnt them a bit, but they should be okay." Anna shrugged.

"I did not!" Mary's cheeks burned.

With a smile, Anna elbowed her. "I'm just teasing. You make it so easy."

Isaac was near the table, so he picked up one of the pale cookies and took a bite. He didn't have to fake his groan. "These really are good."

"Thank you." Mary beamed.

"All right, we have work to do," David snapped.

Mary's smile vanished, and she stood up straighter. "We didn't mean to keep you from it. Come on, Anna."

"And we don't have work to do?" Anna grumbled as they left.

In the heavy silence Isaac swallowed the last bite of cookie in his mouth. "I was only being nice."

"I know." David scrubbed at his head, sticking his hair up. "I'm sorry. I'll apologize to the girls later." He picked up the hammer. "We can't let that happen again."

"No. We can't. Nothing's changed, no matter how much we want it to." Isaac picked up a metal spokeshave and bent to shape a drawer handle.

The minutes crawled by. The only sounds in the barn were the horses nickering in their stalls, and metal on wood. When Isaac risked a glance across the table, he found David's gaze on him. They both jerked their heads back to their work, and for the first time since he'd gone to work at the Lantz farm, Isaac wished he was anywhere else.

I WILL NOT think of David. I will not think of David. I will not think of David.

Of course as Isaac tried to relax on one of the wooden chairs in the living room, all the best intentions in the world couldn't keep him from remembering the sensation of David's touch—the sweetness of his kisses, and the hot heft of him filling Isaac's mouth. Filling his body. The bliss of being buried in David himself, bringing him to completion and hearing his cries—coming inside him.

Never again.

The weight of that knowledge was unbearable. In only a day, Isaac felt utterly bereft. How would he keep going like this? It was impossible.

"What's wrong?"

Blinking, Isaac focused on little Joseph, who was reading on one of the wooden chairs near Isaac's. "Nothing."

"You keep sighing like...there's no apple pie left, and you didn't get any."

Isaac tried to smile. "I hate it when that happens."

"It's the worst," Joseph agreed.

"Well, it's nothing like that." Isaac had to look away. "Nothing that bad. Don't worry."

He unfolded that week's hefty edition of *Die Botschaft*, which was more than seventy pages and had arrived in the mail that morning. He tried to concentrate on a letter from Fannie Miller of Neillsville, Wisconsin, who wrote of her husband's scramble to round up his cows after the gate wasn't closed properly.

Sighing, Isaac turned the page. Growing up they'd read *The Budget*, the first weekly Amish newspaper founded more than a hundred years ago. But some communities felt it had become too liberal and modern, and Zebulon was one of them. *Die Botschaft* was more conservative, but both newspapers used the same format—dozens of pages of letters from correspondents relaying news and stories from communities all across the country and up into Canada.

Each week, Isaac scanned for news of Red Hills or other towns in Ohio where his cousins lived. Once he had read a letter that mentioned his cousin John Byler and a pitchfork accident. Fortunately John had been recovering nicely, according to the correspondent.

Of course there were no pictures in Amish newspapers, and Isaac had wished he could see what John looked like now. Unable to focus on a report from Aylmer, Ontario, on Levi Stutzman's cataract surgery, Isaac flipped through the rest of the pages, looking without really seeing.

The thump at the door made him jump, and he tore one side of the paper where his fist clenched. His breath caught in his throat, cheeks burning. Around the living room on their wooden benches and chairs, his brothers looked up expectantly.

Father had retired to the outhouse for an indeterminate length of time, as was his usual custom after supper. Isaac folded the paper with shaking hands, and went to the door. He passed the kitchen, where Mother and Katie stood waiting, jars spread out on the table behind them, their canning of the last late autumn squash forgotten for the moment.

It was unusual in Zebulon to have a visitor so late in the day, and Isaac muttered a quick prayer that it wasn't bad news. When he opened the door to a gust of wind and spray of sleet, he saw it was worse.

"Deacon Stoltzfus." Isaac forced a smile that likely was more of a grimace. "Good evening."

There was no hint of a smile from the deacon. "Isaac Byler. I come on official church business." His voice was practically a growl, and although he wasn't the tallest of men, he somehow loomed in the doorway. "I'm sure you know why."

An awful spike of fear sent shivers over Isaac's skin. *He knows. Oh God. He knows!* His breath was shallow. "I don't think I do."

Deacon Stoltzfus regarded him stonily. Wet snow covered the brim of his black hat, and his face was creased in shadow, the lamplight from the living room faint by the door.

Isaac swallowed hard. "Has something happened?" His mind raced. *Mervin told after all.* Isaac's palms sweat despite the freezing air gusting in. *Oh God. Please no.*

"Isaac!"

Heart in his throat, he whirled around to find Mother behind him. "Yes?"

"Let Deacon Stoltzfus inside this instant." She smiled apologetically. "I'm so sorry, Jeremiah. You must be chilled to the bone in this weather. Winter is surely upon us now."

Isaac stood aside, and the deacon marched in. Mother took his hat and coat and hung them, and called for one of the boys to fetch Father.

"May I offer you something warm to drink? Tea?" Mother ushered the deacon to one of the wooden chairs in the living room.

Deacon Stoltzfus shook his head, and remained standing. They all stood as well, waiting. When Father appeared, he shook the deacon's hand solemnly. Isaac gripped the back of a chair, afraid his knees might give out.

"Your son has violated the Ordnung in a most grave way. He has sinned against God, and against our community."

Oh Lord have mercy. Isaac wasn't sure whether to weep or vomit, or perhaps run into the night and never return. How could he face this? For Mother and Father to hear what he'd done—he thought the shame alone might kill him. He had to speak—had to make them understand—but how could they?

He tore his gaze from the deacon's forbidding face. Mother and Father were frozen, watching the deacon and waiting. Before Isaac could say anything, Deacon Stoltzfus shattered the silence.

"Last night, your Ephraim and some of the other boys smoked cigarettes and drank English alcohol. They also enticed three of our young girls to sneak out of their homes and join them in the woods on Jonah Miller's land. He discovered the evidence this morning. His son confessed his part in it."

Terrible relief surging through him, Isaac swung around to gape at Ephraim, who stood by the stairs. Defiance was written on his face, his fists clenched.

"We didn't do anything wrong! It wasn't a big deal. We just wanted to have fun for once."

"Ephraim!" Father exploded. He pointed to the bench along one wall by the wood-burning stove they hauled into the living room for winter. "Sit." His bushy dark brows were a slash across his face. "Children—upstairs."

Isaac tried to catch Ephraim's eye as they passed each other, but Ephraim's gaze was on the floor, his jaw tight. Isaac ushered his sister and brothers up the stairs before him. Naturally they all stopped at the top, and Isaac shooed them around the corner. He was the oldest, and it was only fair he have the best eavesdropping spot.

He gingerly sank to his knees by the top of the stairs, just out of sight should anyone glance up. Katie, Nathan and Joseph crowded against his back. It was dark on the second floor, and the glow of the lamps below died halfway up the stairs.

Deacon Stoltzfus's gruff, powerful voice was certainly easy to hear. "As you know, the Ordnung says when youngies are seventeen they may attend the singings and date each other in the proper manner. This was not proper. This wild behavior will not be tolerated."

After a beat of silence, Father spoke, his steady voice seething. "No. It shall not."

"Hannah Lambright has confessed her impure actions, and named your son as an accomplice in her sins."

Isaac felt sick. What would the deacon and his parents say if they knew *his* sins?

"We just kissed!" Ephraim exclaimed. "It was nothing."

"Nothing!" Mother's voice echoed through the house.

She sounded furious and close to tears. Normally she would stay silent and let Father handle problems like this. Again, Isaac imagined how she would react if she knew the sins he'd committed in recent days. He took a shuddering breath, staring at the shadows of the stairwell.

Deacon Stoltzfus went on. "This behavior is a sin against God and our people. We must guard against temptation lest Zebulon disintegrate into the ruin that has befallen too many other communities."

Trembling against Isaac's back, Katie whispered, "Why would Ephraim do that, Isaac?"

Nathan shushed, but Isaac reached an arm out and pulled her to his side. "It's okay," he whispered. "It'll be okay."

Katie's eyes swam with tears. "But why would he break the Ordnung?"

"You'll understand in a few years." He pressed a kiss to her forehead and held her close. Even if it wasn't their way to be affectionate, it felt wrong not to comfort her. "He didn't mean to do anything really bad."

Ephraim's voice rang out again. "We were just having a little fun!

Jacob Esch's cousin in Pennsylvania has his own car! They go to English parties every weekend. We don't get to do anything, and it isn't fair!"

"You know very well what kind of tragedies are born of wild rumspringas when communities turn a blind eye and hope their youngies will return to the righteous path." Father's anger sounded as if it was giving way to sorrow. "We came to Zebulon to keep our children safe. We only want the best for you."

"Then can't you see that the more you try to stop us from learning and exploring, the more—"

"*Learning?*" Father exploded. "You do not know anything if you think running wild is the way. In these learning years you should do your chores and listen to your elders. You shame our family and community. You disrespect God when you sin like this. You will do as I say! You will do as the Ordnung says! There is no other way. There will be no other arguments."

When Ephraim spoke again, he was defeated. "Yes, Father," he muttered.

"Samuel, we trust you and Ruth will help your son face his sins and pay penance for them," Deacon Stoltzfus intoned. "That you will make him understand the importance of obedience."

"We shall. Thank you for bringing this grave matter to our attention, Jeremiah. Let me show you out."

The floors creaked with their heavy footsteps, and Isaac breathed a sigh of relief that the deacon was leaving. He squeezed Katie close, Joseph and Nathan crowding against them as they all waited. The front door shut with a reverberating thud. Then Father's slow steps back to the living room.

Silence.

"Father, I—"

"Stop." Father didn't raise his voice this time. "Ephraim Byler, you have disrespected the Ordnung and your community. You have disrespected Hannah Lambright. You have disrespected your family. Most of all, you have disrespected yourself. Your sins bring your mother and I great shame and sorrow. At church on Sunday, you will stand before Zebulon and repent these sins. You are no longer permitted to leave this farm unless we're with you."

After a few moments, Ephraim spoke, choking back emotion that was likely anger. "For how long?"

"Until we can trust you again. Do you understand?"

"Yes." Ephraim's voice was barely more than a whisper.

"Tomorrow night we will begin extra Bible study together. Now go to bed."

As quietly as he could, Isaac herded his younger siblings into Katie's room, and lit a lantern. Nathan opened his mouth to protest, but Isaac glared and pulled Katie's door almost shut. He lit another lantern, and waited for Ephraim in their bedroom.

Eyes blazing, Ephraim stalked through the door. When he yanked back his arm, Isaac lunged for the door, grabbing it before it could slam shut. He closed it gently. "That won't help things," Isaac hissed.

His hands in fists, Ephraim paced through the yellow glow of the lamp and the dark shadows that stretched into the corners of the room. "It isn't fair. We hardly even did anything! Shared a few cigarettes and some whiskey Daniel got in town. Now I'll be even more of a prisoner here than I am already!"

"I'm sorry." Isaac wanted to reach out to his brother and soothe him, but it wouldn't do any good.

Ephraim roughly ran a hand through his sandy curls. "And I don't know what Hannah told them, but I barely touched her."

"You know you aren't supposed to be dating girls at all yet, let alone kissing them. Couldn't you have just waited a little while longer? It's only two months until you're seventeen. Then you're allowed." But Isaac knew he was a hypocrite.

"Of course you'd say that!" Ephraim rounded on him. "My saintly brother. You never do anything wrong. You can take out all the girls you want, but you still don't. So pious and perfect," he spat.

"I'm not perfect, Ephraim. Not even close." He stepped in Ephraim's path and whispered, "I've broken the Ordnung too."

"No way," Ephraim scoffed. "*You?* What could you have done?" But he stopped pacing, and waited with obvious interest.

With a finger to his lips, Isaac crept over to the door. When he jerked it open, Nathan tumbled into him.

Nathan righted himself, pimply cheeks ruddy. "I'm not some little kid. I'm almost done school. I want to hear!"

"Go back to Katie's room until I come get you. Ephraim and I need to talk. You are too a kid, and no kids allowed!" He closed the door again, listening to Nathan's huffs and retreating stomps.

Ephraim was still waiting with keen interest. "What could you have done?"

I sucked a man's cock in my mouth. I fucked a man, and let him fuck me. I loved every second of it, and I want more. "I watched a movie. I did worldly things."

Ephraim's eyebrows shot up. "Really?"

"I'm not as perfect as you think." *Not even close.*

"But you didn't get caught." Ephraim's anger seemed to be burning itself out, and he slumped onto the side of the bed he shared with Joseph. "We didn't think anyone would find the bottle. I guess we left the burned-out cigarettes too. Have you ever smoked?"

Isaac shook his head and sat beside him.

"I hardly even finished one. It was pretty gross. I just…Isaac, don't you feel trapped here sometimes?"

"I didn't really think about it much before." Isaac pulled a loose thread from the cuff of his navy shirt. "But lately I've been more…curious."

"I know what happened in Red Hills was terrible. Doing drugs and all that. But the more they try to keep us away from the world, the more I want to see it." He laughed ruefully. "If cigarettes and alcohol are anything to go by, it's not all that exciting. My head hurt something fierce this morning."

"You like working on the farm, don't you? You're good at it. Better than I ever was. You have a way with the cows. I always thought you'd be happy with a farm of your own."

"I would be. But that's years away, Isaac! Boys in Red Hills got their own buggies when they were sixteen more often than not. But here in Zebulon living these older ways, hardly anyone has enough money. You're eighteen and you don't have your own buggy yet. You have to get one first. You have to do *everything* first. I'm already sick of waiting. I want a farm of my own." He flung out his hand. "A *bed* of my own. I sure wouldn't mind sharing it with a wife, but not my brother."

Isaac grimaced. "I know how you feel." Of course he didn't want to share with a *wife*, and his imagination spun wildly with thoughts of David—both of them naked, skin slick, flesh fevered as they came together in a proper bed with hands and mouths and bodies. Nestled there together afterwards under a quilt, safe in each other's arms, he would listen to David's breathing—

"Isaac?"

He blinked. "Uh-huh?"

"Can I tell you a secret?" Ephraim whispered.

Isaac nodded.

"I don't think I want to stay in Zebulon."

He took this in. "Where do you want to go? Into the world?" Isaac felt sick at the thought of losing another brother.

"Maybe? I don't know. I just want to see what's out there. I feel so closed in here. I love farming. But I hate all the rules. I hate how controlled we are. Not even just the youngies—the adults too. Does God really care how wide the brims of our hats are? Or whether a girl's dress goes to her shins or the tops of her shoes? The rules are different everywhere. How does it work? When you really think about it, none of it makes any sense. There are so many English people out there. Are they all going to hell?"

"I don't know." Isaac rubbed his face. "I don't know anything any-more."

"So…it's not just me?" Ephraim's eyes lit up. "Sometimes I feel like

I'm the only one with questions."

"It's not just you. Believe me."

Ephraim sighed. "There's no point even talking about it with Mother and Father. You heard him tonight. We can't even ask questions. I feel like it's all or nothing. When I was little, I didn't understand why Aaron left. I do now."

"Me too." Isaac couldn't remember ever hearing his brother sound so...grownup. "I'm sorry we haven't talked more. I've been wrapped up in myself." *And David.* "I wish we could ask more questions, and talk to Mother and Father about how we feel, but…"

"It won't do any good." Ephraim ran his hands over his thighs. "I've been thinking. I'll stay for another year or so. See what it's like once I can go to the singings and date. I can't leave Father with all the farm work. I have to wait at least until Nathan is finished school."

Isaac's throat was dry. "And then?"

"I don't even know if I want to live in the world. But I'll go back to Red Hills, maybe? Abigail or Hannah would let me stay, I'm sure. Or I could go somewhere else in Ohio. Or Indiana, since those blue bloods in Pennsylvania would look down their noses at me. Maybe I could stay in Minnesota—in one of the settlements in Polk County. We were lucky Father found a dairy nearby willing to pick up our milk. There are farms down there that work with the English and do really well. They're not so strict as we are, but they're still Amish. I could try it out. I'm a good worker. I don't have any money, but if I go to another Amish town, they'll help me as long as I haven't followed church here. I could see what it's like somewhere else and figure things out."

"You've really thought about this."

"More and more lately. Don't you think about the future?"

"Sometimes." *It's impossible to have the life I want.*

The door burst open, and Nathan stomped in, followed by Joseph. Nathan went to his storage chest and flung up the lid. "It's bed time, and this is *our* room too."

Joseph went about his business, not appearing too fussed. Isaac hesitantly patted Ephraim's leg. "We can talk more later. Whenever you want, okay?"

A small smile lifted Ephraim's lips. "Okay."

Before long, the lamp was out and they were all in bed, Nathan snoring almost as soon as his head hit the pillow. Isaac stewed as the rattling racket grew, finally jabbing Nathan in the side to get him to roll over. Staring at the black square of darkness of the window in the temporary peace, Isaac tried to imagine his future.

Where his mind had always been a curious blank when it came to living in his own house, now he could envision it so clearly—a welcoming kitchen, and twin rocking chairs by the fire in the living room. A cozy bed upstairs where he'd eagerly retire each night to a warm embrace. No wife by his side, but his David.

Throat tight, Isaac squeezed his eyes shut, wishing he could unsee this future that could never be.

Chapter Twelve

"DAVID, CAN YOU take this pie to Eli Helmuth's this afternoon? He's been under the weather." At the kitchen counter, Mrs. Lantz wrapped the pie plate in a cloth as a log in the stove hissed and crackled.

With a glance at Isaac, David swallowed his forkful of pot pie. "I can't. Isaac and I have to go to town for new tools. Didn't I mention it?"

Across the kitchen table, Anna piped up. "Nope."

It was the first Isaac had heard of it, but he stayed silent and finished his last bite of flaky pastry.

Mrs. Lantz waved her hand. "Perhaps you did. I'm so forgetful lately. It's all right, dear. I'll take it to him myself." Smiling, she went about stacking the pots and pans before picking up the pail and disappearing out the side door to the well.

Anna smirked. "She was hoping you'd say no, David."

"Why?" David frowned.

Glaring at her sister, Mary snatched up some dishes from the table. "*Anna.* That's enough."

"What?" Anna grinned mischievously. "You know it's true."

Isaac watched the exchange silently, gaze darting back and forth between the players. David was tense beside him.

"What's true?" David asked.

Anna leaned across the table and lowered her voice. "Mother has the hots for Eli Helmuth."

"Anna!" The dishes rattled as Mary dumped them on the counter. "Where did you hear such language?" Sighing, she addressed Isaac. "Please excuse my sister."

"I'm sure Isaac can handle it, Mary." Anna rolled her eyes. "He's heard worse, I imagine."

"Not in our home he hasn't." Mary could barely get the words out through her clenched jaw.

"It's all right. Really," Isaac held up his hands. "I should go back to work and let you all…talk." He stood up.

"Girls, that's enough." David's tone brooked no argument. "Anna, I'm sure Mother is only showing a neighborly interest in Mr. Helmuth."

Anna pressed her lips together. "She's widowed, not dead. Why shouldn't she show any kind of interest she wants in Eli Helmuth? He's alone now too. There's nothing wrong with it."

"Of course there isn't," David agreed. "But you shouldn't talk like that, Anna. You know it isn't right. If Mother heard you—"

The kitchen door swung open with a frigid blast of air, and they all spun to see Mrs. Lantz in the doorway, water sloshing over the pail. She blinked. "Why do you all look so guilty?"

"Nothing!" they chirped in unison.

Mrs. Lantz raised an eyebrow. "Mmm-hmm. All right then, there's work to be done. You boys should go now so you're back before dark."

"Yes, Mother." David grabbed a cookie from the cooling rack on the counter, tossing another to Isaac.

Chuckling, she wiped her hands on her apron. "Off with you, then. Isaac, keep him out of trouble. He drives that buggy too fast."

"I will!" Isaac waved and hurried after David to gather their coats and hats.

He and David didn't speak until they were driving toward the county road. Snow banks lined the lane in heaps where it had been shoveled away.

David sighed. "I hate being like that with the girls. But with Father gone, I feel like I have to try to do what he would have done."

"Of course." Isaac stroked David's thigh with his gloved hand before he knew what he was doing. He whipped his hand back. "Sorry."

David glanced around as Kaffi clomped onto the road, the buggy creaking. "I'm not. Come closer."

Heart skipping, Isaac slid over until their hips and shoulders touched.

"I know we said we wouldn't, but I thought…it's just for a few hours. We've been so good. We deserve an afternoon. No one will know. What do you think? If you don't want to, we can—"

"I want to." Isaac gripped David's hand, the leather of their gloves squeaking together. "Lord, I've missed you. We'll be careful." He knew it was irresponsible. Stupid, even. But sitting close to David and feeling the heat of his body, Isaac couldn't bring himself to care.

"You have no idea how much I've missed you." David glanced at him. "How much I want to kiss you again." He looked back at the road. "It's torture, Isaac."

"We'll be careful," Isaac repeated. He returned his hand to David's strong thigh, wishing it was bare skin he caressed.

David nodded vigorously. "We will. We'll make sure we're alone. That no one can catch us this time. We were reckless before. We won't let it happen again. But every so often, we can sneak away, and they'll never know."

Isaac heard an approaching car and slid across the bench, snatching his hand from David's leg. "We'll make it work." He smiled, feeling happier than he had in weeks. "Do you really think your mother likes Eli Helmuth?"

David huffed out a laugh. "I don't know what to think. It never even crossed my mind."

"Would it bother you?"

David reined in Kaffi as they came to a stop sign. He looked both ways and got Kaffi moving again. "I guess not. It's strange to think of her with anyone but my father. But I want her to be happy. She deserves it."

It occurred to Isaac that if Mrs. Lantz remarried, David wouldn't be responsible for his family anymore. Of course bringing old Eli a pie was a far cry from getting married. Still…

"Anna's rarely wrong when it comes to things like this. We have to be extra careful around her. She has a sharp mind, and a sharper tongue. It feels like she's growing up very fast all of a sudden."

"Same with Ephraim. Did you hear about the party he and his friends had? Drinking and smoking?"

David huffed out a laugh. "Of course. Mrs. Kauffman—Josiah's Rebecca—dropped by on some made-up errand to tell Mother the news. How's Ephraim?"

"Angry. Frustrated. He was talking about leaving next year."

David looked at Isaac sharply. "Really?" He glanced back at the road. "Do you think he will?"

"Yes. Sooner or later."

"He doesn't have any money, does he?"

"No. But he's chomping at the bit. The more Mother and Father try to control him, the more frustrated he'll get."

David reined in Kaffi as he made a turn. "I can't imagine what that's like."

"Leaving?" Isaac felt as though his heart was stuck in his throat.

"Having the freedom to actually do it." David stared at the road.

"But…" Isaac took a deep breath. "We all could if we really wanted to."

"No," David bit out. He cleared his throat. "Some of us have too many responsibilities."

"I suppose we do." It was all Isaac could say. "No choice."

David's hands were still fisted around the reins as he exhaled. "Ephraim's young. The world seems so black and white when you're sixteen."

"Isn't it black and white according to our parents? To the Ordnung?"

"I suppose it is. Once we make the vow to follow church, then we have to follow all the rules."

"And in the meantime?"

"We'll pray for forgiveness." He nodded. "Baptism will wash our sins away."

"Do you really believe that?" Isaac wasn't sure if he could anymore.

David smiled sadly. "I have to." He shook his head. "But let's forget everything for today. It's just you and me. Nothing else matters. Not for the next few hours, at least."

Isaac was all too willing to push the unsettling questions away. "Are we going to the hardware store on the highway? I didn't know we needed new tools."

Beneath the brim of his hat, David shot Isaac a sly glance. "Well, we could use a few things." He nodded behind to the small storage area in the back of the buggy. A plastic bag sat there, a level sticking out of a pile of hand tools.

Isaac laughed. "So where are we really going?" Exhilaration surged through him. It was wrong, but he couldn't help himself.

The dimple creased David's right cheek. "You'll see."

"A *MOTEL*?" ISAAC craned his head as they turned into the parking lot of the Wildwood Inn. There was a car on the quiet stretch of country road behind them, but no other buggies in sight. "Are you crazy?"

David just laughed. "Probably." He drove around to the back of the long one-story building. "No one from the road will see the buggy back here."

"But, but—" Isaac sputtered. "What about the motel people? What will they think?"

"They'll think we're having sex." David smirked. "And they won't care as long as we pay. Come winter they don't get much business. It's okay, I know the girl at the desk. She said I could hitch up Kaffi and the buggy back here to that pole." He pulled the hand brake and reined in Kaffi.

"How do you know her?"

"The drive-in. Jessica from the snack bar, remember? After I picked up the tools the other day I stopped by here and asked her about getting a room."

The pole at the back of the lot was wide and wooden, near the edge of the forest beyond the motel. The area had been plowed recently, the snow from yesterday pushed cleanly from the pavement into banks.

"So she *knows* about us?" Isaac perched on the edge of the bench, his knee vibrating as he fidgeted.

"I didn't tell her anything." He put his hand on Isaac's knee. "I'm sure she guessed I'm bringing someone here, but I didn't say who. I'll ask for a room back here, and she'll never even see you."

"But I'm sure she saw me when we came in." Isaac yanked off his gloves and pulled at the dry skin around one of his finger nails.

"Maybe, maybe not. The buggy has a roof, and the office is on the far side. But even if she did, she's not going to tell anyone." David sat back with a sigh. "But if you want to leave, we will. I didn't mean to upset you. I should have told you where we were going. I'm sorry, Isaac. I just wanted to be with you. I thought we'd be safer here than anywhere in Zebulon."

Isaac's anxiety faded away in the face of David's disappointment. "Well, we've come this far, and you're right—we're hidden back here. We're far enough away from Zebulon too." He buzzed all over as he thought about having a room to themselves. *Just this once.* "What are you waiting for? Go get a key."

With a grin, David hopped down and tied Kaffi to the post. "I'll be back in a minute."

It was actually four minutes before he returned, and Isaac thought he might vibrate out of his skin as he waited. He flipped his pocketknife open and shut, open and shut, open and shut. Then David appeared, waving him over to one of the rooms—number sixteen.

"Bring the bag," he called out.

Isaac glanced behind him. The only bag he could see was the plastic one holding the new tools, so he grabbed it and hurried across the salted concrete. The cutting wind made the hair on his neck stand up, although he couldn't be sure it wasn't the excitement of knowing what was to come.

Room number sixteen at the Wildwood Inn was musty, but clean. David flicked on the overhead light and closed the brown curtains. The room was mostly beige with orange and yellow here and there. A painting of wheat fields rippling in the wind hung over the double bed on the opposite wall.

A real bed.

Isaac's pulse raced. For all the times he and David had already sinned, this felt more real somehow. For all the times he'd dreamed of it, they were actually going to share a bed. *You shall not lie with a man as with a woman...*

The wooden dresser opposite the bed was worn but well shined, and a TV sat on top of it. Beside the dresser was another smaller one, and above it was a huge mirror. Isaac stood frozen in the doorway. "There's a mirror."

David glanced at the dresser, and then back to Isaac. "Yes." His brow creased. "Surely you're not worried about *that* rule right now considering..."

Heat washed through him, and Isaac wasn't sure how much was lust, and how much was shame. "I don't want to see myself."

"Isaac." David's face softened.

"I can't." Maybe it was silly, but the thought of looking at himself when he was going to sin so thoroughly made him unbearably anxious. His chest tightened. "Please."

"Okay." David pulled down the yellow cover on the bed and yanked the sheet off. He draped it over the mirror. "Is that better? I'll cover the one in the bathroom too." He came to the door and took Isaac's hand. "But if you want to leave, we can."

Isaac stared at the rusty orange squares on the carpet. "No. I want…I want you so much. But I shouldn't, David." He felt David's fingers gently tipping up his chin, and met his tender gaze. "It's stupid about the mirrors, I know."

"It's not stupid." David brushed their lips together. "It's all right. No one will see. Not even our reflections. It's just you and me, remember?"

At the feel of David's lips against his, Isaac's fear and guilt faded away. He kissed him desperately, tugging the length of David's body against him. David tasted of pot pie—meat and butter and warmth. *It's just us.* Suddenly Isaac couldn't stand the thought of anything between them, and he tugged at their clothing.

They both breathed loudly in the silence as they stripped off their clothes, fingers flying over hooks and fastenings. Gloriously naked, Isaac rolled on top of David on the bed, inhaling the faint whiff of sawdust that clung to both their skin. The thought that they smelled alike made his blood hot for some reason.

David's breath fluttered on Isaac's face as he gasped. "God help me, Isaac. I've missed you so much. It's torture being around you and not being able to touch you." He pressed messy kisses to Isaac's face.

Rolling his hips, Isaac rutted against him, their cocks growing hard and their skin becoming slick with sweat. An English heater rattled by the wall, making the room as warm as summer. "Yes, yes," Isaac muttered mindlessly.

"Where's the bag?" David kissed him again.

"Oh, um…over there somewhere. I'll get it."

But David was still kissing him, hands tangling in Isaac's hair.

Smiling around David's searching tongue, Isaac nipped him. "If you want the bag, you have to stop kissing me."

David groaned, unhooking his legs from Isaac's. "Hurry."

The plastic bag sat on the floor by the dresser, and Isaac scrambled off the bed and snagged a finger in one of the handles. The tools clattered as he hauled it up. "What do you have in here?" He crawled across the mattress and poked through the bag, pulling out a jagged fret saw with a plastic guard on its blade. "Are you going to fuck me with this?" he teased.

"No!" David laughed. "Look again. There's a tube in there."

Isaac poked through the bag and found a plastic tube. He read the label. "Personal lubricating jelly." He glanced at David. "This is what the English use instead of grease?"

David was already spreading his legs, pulling his knees back and exposing his hole. Not needing to be asked twice, Isaac fumbled with the cap and squeezed. Nothing came out. He shook the tube, but still nothing.

"The seal. You have to break the seal." David licked his lips.

Once Isaac had the jelly on his fingers, he pushed them into David, knowing he should be patient but wanting desperately to impale himself, shove into David's body and come inside him, hidden away where no one would see. The slick jelly was just as messy as saddle grease, but when he smeared it over his cock, the smooth slide of it had him gripping the base of his shaft, breathing deeply as he regained control.

Nostrils flaring, David hauled Isaac on top of him. "Fuck me, please," he gritted out.

Isaac moaned as he fit his cock into the heat of David's ass. It was so tight, and he inched in, kissing David's face. David smiled, squeezing around him. As Isaac began to thrust in and out, he panted words and sounds that sounded loud in his own ears. *"Oh, oh, yes, oh, yes, oh, oh."*

Sweat glistened on David's forehead, his hair sticking up in all directions as he turned his head back and forth on the pillow. "Yes, just like that. Right there. I never want to stop. Isaac, we can't stop. I need this. Need you." He dug his fingers into Isaac's hips, his heels on Isaac's back. "I love you."

Isaac's breath caught, and emotion swelled in him. He stopped his thrusts, buried deep in David, his arms straining as he held himself up. "Do you really?"

David took Isaac's face with shaky hands, his eyes bright. "Yes. I love you, Isaac. No matter what happens, I'll always love you."

"We'll never stop," Isaac muttered, gasping as he pulled back and rammed into David. "I love you so much." Isaac had never even had a sip of moonshine, but he couldn't imagine anything was more intoxicating than the fever gripping him. He thrust back into David's body and bit his lip to stop from crying out.

"Do it. Scream. No one's listening."

So Isaac screamed.

His shouts filled the air as he slammed into him, David's cries filling the spaces between until it sounded like strange and wonderful music. There was pleasure in every pore as Isaac grunted, eyes locked with David's. He wanted to make David come, but he couldn't control himself as David squeezed around him, lips parted.

"Do it, Isaac. Fill me up." He clamped down.

Shouting to the heavens, Isaac let go, jerking as he shot into David's ass. They kissed, mouths open, tongues searching. He wanted to stay inside David forever, but David was still hard between them. He pulled back, his softening cock slipping out.

Isaac ducked his head to suck David, but David wriggled out from beneath him. He swiped his fingers into the seed dripping out of him and got behind Isaac. Isaac leaned forward on his elbows, offering himself up eagerly.

He groaned when David rubbed his slick fingers over Isaac's hole, straining his neck to watch as David transferred the slippery mixture from his own ass to Isaac's. It was utterly depraved, and a phrase from a long-ago sermon popped into Isaac's mind.

Carnal sin.

If hell waited one way or the other now, then let it be like this. "Yes," he moaned. "Give me all of it."

He hung his head against the cheap sheets as David squirted an extra dollop from the tube and pushed inside. Isaac closed his eyes, panting as his cries mingled with the squeak and bang of the bed as it hammered the wall.

It was all sound and sensation—his body open as David fucked him like a dog would, with harsh grunts that were practically barks, his wet fingers gripping Isaac's hips so hard they were sure to leave bruises that would make him blush and smile.

He imagined he could smell the hay and sawdust and manure of the barn along with their sweat as David's hips slapped against his ass. Isaac's spent cock twitched to life as David rubbed against the sensitive spot inside him, but Isaac only cared about David reaching the breaking point. Squeezing, he rocked with David's thrusts, pushing back and meeting him.

It wouldn't be long, and sure enough David cried out, shuddering as he came. Isaac could feel it deep within him, and the thought that their seed was mixed inside him made him whimper. He wanted to plug himself up and keep it there forever. *I must truly be sick.*

But as he collapsed with David on him, still buried *in* him, pressing little kisses to his neck and murmuring tender words of praise and love, Isaac didn't care.

Let it be like this.

THE STORM ARRIVED so fiercely that Isaac could hardly believe that minutes ago the pavement had been clear, and the late-afternoon sun had even peeked out. Now the snow whipped across the road, striking their faces and making Isaac's eyes water. He kept his head low, but his hat could only do so much. But worse than the bitter cold was that the world had become white.

"Light the lantern!" David shouted above the howling wind.

Isaac did, knowing the lantern in its box would do little to make them visible in the blinding snow. "Can you pull over?"

"I'll try!"

Even with his gloves, Isaac's fingers were numb as he gripped the seat. The next road was someone's driveway judging by the mailbox.

The lane was narrow and long, but there was another road that split off it, and using the extra space, David was able to get the buggy turned around.

"If it comes down too much, we'll get stuck." He wiped snow from his chin. "But better to wait here, don't you think?"

Isaac nodded as a gust rattled the buggy. There was forest on either side of the lane, but it didn't seem to offer much protection. "Guess we should have stayed in bed for a while longer." Isaac could have spent all day hidden there.

He hadn't even been tempted to peek at the TV. Cuddling with David under the covers was everything he wanted and more. David had told him stories about his father, and Isaac had shared his memory of the time the chickens had gotten loose and laid eggs in the most unexpected places. To be together miles away from home and without having to listen for footsteps was a dream.

If his hair wasn't still damp from the shower they'd shared, Isaac would think he'd imagined it entirely. It had been so warm and safe, and now they were back in the real world, and winter was baring its fangs. The ends of his hair were brittle and frozen.

David's teeth chattered. "Whoever thought our buggies shouldn't have windshields didn't live in Minnesota."

They huddled together, the brims of their hats bumping. They seemed to be alone among the trees, but at least if anyone happened by, they had a good reason for pressing against each other.

But before too long, the snow cleared and the wind died down, almost as if by magic, or the flick of an English light switch. Winter could be like that in Minnesota—a lion and a lamb. Mostly lion, though.

David snapped the reins and they ventured back to the main road, the buggy wheels groaning in the drifts. Snow still swirled in the air, but at least they could see now. "Let's just get home," he muttered.

As David urged on Kaffi, Isaac lit the lantern again, glad that there weren't many cars out. It was slow going on the snow-covered road, and it was almost dark when he pointed to the bend ahead. A red light flashed over the snow on the far side of the road. "What's that?"

Then they came around the curve and saw for themselves. The red lights of three state police cars spun over the scene, and orange-red flares sparked on the road. A small blue car had skidded to a stop, its tail almost in the ditch.

Ahead a buggy lay crumpled on its side, the wheels in the air rocking in the wind.

Isaac's lungs wouldn't expand. *Please God. Please no.* He looked to David, whose eyes were wide as he pulled the hand brake and hauled on the reins, jerking Kaffi to the side of the road. They both leaped out, slipping and sliding on the patches of ice as they ran.

That it was someone they knew was certain. His family's faces flashed through his mind—Mother and Father and Ephraim and Nathan and Katie and Joseph—and he mumbled a prayer. "Please, please, please." *Don't be them. Don't be them.*

A police officer held up his hands and stepped in their path. "You need to stay back, boys. I'm sorry."

Isaac ignored him, desperately trying to get a closer look at the horse and buggy. He sagged in relief as he took in the coloring of the animal, which lay broken and unmoving, blood seeping into the snow. It wasn't Roy.

But still, he recognized that horse.

He reached for David, who was already scrambling toward a slash of black on the ground. Mrs. Lantz's eyes were shut beneath her black bonnet, and her bloody leg was twisted horribly, her long cloak and dress torn. Police officers knelt over her. The policeman who tried to block their way, an older man with a gruff voice, held David's shoulders.

"Son, you have to stay back. The ambulance is almost here."

David couldn't seem to speak, little gasps escaping his lips as he stared at his mother's crumpled body.

Nearby, a middle-aged man shouted as he paced around. "It wasn't my fault! I couldn't see them until it was too late! Oh my God, oh my

God." Blood trickled down his face, and he ran a hand through his thinning hair, making it stand on end. "I'm sorry. God, I couldn't see them! There were no tail lights for fuck's sake! How was I supposed to see them in this?"

David was motionless, eyes locked on his mother. The policeman tried to ease him back.

"They're doing everything they can, son. Do you know her?"

When David didn't answer, Isaac did. "That's his mother." His voice sounded strangely far away, as though there was a buzzing in his ears. He clutched David's hand, the leather of their gloves sticking together. *This isn't real. This isn't real.*

He screwed his eyes shut for a moment, praying that when he opened them he'd have fallen asleep, and he'd still be in that motel bed with scratchy sheets and David wrapped around him. He wanted to weep when he looked around again, but he couldn't. David was frighteningly pale and still.

"Then Mary's your sister?" the officer asked David.

But David didn't seem to hear him, his gaze riveted to his mother on the ground a few feet away.

Isaac's stomach curdled sickeningly. The driver's plaintive shout echoed through his head. *How was I supposed to see them?* Oh Lord. *Them.* Isaac whipped around. "Mary! Mary!"

The officer raised his hands. "She's all right. It was a miracle, I tell you. Got thrown clear into a snowbank. Missed hitting a tree by inches. She's over there." He called to another officer. "Bukowski! Take this kid to see the girl."

Isaac exhaled a long breath and murmured a prayer of thanks that at least Mary was all right. He turned to David, peering at him closely. He shoved his gloves in his pockets and tipped David's chin toward him. But David's eyes never left his mother. "David, do you want to see Mary? She's all right. Did you hear what the policeman said?"

But Isaac didn't think David could hear anything. He looked at the officer. "I don't know what to do."

"It's all right, I'll watch him. Go see the girl. Poor thing's in shock too."

Isaac squeezed David's hand so tightly it had to hurt. "I'll be right back. I need to make sure Mary's all right. Can you hear me?" He wanted to hold David close, kiss him and tell him everything would be fine. But he stepped back, aching as he walked away, somehow putting one foot in front of the other.

A policewoman—Bukowski, Isaac assumed—smiled kindly and led him to one of the cruisers. On the other side of the road, an officer directed traffic with flashing sticks as a few vehicles crawled by, full darkness settled in now aside from the eerie colored lights casting everything in a bloody hue.

Officer Bukowski opened the back door of the car. "Mary, honey? Someone's here for you." She stepped back.

Mary was wrapped in two blankets. As she turned her glassy stare to Isaac, he crouched down and took her gloved hand. It was slick and sticky, and he realized with a wave of nausea that it was blood. But he didn't let go. "Mary? It's me. Isaac. It's all right. You're going to be all right."

Her black cap and bonnet were gone, her blonde hair spilling loose from its pins. Through puffy red eyes, fresh tears slipped down her cheeks, cutting a line through smears of red. "Isaac?"

"Yes. I'm here. David's here too. He's looking after your mother." Not quite true, but close enough.

Mary's face crumpled. "She was screaming, Isaac. I couldn't help her. And old Nessie too. When the police came, they shot her in the head. But mother isn't screaming anymore either." She shuddered, gasping. "Is she dead?"

"No, she's alive."

"Really?" she whispered.

"Yes. The ambulance is coming. She's alive."

Mary nodded. "All right. I know you wouldn't lie to me, Isaac."

His stomach, already churning with horror and fear, roiled even more as guilt poured in as well. "I'm so sorry this happened, Mary."

"She was nervous to take the pie, so I went with her. Anna was right, she likes Mr. Helmuth. I think he likes her too. He was so happy to see her." Mary's words spilled out, and her eyes went unfocused. "When we left it wasn't even snowing. We were going to pull off the road, but there was nowhere to go along this stretch. Then it was so loud, and I was flying. I was buried in the snow, and everything hurt. I couldn't see out. But I could hear the screaming." A sob burst free, and she bowed her chin to her chest, hair draping her face.

Isaac stroked her head helplessly. "It's all right," he murmured. "It's all right."

At first he thought the faint wails were coming from Mary, but as they got louder he realized it was the ambulance approaching. "I'll be right back. The ambulance is here. Hold on." He made sure she was tucked in safely before he gently closed the car door.

As the ambulance roared up with red lights flashing, Isaac hurried back to David. He wrapped an arm around David's back, not caring what anyone might think. "Mary's all right. David? Can you hear me?"

David still stared with empty eyes. White flakes dusted his hat and coat, and Isaac was struck by the thought that if they left him there, by morning he'd be buried in snow and lost forever. Isaac brushed off the flakes, suddenly frantic in his need to see David's hat and coat unblemished again.

"It's okay. He's in shock." The same policeman from before spread a blanket over David's shoulders. "It's very common. He can ride in the ambulance. You go with his sister, and we'll take you to the hospital."

Isaac nodded dully as the paramedics crowded around Mrs. Lantz. He was tempted to ask if they thought she'd make it, but wasn't sure he wanted to hear the answer. A thought occurred to him. "Our buggy is still on the road. I can't leave it there. I don't think we tied the horse…" He looked back for Kaffi.

"We've moved it already. Don't worry about it, son. The horse is just fine."

"Thank you." Isaac watched as the paramedics rolled over a stretcher. He stood close enough to David that he could press against him so David might know somewhere in his mind that he wasn't alone.

Suddenly the driver of the car was in front of them, his eyes wide as he clutched at Isaac. "I'm so sorry. You have to believe me! It was an accident!"

The policeman stepped in, pulling the man away firmly. "It's best if you don't talk to anyone, sir. Go back over there and wait."

The man reached for Isaac again, eyes shining. "Please, you have to understand. I couldn't stop in time! I couldn't see anything. I didn't know they were there, and I slammed on the brakes but—"

"I believe you." Isaac touched the man's arm. "We don't blame you."

The policeman led the driver away, and Officer Bukowski helped nudge David to the ambulance as the stretcher was loaded on. David walked like one of the creatures in Aaron's old comics—a zombie they were called. He climbed into the ambulance, and Isaac squeezed his shoulders.

"I'll be right behind you. I'm going to the hospital with Mary. All right? David?"

But David only stared at his mother, who now wore an oxygen mask, her skin distressingly pale. Her leg was in a splint, and a bone protruded sickeningly beneath her knee.

Choking down a rush of bile, Isaac stepped back as they closed the doors. Bukowski shepherded him along, and he was vaguely aware of getting into the police car and sitting beside Mary, who leaned against him, whimpering.

Isaac held her close and watched the world go by, the siren piercing the terrible night.

Chapter Thirteen

T HE FLOOR BENEATH Isaac's boots was the color of February—merciless gray. It was everywhere in the hospital, as though it had seeped into the other people in the waiting room as well. The lights overhead were too bright, and he wished they'd turn them down.

It had been a decade since he'd seen a doctor. The chicken pox had spread through the community like wildfire, and Mother had taped mittens to his hands so he couldn't scratch at his face. They'd visited the doctor in Red Hills who dealt with the Amish, but in Zebulon they didn't even have a doctor. The Amish Isaac knew only went in emergencies. Otherwise they used the home remedies in the paper or visited a chiropractor in Warren for their ailments.

He shifted in the thinly padded chair and flipped his knife over in his hands. His hat balanced on one knee, and when he glanced up at the clock on the wall—which had seemed to stop telling time it moved so slowly—a few people jerked their heads away.

Isaac smoothed his fingers over the handle of his knife, the blade folded neatly inside. He obviously had no wood to whittle, so he examined the old metal. He'd looked at the knife a million times in the years since Aaron had left it on his pillow, but now it seemed strangely new. From the outside it was nothing—an object like any other. But the truth hidden inside could slice to the core.

Bible passages unfurled in his mind, as if Bishop Yoder and the preachers hovered over him, their breath harsh in his ears.

For if we go on sinning deliberately after receiving the knowledge of the truth, there no longer remains a sacrifice for sins, but a fearful expectation of judgment, and a fury of fire that will consume the adversaries.

He slid his fingertips along the knife's innocent seam.

But each person is tempted when he is lured and enticed by his own desire. Then desire when it has conceived gives birth to sin, and sin when it is fully grown brings forth death.

Isaac flicked open the knife, the silver blade gleaming above the endless gray.

If anyone does not abide in me he is thrown away like a branch and withers; and the branches are gathered, thrown into the fire, and burned.

"Sir!"

He jolted, looking up at a young nurse standing over him, her lips compressed in a thin line. "Huh?"

"No weapons allowed in the hospital. Either you put it away immediately or I'll have to call security."

"Oh. I'm sorry." He snapped the knife shut and returned it to his pocket. "I didn't mean any harm."

The nurse sighed, face softening as she brushed away a strand of brown hair that had escaped her ponytail. She had dark skin, and her green uniform stretched over her swelling belly. "I'm sure you didn't. How are you holding up?"

"Do you know where my friend David is? He rode in the ambulance with his mother. I haven't seen him, and no one will tell me anything." They'd whisked Mary away for an examination as soon as they'd arrived, and ushered Isaac to the waiting room with no sign of David. "Is his mother all right?"

"Are you family? I'm not supposed to tell you anything if you're not."

"Yes." Another lie to add to his collection—so many there was no sense in counting now.

The nurse arched an eyebrow but took the seat beside him, lowering herself with a hand to her back. "What's your name?"

"Isaac."

"Nice to meet you, Isaac. I'm Danielle." She rooted in her pocket and pulled out a colored tube. "Lifesaver?"

He nodded and lifted his palm. She tapped two candies onto it, one orange and one green. He sucked the green one first, and the lime flavor spread over his tongue. "Thank you."

"No prob." Danielle popped a cherry circle into her mouth. "So, Mrs. Lantz is in surgery. It'll likely be quite a while yet."

"What about Mary?"

"Bumps and bruises, and they'll keep her overnight for observation. But she should be just fine. She was very, very lucky."

He thought of Mary in the back of the police car, her cap gone, blood and tears staining her face. "Where's David? Mrs. Lantz's son."

"We put him in a quiet room to rest. He's in shock. I can take you to see him for a few minutes if you want."

Isaac sat up straighter. "Yes! Please."

"I'll show you the way." With a soft grunt, she levered herself up.

He wasn't sure if he should offer to help or not, but then it was too late and she was leading him down the hallway surprisingly quickly given her condition, her sneakers squeaking on the floor. She clearly wasn't trying to hide that she was pregnant, and even rubbed her palm over her protruding belly as they walked.

They passed gurneys, some empty and some not, and people with clipboards brushed by, rushing here and there. Isaac carried his hat, trying not to stare at any of the patients as he sucked on the orange Lifesaver. Orange had been his favorite years ago, but today the taste was cloying and too sweet. All wrong.

After an area of many beds separated by curtains, they reached several doors. At the last, Danielle twisted the handle, knocking lightly and calling out. "David? You have a visitor."

Locked cabinets lined the left side of the dim, narrow room above a counter and sink, the only light coming from beneath the cabinets. Against the right wall rested a gurney, where David sat on the side. His hat and coat hung from a hook on the wall, and his blue shirt was half untucked from his pants. At least now he was awake enough to meet Isaac's gaze, although Isaac's throat tightened at the grief shining from his pale eyes.

"A few minutes, okay?" Danielle gave Isaac's shoulder a gentle squeeze, closing the door behind her.

"God, David." Isaac dropped his hat and wrapped him in a hug, moving between David's legs. "I was so worried. I *am* so worried. But Mary's all right, and they're looking after your mother. She'll be fine. I know it." *Another lie.* He longed to feel David's arms around him, but David was limp.

David said something, his words muffled against Isaac's shoulder.

"What?" Isaac drew back and caressed David's hair.

A tear dangled on his lashes. "It's my fault, Isaac. I should have gone to Eli's like she asked. She and Mary would be safe at home."

"No, no. You couldn't have known. It isn't your fault." He pressed a kiss to David's cold forehead.

"I should have gone. Instead I was—" He broke off, eyes squeezed shut.

"I know." *Sin when it is fully grown brings forth death.* Isaac choked down a sob. "I wish we could go back and take the pie instead."

"I wish I'd never met you."

Isaac staggered back as if he'd been struck, an iron band squeezing around his chest.

David reached for him, stumbling off the gurney. "No, I didn't mean it. Forgive me. Oh God, forgive me."

The counter rammed Isaac's lower back as David desperately threw himself against him, fingers digging into Isaac's skin.

"I didn't mean it." David's words were hot on Isaac's cheek. "I should wish it, but I don't. I couldn't. I can't even be truly sorry for the things we've done. I know I'm a sinner all the way through. But I can't be sorry when I love you so much."

Isaac wasn't sure whose tears he tasted. He shuddered as he forced his lungs to expand. David was shaking in his arms. "I love you too. We'll find a way. We'll fix this."

With a long exhale, David went still. For a minute they only breathed, holding each other. David's hair tickled Isaac's cheek, and he rubbed against it. A clock ticked the seconds by, the world beyond them miles away. *We'll fix this.* They had to.

The branches are gathered, thrown into the fire...

When David straightened, he gazed at Isaac tenderly, brushing his fingers over Isaac's cheek. "I wish I could have a picture of you, my Isaac." He pressed their lips together.

The kiss was achingly gentle, David's dry lips softened by his tears. He cradled Isaac's head as he opened his mouth and slid their tongues together. Isaac melted against him, quaking. They had to find a way to be together. *He loves me. We love each other.*

David whispered against his lips. "Always so sweet."

Isaac was going to explain about the candies, but he just kissed David instead, leaning their foreheads together. "We'll find a way."

As he stepped back, David shook his head. "I wish that were true."

Dread uncoiled like a serpent in Isaac's belly. "It *is* true. It has to be." He grabbed David's arms.

"Don't you see? God is punishing me. I must repent or my mother will die. Everyone I love will pay for my sins. Including you."

"No." Isaac's heart pounded.

"You need to stay far away from me."

"No! You don't know what you're saying. We'll get through this together." David was passive in his grasp, and Isaac wanted to shake him.

"We were never going to, Isaac. We've been lying to ourselves. Pretending it wouldn't have to end."

"Don't say that!" Isaac trembled even as he recognized the truth in David's words. "I love you, and you love me. Don't you?"

A tear slipped down David's cheek. "I love you more than anything. That's why it has to be over. We were fooling ourselves, Isaac. Thinking we could break the rules and not face the consequences. You know it's true."

He clutched David's hands. "It isn't fair."

An awful grimace contorted David's face. "Perhaps that was God's lesson for us all along."

As if he'd been hollowed out with the scrape of a spoon, Isaac sagged against David, their lips finding each other for a last kiss. *No. This can't be all there is.*

Light and distant noise from the hallway washed over them, and Isaac jerked back, blinking at Danielle, her fist still raised where it had struck the door. She smiled sadly. "I'm sorry to interrupt. But there are some people here to see you. They're very concerned. David, are you up to it?"

David scrubbed a hand over his face and hair. "Yes. I'm fine." He tugged on his shirt, straightening it, and running his thumbs under his galluses.

"We were just..." The words tumbled out, and Isaac's cheeks burned. "We weren't..."

Danielle held up her hands. "You don't have to explain anything to me, hon. And I won't say anything to anyone, so breathe, okay?"

He nodded jerkily, picking up his hat from where he'd thrown it aside on the floor. "Thank you."

She opened the door wider. "Ready?"

Gaze on the winter tiles, Isaac followed, David close behind but already beyond reach.

ISAAC HAD BARELY entered the waiting room when he was knocked back, stumbling as Mother threw her arms around him. He couldn't remember the last time she'd hugged him. Closing his eyes, he was a child again for a moment even though he had to stoop to lay his head on her shoulder. He inhaled deeply for her scent—usually a mix of flour and sweat—but her cloak only smelled of the frigid air. Snowflakes melted beneath his cheek.

"Josiah Raber came to tell us he'd heard there'd been an accident with the Lantz buggy. He saw you and David out on the road earlier, and we thought..." Mother stepped back, dropping her arms and glancing around. She took a deep breath, clearly gathering her composure after her outburst.

Nausea washed through him, and Isaac kept his gaze on Father's old boots a few feet away. "We're fine." *Where did Josiah see us? Near the motel?* He shoved away the panicked thought. It was shameful to even care about his secrets when Mrs. Lantz could very well die. "It was David's mother, and his sister Mary."

Father stepped forward and clapped a hand on Isaac's shoulder. "Yes, we know that now. We went to the O'Brien's up the road right away, and they drove us here. Praise the Lord you're all right."

Isaac forced himself to look up. He imagined his parents could see straight through him to the horrible truth, but they only watched him with quiet compassion. It somehow made it worse. Although he'd assured David it wasn't his fault, Isaac couldn't deny that if they'd gone to deliver the pie themselves it wouldn't have happened. But maybe it would have. Perhaps it would be David on the operating table. Or dead.

He concentrated on breathing—in and out, in and out—until the dread loosened its grip. If not for Father's steady hand on his shoulder, Isaac thought he might fly apart. But he had to be strong now. He stepped back, holding his head up. For the first time he was aware of several other people from Zebulon, a wall of black beyond his parents, Bishop Yoder and Deacon Stoltzfus among them. The scattered English people about stared with sympathetic curiosity.

Isaac watched David nearby, itching to hold him. He forced his gaze away, stomach lurching as his eyes met the deacon's. Deacon Stoltzfus watched him with his usual stony expression, and Isaac looked down at his hands, realizing with a start that they were still bloody.

"David, we're all praying for your mother," the bishop intoned. "The Lord tests us, and His will is at times a mystery."

David had left his hat and coat in the little room, and his hair stood up this way and that. No one approached him, and Isaac could see why. The tension seemed to vibrate from him. The shock had melted away and seemingly left anger and grief in its wake. David cleared his throat, and Isaac could sense the room holding its breath.

"Anna and the girls?" David asked, his voice raw and flat.

Joseph Kauffman stepped forward. "My Katie is with them. Don't worry."

"Thank you. You all didn't have to come."

A murmur of disagreement rippled through the room, and Bishop Yoder spoke again. "Of course we've come. Let us go visit Mary and pray with her. She is undoubtedly in need of comfort from the Lord."

Danielle stepped forward. "I'll take you to her."

Isaac willed David to look at him before he went, but David merely shuffled along after Danielle and the bishop, vanishing into the depths of the hospital. Isaac's head throbbed, and he let Father guide him to a chair. Beyond the waiting room there was a constant clamor of shouts, beeps and activity.

Leaning over Isaac, Mother fussed with his hair. "We should get you home. You're exhausted."

"No, I'm fine. I want to stay." He squirmed away from her touch. "At least until…" *At least until we know if Mrs. Lantz is dead or alive.*

"Where were you and David going?" Father asked.

Isaac hitched a shoulder, concentrating on breathing steadily while part of him wanted to fall to his knees and confess. "Just to the hardware store. Needed a few tools." He couldn't bear to look his parents in the eye. He gripped his knife inside his pocket.

Fortunately Mrs. Yoder called his parents over to where all the Amish folks were huddled together, discussing something intently. Isaac squeezed the knife and closed his eyes, wishing more than ever that Aaron was there. He tried to imagine where Aaron was right that moment. Did he live in a city? A town? Was he married? Isaac tried to imagine him almost ten years older, but couldn't.

But what could Aaron do? He couldn't fix David's mother. He couldn't turn back time for David and Isaac to make another choice. What would he say if he knew the truth? The Bible's teachings were the same out in the world—lying with another man was an abomination. Even though Aaron had turned his back on the church, he could never accept Isaac's true nature. Could he?

A tentative hand rested on Isaac's arm, and he blinked at Danielle sitting beside him.

"Hanging in there?"

He nodded. It was a wonder that she had seen him and David kiss—had witnessed their sin—yet there was no judgement in her gaze. *Maybe Aaron would be the same.*

"Can I ask you something?"

"Uh-huh," he replied.

"How did they all find out so quickly? I thought you didn't have telephones."

A ghost of a smile lifted Isaac's lips. "You'd be amazed how fast news can spread on the Amish grapevine. And when there's an emergency, we get our English neighbors to drive us. We—" He broke off as June walked into the waiting room with Eli Helmuth. Isaac was on his feet and moving toward her before he could think. "June."

"Hello." She smiled. "Isaac, isn't it? You're the young man who works with David."

"You've met?" Mother asked, her gaze sharp.

It seemed as though his well of lies had run dry, and Isaac simply nodded. He realized he'd also used her first name, which was sure to set off alarm bells with Mother.

"Just once," June said. "David was giving me a hand with my fence, and Isaac was a big help too." She shook snow off her brightly colored scarf, which matched the red in her long coat.

Isaac had been back to June's several times with David since the first, life-changing night, but it was true enough that they had once fixed a broken gate. "I'm sure David will be grateful you came."

Eli's voice was gravelly. "As I am grateful for the ride."

"Oh, of course." June waved her hand. "It's the least I could do. I drove by the accident scene and pestered the cops until they told me the name. I went over right away. Anna thought Mr. Helmuth would want to come to the hospital."

Eli was an older man now, probably sixty, but he was still fit and strong, his long beard only a little silvery. "Is there news?" he asked solemnly.

As the others filled him in, June made her way to Isaac. Danielle was gone, and Isaac and June sat together. "How's Anna?" he asked.

"Upset. Angry. Worried to death. The little ones hardly made a peep." June sighed, fiddling with the plastic clip in her light hair. It was painted to look like a butterfly's wings. "It doesn't seem fair, does it?"

Isaac shook his head.

"How's David?"

"Not good." Isaac shivered. "He blames himself. If we'd...if we hadn't...Mrs. Lantz asked us to take the pie for her, but we were too busy, so she and Mary went." He whispered, "We were selfish."

"It was an accident, Isaac. It doesn't matter what you and David didn't do." She paused. "Or what you did do."

Eyes on his knees, Isaac jerked his head in a nod as he concentrated on breathing. *Does she know? Can she tell?* He shuddered.

"You should get a good night's sleep. I can drive you and your parents home if you want. They're calling for more snow overnight, so we should go soon."

"I can't. I need to stay with...I need to stay." He glanced up as a hush washed over the room. David and Bishop Yoder were back, accompanied by a small man in the same kind of green uniform Danielle wore, although he had a cap over his black hair. Scrubs, Isaac thought they were called, although he couldn't remember for the life of him how he knew that.

The man cleared his throat. "I'm Dr. Ling. David's asked me to speak to you about his mother. She's in very serious condition, but we've stabilized her and performed surgery on her leg. She suffered a compound fracture in her right leg as well as other internal injuries, and a concussion."

As Dr. Ling continued speaking, Isaac's head filled with a strange buzzing, as if he was watching everyone around him from a distance even though he was sitting right there. David kept his gaze down, and Isaac silently willed him to look up, just for a moment. He could hear David's voice clearly in his mind.

I can't be sorry when I love you so much.

Yet standing there with Bishop Yoder's hand heavy on his shoulder, David looked the sorriest man Isaac had ever seen.

"We should get home," June said.

Isaac blinked. Joseph Kauffman and Eli Helmuth were speaking to David now, and David nodded blankly. Isaac blinked again at June beside him. "Is she going to be all right? I didn't hear."

June touched his arm lightly. "We don't know yet. It'll be touch and go for a while, but the doctor's hopeful."

"Touch and go," Isaac repeated, his tongue thick.

Then Mother and Father were there, urging him gently to his feet. "Come along now, Isaac. There's nothing we can do tonight but pray. You need to rest," Father said.

Mother pressed her hand to his cheek. "You're very pale."

"I'll give you a ride home," June told Isaac's parents.

Mother and Father shared a glance, and Father nodded. "Thank you."

Then somehow Isaac was moving, and they were leaving the waiting room. "No. I need to stay." He dug in his heels as they led him to the glass doors that swooped open and shut with each person that went in or out. "David...he needs..."

"Eli's staying with him, and Martha Yoder as well." Mother didn't slow her pace. "There's nothing more you can do tonight."

"There is!" Isaac's pulse raced, and the bright lights all around blurred. Was he crying? Why was he crying? "David!" He struggled to escape their grasp. He had to see David! Didn't they understand? He couldn't leave him alone. They loved each other. "I can't go!" He looked back the way they'd come, but David was already out of sight. "No!"

"Isaac, my goodness!" Mother gripped his arm. "It's all right, we can come back in the morning."

But he was filled with a terrible dread that he'd never see David again. "I have to stay!"

Then Danielle was there, her hands on his shoulders, hard yet somehow gentle. "Isaac, you need to breathe. It's been a very traumatic day, and it's normal that you're overwhelmed. Go home and rest, and I'll tell David you asked about him. Sound good?"

Somehow Isaac found himself nodding, her calm voice settling him.

She smiled. "I'll make sure David and Mary are okay. Go on now."

It was snowing again, the flakes sticking in Isaac's hair. He must have left his hat, but a moment later Mother was placing it on his head. They all squeezed into the front seat of June's big truck, Isaac in the middle with Mother and Father on his right. June leaned over him and buckled his seat belt around his waist. She smelled like a flower, but he wasn't sure which one. Lilac, maybe.

"There's another belt there on the right, Mr. Byler."

"It's all right. We put our faith in the Lord's protection," Mother said. "But thank you."

Isaac wondered if Mother would actually ask him to take off his seat belt, but she didn't. June seemed to want to say something more, but turned the key instead. The engine roared, and Isaac could feel cold air on his face from the open vents. June fiddled with a few knobs, and the air slowed. She turned on the wipers, and they squeaked across the windshield, pushing the fresh snow away. Isaac crossed his arms in front of him so he wouldn't dig his elbows into June or Mother.

The digital clock above the radio said it was after ten, and there were only a few other vehicles on the road. Isaac watched the lights coming toward them, the wipers slowly waving back and forth. There was warm air coming from the vents now, but he shivered.

The world felt muffled, and if he closed his eyes, he could almost imagine he was at home in bed, and that the next time he woke Nathan would be snoring in his ear, the warm scent of fresh biscuits wafting up as Mother went to work, always the first one awake.

But of course he was still in June's pickup truck, where he and David had eaten popcorn and Pepsi, and been tempted by the world. Although their true wickedness had come later that night—and almost all the days to follow.

"We should check on Anna and the girls." Mother's voice was too loud. "Tell them the news."

"Yes, I told Anna I'd go back and give her an update. But if you'd rather go yourselves, I can take you." June tapped the blinker and slowed to make a left turn.

Mother and Father looked at each other, having one of their silent conversations. *Tick, tick, tick.* A green arrow flashed in front of the steering wheel.

Father answered. "If you don't mind going without us, we would be grateful. We want to get back and check on our children, and the snow seems to be worsening again."

"I don't mind at all. It only takes me an extra few minutes to stop by." June slowed and made another turn toward Zebulon.

Isaac held his hands to the vent in front of him, thinking of the drifting snow that would block the outhouse door and need to be shoveled. He thought as well of the nip that would be in the air in the small hours of the night when the big stove downstairs needed more wood, everyone huddling in their beds with noses cold and feet bundled in the thick socks Mother knit.

As they neared home, Isaac tried to imagine David back at the hospital, perhaps sitting by Mary's bedside. But he could only think of him in a reckless room of beige and orange, their bodies flushed and fervent in another life.

Chapter Fourteen

THE LANTZ HOUSE was unchanged from the previous morning, although the snow on the lane wasn't marred by the little footsteps of David's sisters as they skipped off to school. Isaac slowed Silver as they reached the house, and when the door opened, it was Anna who peered out.

She disappeared again, but the door was ajar, so Isaac unhitched Silver and hurried over, straightening his hat. At the threshold he paused. He was about to take off his glove and rap his knuckles on the door, but then Anna was there again.

"Just stay put and finish your breakfast. I told you, it's only Isaac," she called over her shoulder before pulling her dark cape around her and stepping outside. Her white cap was askew over her light hair, and she reached up to straighten it. "Sorry. It's taken forever to get them to even take a bite. I made Mrs. Kauffman go home around midnight, and if I don't at least keep them fed I'll never hear the end of it."

"It's all right."

There were dark smudges under her eyes, and she smiled grimly. "I don't suppose you have any news." She held up her hand. "Wait…" She opened the door again and closed it after peeking inside. "Just making sure. So, news?"

"No. I wanted to go back to the hospital, but I thought I should come and make sure everything was okay here first. I figured that's what David would want me to do."

"That's good of you, Isaac. We're fine. Just waiting. That English woman from down the road said she'd bring Mary home this morning. She's been very kind. You don't look like you got much sleep either. Did you have breakfast? I have a fresh pot of coffee on."

"No, I'm fine. My mother already made me eat too much." He flushed. "Not that I'm complaining."

Anna smiled sadly. "It's all right, Isaac." She straightened up, taking a deep breath. "Now tell me. Do you think my mother's going to die? You were there, right? The policeman said David and another boy were there on the road, where it happened. And you were at the hospital too. June said they were hopeful. Are you hopeful, Isaac?"

"Of course! And...and I prayed most of the night, and everyone's praying—"

"I don't care about prayers." Anna huffed. "I know I shouldn't say that, but it's the truth. I've been praying, too, but it won't change anything. I know I'm supposed to trust in God. That it would be His will. But it's not fair. It isn't."

Isaac swallowed hard. "I know. But I think it was a good sign she lived through surgery. I was afraid she wouldn't. They said it would be touch and go. Whatever that means."

Her eyes wet, Anna blew out a breath. "Okay. Thank you. And you saw Mary? She's really all right?"

"Yes. Physically, at least. She was in shock, but she's okay."

They both turned at the rattle of an approaching buggy. Isaac's stomach lurched when he saw Mervin at the reins, Mervin's mother beside him.

Anna sighed. "I know everyone means well, but..." She pasted on a smile as the buggy drove up. "Good morning, Mrs. Miller, Mervin," she called.

Isaac nodded to them as they climbed down and approached. He was afraid to meet Mervin's eyes, heat in his face as he thought of the last time they'd spoken, and what Mervin had heard in the barn. Mervin kept his gaze locked on Anna, his arms heavy with baking dishes.

"Hello, Anna." Mrs. Miller held another dish. "I just wanted to make sure you had enough food, and Mervin insisted on driving me since the roads are still slippery this morning."

"Thank you—that's so kind. Please come inside. Let me help you with that." Anna took the dishes from Mervin and ushered his mother into the house.

Mervin didn't follow, and Isaac shuffled his boots in the snow as the silence drew out, their breath clouding in the winter air. Mervin had always had too many words to say in not enough time, but not this morning. Finally Isaac opened his mouth, and blurted the first thing that popped into his head. "How's Sadie?"

Pale eyebrows disappearing under his black hat, Mervin answered, "She's fine."

"Good. That's good." Isaac floundered, his mind spinning uselessly. "Are you driving her home from the singing on Sunday?"

"Isaac, please stop."

His lungs felt as though they were full of lead. "I know things have changed, but...I still...you're my best friend," he whispered.

Mervin lowered his voice, words urgent. "You know that if you repent, God will forgive you. There's no sin too great. Have you tried to overcome this? If you pray hard enough, I know you can do it."

Isaac thought of his silent prayers that morning. The first was for Mrs. Lantz, but the second was hopelessly selfish and weak—a plea that he could be with David again. That they would find their way through this together, even though he knew in his heart the only possible life in Zebulon was apart.

Mervin went on with a glance at the house, his voice low. "I know you think you're different, but you're not! He has you thinking crazy things. You remember how his brother influenced those girls? They died because of him! I know this isn't you, Isaac. It can't be." He clasped Isaac's arm.

Regretfully, Isaac stepped back, and Mervin's hand fell away. "I wish I could tell you what you want to hear. But it is me. David only helped me see it."

"*Helped* you? He—" Mervin flushed. "Isaac, you know what the Bible says. You know how things are supposed to go. You have to join the church. Get married. I should tell the bishop everything. I might go to hell myself for keeping your secret! And what about your parents? Think of them!"

"Please don't tell!" Isaac glanced around and lowered his voice. "Please, Mervin."

"What are you going to do? Just keep lying to everyone? For how long?"

As Mervin's words bore down on him, Isaac felt like the snow at his feet was quicksand. He turned and stumbled to the barn, blood rushing in his ears. He grabbed a shovel, and began clearing a path back toward the house where Mervin still stood, his shoulders slumped.

For how long?

Isaac threw the fresh snow atop the banks that already lined the walkway. *Bend, lift, throw. Bend, lift, throw.* Before long he panted, and sweat dampened his hair beneath his hat. He heard the clatter of Mervin and his mother leaving, and Anna called to him, but he didn't falter. *Bend, lift, throw.*

What are you going to do?

As the drone of an engine approached, Isaac stopped, hands gripping the shovel so tightly the handle creaked. His chest heaved, the puffs of his breath filling the air like smoke. What would he do? For the first time he knew the answer. For the first time he said it out loud.

"I'm leaving."

June's truck rumbled into sight, and Isaac's words faded on the wind. He spotted David's hat through the windshield, and he rushed forward, slip-sliding back to the house, the shovel forgotten in a snow bank. Anna burst through the door, jabbing a finger behind when her sisters would have followed. The three girls crowded the threshold, jostling for position.

Isaac's heart thudded as David climbed down and gave a hand to

Mary, who seemed very small under her black cape. Anna flew at her sister, skidding to a stop by the truck and hugging her with care. Isaac hovered several feet away, and June got down from behind the wheel in her long red coat, giving him a little smile.

Anna kissed Mary's pale cheek. "I'll heat up the water for a bath, and there's lots of food. Mrs. Miller and Mervin brought apple bread—your favorite." She blinked back tears. "And I'm sorry for what I said yesterday morning. I didn't mean it."

Mary smiled wanly. "I know."

Anna looked to David. "Well?"

He nodded. "She's going to be all right. She won't be able to walk for months, and she'll be in the hospital until next week at least, but she's going to make it."

The relief was blissfully warm as it swept through Isaac.

Taking a shuddering breath, Anna blinked rapidly, and David kissed her forehead. Then his gaze met Isaac's, and his jaw tightened.

"What are you doing here?" David asked shortly.

Throat like sandpaper, Isaac answered, "Shoveling."

"You shouldn't be here."

Mary's brow creased. "David, what's the matter?" She turned to Isaac. "I'm glad you're here. I wanted to thank you for yesterday. I've never been so scared, and you made it better."

"But I didn't do anything."

She smiled softly. "You were there. That was all I needed."

Isaac had to look away as guilt congealed in him. "I'm glad I could help."

David spoke again, his tone even. "I only meant that I can't pay you. I don't know what's going to happen. The hospital bill's going to be huge."

Taking a deep breath, Isaac looked into David's pale blue eyes, willing his voice to remain steady. "I don't expect you to pay me. I just want to help."

"We all do," June added. "I'm sure David appreciates it, Isaac."

David nodded stiffly and turned on his heel, striding toward the house where his littlest sisters still waited in the doorway.

"Anna, if you'd like to visit your mother, I can drive you back with David once he gets cleaned up," June went on. "We left Mr. Helmuth there in the meantime, and of course I can bring you home later."

Anna nodded eagerly. "That'll be all right, won't it?" she asked her sister. "I know we're only supposed to ride in cars in an emergency, but this still counts, doesn't it?"

"I'm sure Bishop Yoder would agree," Mary said. "It would take too long in the buggy, and there's still a lot of snow on the roads."

Isaac watched David open his arms to his little sisters, who crowded around him. He crouched down and spoke to them, kissing them and hugging them as they sobbed in obvious relief.

Feeling as though he was intruding, Isaac backed away with a nod to June, kicking through the snow until he found the shovel. The longing to get David alone and hold him close was unbearable. But David had made it clear he didn't want that.

"Isaac?" Mary called out.

He trotted back. "Yes?"

She was still so pale, but her eyes were warm. "You really did help. Thank you. I hope…" She lowered her head, shrugging. "I hope I'll see you soon." She turned on her heel and returned to Anna before disappearing into the house.

Isaac turned to the barn and dug into a fresh mound of snow, keeping his head down and his mind blank.

Bend, lift, throw.

DAVID'S WEIGHT PINNED *him over the side of the worktable, his palm against Isaac's mouth to stifle his cries. Isaac couldn't move, and as David slammed into him, every thrust stretched Isaac more, deeper and deeper until*

he thought he might shatter in the best possible way. He closed his eyes and felt both in his body and outside it at the same time. His focus narrowed on his ass, as if his arms and legs didn't exist anymore, and his whole being was that center of burning pleasure.

But then David was gone, and Isaac was alone, goose bumps on his naked flesh, the table like ice beneath him where he was bent over. He tried to stand up, but his legs gave out each time. He pushed with his hands, but now the table really was ice, and he was helpless. The ice was cracking. He called for David, but there was no sound.

With a gasp, Isaac woke. He'd flailed an arm out and hit his brother, and Nathan snorted and mumbled before flopping over. Isaac froze, waiting. In the other bed, Ephraim raised his head.

"Isaac?" he asked blearily.

"It's fine. Go back to sleep," Isaac whispered.

"But—"

Isaac snapped, "I said go back to sleep."

With a little huff, Ephraim flipped over. Joseph still seemed out like a light, and as the low growl of Nathan's resumed snores filled the air, Isaac exhaled. He shouldn't be short with Ephraim, but all he wanted in that moment was to be alone. *I'm a terrible brother.*

He'd promised Ephraim they'd talk more, but had been wrapped up in his own world. A few times he'd snapped to attention while doing chores in the barn, finding Ephraim waiting expectantly and realizing he had no idea what Ephraim had said. The last time Ephraim had muttered for him to forget it.

I'll make it up to him. Later.

After his dream, Isaac was half hard beneath his nightshirt, and he wondered if he could be quiet enough to find release and sleep again. It had been days since the accident now, and he still hadn't seen David again. Each morning when he arrived at the Lantzes' to work, David had left before dawn for the hospital.

Not that Isaac begrudged David seeing his mother. But he felt utterly adrift. Mary and Anna had their hands full taking care of their sisters when they weren't at the hospital. Isaac never went to the house for lunch anymore, although they brought him food most days, Mary lingering as Isaac feigned great interest in whatever he was working on.

If she only knew. Isaac rubbed himself with the heel of his hand through his nightshirt. He was strung tightly, like a horse whose master was yanking too hard on the reins. It was as though his body couldn't understand David's sudden absence after feeling his touch so often. Isaac needed release, but the thought of trudging through the snow to the frozen outhouse for privacy was enough to dampen the tense desire.

He pulled the quilt up to his chin and curled toward the window, knees to his chest. It was a dark night, and he could see little more than blackness through the square of glass. He needed to close his eyes and go back to sleep, for dawn would come all too soon.

In the morning he'd get dressed, and eat breakfast, and do his chores, and hitch up Silver to the old buggy. He'd wave to the Lantz girls as he arrived, and shovel any new snow to make sure Mary and Anna had a clear path to the washhouse and well.

Then he would work in the barn where he'd known such incredible joy. Not only the pleasure of his furtive coupling with David, but the companionship they'd found—the hours talking of nothing and everything, and the easy silences. They'd been virtual strangers, and now they'd shared so much.

He'd finished the projects David had abandoned, doing his best to remember what he'd been taught. He wished with all his heart that David would appear and tell him everything was all right. That David would kiss him and touch him and whisper he loved him, and they'd bolt the door and hide away.

But David didn't come. At the end of the day, Isaac would climb into the hayloft and light the lamp to heat the water for the shower. He'd stand naked and trembling in the shower stall, one hand braced on the icy wall as he jerked his cock, closing his eyes and pretending David was there. When the burst of pleasure faded into nothing, the ache was always somehow worse than it was before.

You need to stay far away from me.

Shivering, Isaac watched the sky lighten by inches as David's voice echoed in his mind. He knew he should do what David asked. But if he stayed away from David and the Lantz farm…where would he go? He would be stuck at home. There were no other jobs for him in Zebulon. He would be back where he started, as if he'd never left. As if none of it had meant anything.

The wind whistled by the window, and Isaac could almost imagine it was a train. The idea he'd only dared speak once filled his mind, pushing at the fear and guilt and hopelessness until it was the only thing left. He burrowed his face under the quilt and mouthed the words.

I'm leaving.

Chapter Fifteen

"I SAAC."

His belly flip-flopped as he looked at David in the entrance of the barn. He'd been sawing so intently he hadn't even heard the door heave open. It was mid-afternoon, but gloomy and damp as January often was, although the lantern beside him on the worktable gave off not only light, but heat. He'd been working so hard he'd hung his hat and shoved up the sleeves of his coat. He wiped his brow before peeling off his gloves.

"I finished the bed frame for the Hooleys. This is the side table. And the new kitchen table for Bishop Yoder's daughter is ready to be delivered. I'll take it tomorrow. Then there's the—"

"Isaac, stop. Please."

No. Don't say it.

David pulled the door shut behind him, and heat flowed through Isaac, his body humming as if it remembered the things they'd done behind that closed door. The urge to throw himself at David and finally touch him again had Isaac's head spinning. But David didn't pull the beam across, and the gulf between them felt like miles and not feet. There were dark circles under David's eyes, and a weariness that made him smaller somehow.

David took off his hat and circled it in his hands, head down. "Isaac—"

"How is she settling in? Is the ramp okay? My father and Ephraim came over yesterday to help me with it." Isaac fiddled with the tools spread out on the table, picking them up and putting them down.

"They didn't have to do that. I was going to build it. But yes, it's perfect. Thank you. And thank you for all the work you've done without me. I'll find a way to pay you."

Isaac shook his head. "I don't care about that." Before David could argue, he plowed on. "Your mother must be glad to be home. Must have been strange to be there for Christmas with all those bright decorations. Do they do that in the hospital? Put up all the sparkling lights? I remember in Red Hills there was this English house out by the highway that had the biggest tree in front of it, with so many lights. Once I asked Mother why we couldn't decorate, and she said candles in the window were quite enough for Jesus, and anything else was prideful and that the English had forgotten the true meaning of Christmas. Although Mother and Father always give us a little something. Joseph got a yo-yo this year, and he can't put it down." Isaac ordered himself to stop babbling.

In the silence, David blew out a long breath and placed his hat carefully on the table. "Isaac, you can't come here again."

He gripped the side of the table, his head feeling as though it might pop off his shoulders. He forced himself to look at David, the wide table still between them.

"I told you I can't pay you. And I told you that you need to stay away."

Isaac swallowed hard. "You don't really think the accident was God's punishment, do you?"

David rubbed a hand over his face. "I don't know. It doesn't matter now. What's done is done. Either way, you know we can't go back to the way things were. It's impossible. We always knew it, even if we didn't want to admit it. Now we have to be men, and face our responsibilities. We've had our rumspringa."

Fury shot through Isaac. "It was more than that!" He slammed the hammer down, cracking a piece of oak. Kaffi startled in her stall, snorting and sidestepping, Silver whinnying nearby. Isaac flattened his palms on the table. "And you know it's not impossible. You know there's a way."

David shook his head, defeated.

Isaac took a deep breath and said it out loud. "We can leave. We can go into the world, where there are other people like us. Where there are people who won't judge us. I love you, David. More than anything. We can be together. We can be free."

The bark of David's bitter laugh echoed in the rafters. "I'll never be free, Isaac. How could I walk away from them after all they've lost? Especially now? Mother will be in a wheelchair for months. We can't even come close to paying the hospital bill. The community's helping, but it's not enough. They're my responsibility."

"What about Eli Helmuth? Surely he plans to ask your mother to marry him? Anna said he barely left her side."

"Maybe, but even so, I can't leave them. Not after Joshua."

"So you'll be trapped here in a life you don't want, and for what? To atone for your brother's sins?"

"And my own!" David shuddered. "You know all the things I've done. I have to make it right."

"By being miserable?"

"By being holy. Living a plain life. By joining the church and devoting myself to God. If I pray hard enough…"

Isaac raised his hands before letting them fall to his sides. "If you pray hard enough? What will happen? You'll stop being a…you'll stop being gay?" The word still felt foreign on his tongue, but he knew he had to say it out loud.

"I don't know. I have to try." David's chest rose and fell rapidly, and he peered at Isaac, imploring. "If we both try, we could be friends. After enough time."

Fists clenched, Isaac choked down a scream. "*Friends?* So we'll both join the church? Get married? Should I marry your sister, David? She loves me—we both know it. Then what? Would I lie with Mary the way I would with you? The way I *want* to with you?"

David flinched and squeezed his eyes shut.

"Would I touch her the way I touched you? The whole time closing my eyes and seeing your face. Hearing your voice in my ear. Tasting your cock in my mouth. Feeling you inside me. Being inside you. It would be only in my mind, but Mary would know it wasn't her I really wanted, even if she never knew who it was. Is that what you want?"

Shuddering, David opened his eyes. "No," he whispered.

As Isaac took a deep breath and said the words, he realized with a strange sense of calm that they were true. "I'm never joining the church, David. If you have to stay in Zebulon, I can't stop you. But I can't stay. I don't know when I'm leaving, but I know I am."

Pale eyes glistening, David nodded. He inhaled deeply and picked up a saw. "I should get to work."

"You need help with this now more than ever." Isaac waved his arm over the worktable and tools. "I don't care if you can't pay me. At least let me do this."

David's throat worked as he swallowed thickly. "I'm a weak man, Isaac. I can't bear to be close to you without..." He shook his head. "You've done so much already. Thank you. But I don't want you to come back here again."

I'm leaving.

Isaac forced himself to stuff his hands into his gloves and put on his hat. He led Silver from her stall, rubbing her neck and saying a silent prayer that he wouldn't be sick. To know that he'd kissed and touched David for the last time weeks ago—that he never would again—made him feel utterly hollow.

He passed within arm's reach of David, but kept his fingers tight on the reins. At the door, Isaac stopped. His voice was reed thin, and he stared out at the last rays of light beyond the swaying branches on the barren horizon. "But you still want me? You still love me?"

David's voice was little more than a whisper. "Always, Eechel."

Isaac left him behind, not sure if that made it better, or all the worse.

CHICKEN AND POTATOES sat like a lump in Isaac's stomach. Dinner conversation had fortunately been dominated by Katie's detailed rendition of her school project on tadpoles and how they become frogs. More than any of them, Katie had always loved school. Now as Isaac settled himself on the wooden bench under the window in the living room, he watched her curled in Mother's rocking chair, reading a textbook avidly. Katie's black cap had fallen to her shoulder, and she twisted a long chunk of her blonde hair around her finger, her eyes darting left and right as she read.

They'd barely been taught any science in school, and Isaac had no doubt the text took a Christian approach. They'd mainly learned English, and to read and write. Practical math and some history—but Amish history, of course. School taught them enough to get by when they had to interact with the English world, and little else.

He remembered the first time he heard the word *evolution,* and Aaron's shouts of protest as Father snatched the forbidden book from Aaron's trunk and marched downstairs to throw it into the stove. Late into the night in their bed, Aaron had talked and talked, seething quietly and telling Isaac all sorts of things he didn't understand. Isaac had nodded, but surely God had created the universe?

He reached into his pocket to feel the knife, watching his sister and listening to a log crack and sizzle in the stove. Though their beds were never quite warm enough in winter, the living room was too hot. Sweat gathered in the dip of Isaac's lower back.

Father read his old black Bible in his rocker next to Katie, swaying gently with the odd tap of his bare foot. Nathan read his school book listlessly where he sprawled on another bench. In the corner, Joseph stood flicking his yo-yo up and down.

Ephraim flipped through the paper on a chair near the stove, flicking the pages loudly. Isaac wished he could ask Ephraim to come upstairs and talk with him, but of course if he did, everyone else's interest would be piqued, and there would be questions to answer. If not today, then tomorrow, or the day after.

Katie turned another page. Before too long, she'd be finished with school. Her life would be raising children, cooking, cleaning, quilting and canning. Maybe she'd settle into it happily. Maybe not. Not that she had a choice. Isaac tugged at his collar. Not that any of them did. He loved carpentry, but what if he loved something more? How would he even know?

He must have sighed as he fidgeted, because Mother glanced up from the desk, the scratch of her pencil on a sheet of paper stopping.

"All right, Isaac? You're very quiet tonight."

He nodded, but she still gazed at him with a furrow between her brows. One of the strings from her bright white cap was twisted, and she straightened it absently. As she opened her mouth again, he asked her, "What are you writing?"

"An article for the paper about Mrs. Lantz."

"I thought Marvin's Adah already wrote about the accident."

"Yes, but this is about the hospital bills. If everyone who reads the paper sends the Lantzes what they can, it will help. Even if it's a dollar." She turned back to her letter.

It was true *Die Botschaft* did go to thousands of homes. "Wouldn't it be better to just have insurance like the English?"

Father's hand froze where he'd been stroking his gray beard, and he laid a ribbon across his page. "Our insurance is our faith in the Lord, Isaac. In our community." He closed the Bible. "What's the matter today?"

There was no point in putting it off. "I won't be working with David Lantz anymore." In the silence that followed, Isaac could feel all eyes on him. He stared through the charred glass on the door of the stove and concentrated on keeping his voice steady. "You know he hasn't been able to pay since the accident. He said not to come back."

It stabbed at his gut to say the words aloud. To think that tomorrow morning he'd wake and not go anywhere. Back where he started. There were surely fences that needed fixing. He was good at that.

He thought of the acres of their farm, and for an awful moment was struck by the notion that he'd never leave again. That his whole life would be here in this house, Nathan snoring beside him at night, the trains rumbling by out of reach. He took a sharp breath, pain needling under his ribs.

"But he needs your help more than ever. Even if he can't pay, you're still learning from him," Mother said.

More silence. Finally Isaac glanced to Father, who watched him with a speculative gaze Isaac couldn't decipher.

"Did you have a falling out?" Father asked.

"No, nothing like that." It was a half-truth, perhaps. "It's only because David can't pay, and he didn't think it was fair. I told him we didn't mind, but he's decided. I can help around here again. There's always more than enough milking, and we can get ready for planting."

Ephraim spoke up, the paper abandoned across his lap, a frown creasing his face. "But you don't want to farm. Father and I are getting along just fine without you. Nathan and Joseph have been doing more chores as well."

Father gave Ephraim a hard look. "But of course we welcome your help, Isaac."

"Of course," Ephraim added. "I didn't mean...it's just that you love carpentry. Can't you start doing it on your own? We could make a workshop here, couldn't we? Or maybe you could go work for the English."

"Ephraim!" Mother huffed. "Why would you suggest such a thing? You know that men don't work outside the community in Zebulon."

"But what's he supposed to do?" Ephraim asked. "He hates farming, and you know it."

Before anyone could say anything else, Isaac jumped in. "It's all right." He smiled, his chapped lips tight. "For now I want to give farming another go." His chest burned. The urge to get up and run into the night was overwhelming. *I'll hurt them more if I stay and pretend.*

Turned in her chair at the desk, Mother sighed. "You were hesitant to work with David to begin with, but it suited you, Isaac. You've seemed so happy these months. Like you've grown into yourself." She glanced at Father. "We're hoping you'll decide to follow church soon."

Isaac jerked his chin in a nod.

"How's Mary?" Mother asked. "She looked well at the last service. Much improved." She and Father shared another look, and he nodded. "It's time you had a buggy of your own. We know you were concerned about the money, so we've been putting aside all of your pay instead of only a portion. There's a buggy maker in Polk County. If the weather clears, Father could take you down next week."

"Your own buggy!" Nathan's pimply face lit up. "How long until I get one?"

Ephraim rolled his eyes. "I'm before you. You're still in school anyway."

Isaac clasped his hands to keep them from trembling. He licked his lips. "I don't know what to say." *I'm never going to drive Mary or any other girl home. Don't waste the money on me. I'm gay.* "Are you sure we can afford it? You know I don't mind waiting. Maybe in the spring—"

Mother shook her head, clearly exasperated. "But why would you want to wait?"

"Did you hear the police came to talk to Bishop Yoder about using the orange triangles?" Ephraim asked, a challenge clear in his tone. "What do you think about that, Father?"

Father's jaw tightened. "I think the police should stay out of our business."

"But other Amish use them," Ephraim insisted. "It's dangerous on the roads. Look at what happened to Mrs. Lantz. I don't get why it's such a bad thing to be safe."

Mother clucked her tongue. "We follow the Ordnung and put our lives in God's hands. You know this. We don't need English ways."

Blood in the snow. The twist of Mrs. Lantz's leg—white bone sticking out through flesh. The red lights spinning over David's ghostly face.

"So why didn't God protect David's mother?" Isaac blurted. "Didn't she and Mary pray enough?" His words hung in the air, thick like the oppressive heat from the stove.

His family stared at him, even Ephraim silent now with wide eyes. Mother and Father looked at each other, and Father cleared his throat.

"It is not our place to question the Lord. There will be no more of this talk. Do you understand?"

"Maybe if you'd been there, you'd question too," Isaac went on. "If you'd seen the blood, and heard how—"

Father slammed his palm down on the arm of his rocking chair. "No more."

Isaac could only nod, and after a few moments everyone turned back to what they'd been doing. In the weighty silence, he listened to the eventual *snick* of Joseph's yo-yo as the string released and rewound, and Mother's pencil scratching again. Pages turned, and the fire sparked as Ephraim creaked open the door and tossed in another log.

When Father spoke again, his voice was even. "We'll go to Polk County when the weather clears. You've waited long enough, Isaac. A man needs his own buggy."

It was true—an Amish man did need his own buggy. But with each breath, Isaac grew surer that he would be a different kind of man.

Chapter Sixteen

"ISAAC! NATHAN!" MOTHER shouted from downstairs. "They're coming."

Isaac already knew, since the clock showed twenty-nine minutes after eight, and the people of Zebulon were nothing if not prompt when it came to church. He stood at the dresser and swished the water in the basin with his razor. It was the kind English men used, with a plastic handle.

Nathan elbowed him. "I need my galluses." He tugged on his drawer, one near the bottom.

Isaac stepped aside, examining the razor. "Why do you think it is that we can't have rubber rims on our wheels or plastic frames for our glasses, but plastic razors are fine?"

"I dunno." Nathan clipped on his galluses. "Because the Ordnung says so. Bishop Yoder will be here any minute. You can ask him. He'll say the same thing Father would." Nathan pitched his voice lower. "It is our way."

Isaac traced the razor blade with his fingertip.

"What's up with you? You look like you're half asleep."

"I guess I'm tired." Isaac shrugged, swirling the cold, milky water again. "It was freezing last night. And you kept me awake again with your snoring."

Nathan rolled his eyes. "I can't help it if I'm stuffed up all the time lately. I had a nosebleed at school the other morning too. Mother's making me eat lemons sprinkled with garlic. She read it in the paper, and apparently it worked wonders for someone in Indiana. Father said we'll go to the chiropractor if it happens again."

Isaac frowned. "Maybe you should go to a real doctor."

"Nah. I'm probably allergic to something." Nathan smirked. "Maybe I'm allergic to *you*."

"Ha ha."

"But you seem distracted a lot, Isaac."

Isaac blinked down at his brother, realizing with a jolt that Nathan stood above his shoulder now. "You're getting taller."

"Yeah, that's usually what happens, Isaac." Nathan's brow creased. "Are you okay?"

A swell of affection for his brother warmed his chest. "Yeah. I'm okay. Hold still for a second." He dipped his finger in the clearest part of the water in the basin and tamped down an unruly lock of Nathan's hair.

"Do I look okay?"

Isaac fiddled with the part on the crown of Nathan's head, trying to get the hair to lie flat. "It's just this one piece sticking up."

"No, I mean..." Nathan bit his lip. "Jeremiah and Ira said I have pimples, and I can feel bumps. Does it look really bad? Because Samuel Yoder's face is gross, and I don't want to look like that."

There were some angry red marks on Nathan's chin and cheeks, but Isaac had seen worse. "You don't look bad. We all get pimples sometimes. You'll grow out of it."

Nathan sighed. "I know it's vain to care what I look like. You missed a spot, by the way. Here." Nathan took the razor and dipped it in the basin before carefully scraping it over Isaac's chin. "But why can't we have mirrors just to make sure we don't look stupid?"

"Bishop Yoder will be here any minute. You can ask him." With a wink, he nudged Nathan's shoulder.

Nathan grinned. "You can ask him about the razors first. Come on, we'd better go."

"Nathan—" Isaac grasped his brother's shoulder. "It's okay to feel that way. To worry about how you look. It's okay to be curious about stuff. So don't feel bad about it. No matter what the preachers might say."

He nodded. "Okay."

Feet thundered up the stairs, and Ephraim appeared in the doorway. "Are you deaf? People are here. We have to get out to the barn."

Of course Ephraim was right, and they hurried downstairs, stepping over the benches crammed into the main room, all their regular furniture pushed aside. Every surface gleamed thanks to Mother and Katie, who had cleaned from dawn until dusk and snapped at anyone who dared leave so much as a fingerprint.

Even in the dead of a Minnesota winter under a leaden sky, the church routine remained the same. The men dropped the women at the house and continued on to park the buggies by the barn, hitching the horses to a long fence. There were quite a few men there already, standing in somber clusters, snow piled around their boots. Isaac straightened his hat and yanked on his gloves, his eyes scanning the figures for David.

He was about to follow his brothers down to the barn when another buggy rolled up close to the house with Mary at the reins. They'd obviously bought a new horse to replace poor Nessie. Isaac's pulse raced as the buggy came to a stop, David a few hundred yards behind in his own buggy with Anna and the younger girls crowded in with him.

Isaac forced his attention to Mary and her mother. Mrs. Lantz grimaced, and Isaac could imagine how painful a buggy ride would be with her leg in a cast.

"Do you mind getting the wheelchair out of the back?" Mary called.

As he went around the buggy, Isaac could see where the rear had been replaced, the new axel looking cleaner than the other dark metal holding the buggy together. Still no orange triangle, of course. He opened the back and hauled out the wheelchair as David hopped down from his buggy.

"I can do that."

"I've got it." Although the fresh flurries had been shoveled in front of the house, the chair's wheels sank a bit in the packed-down snow. Isaac gritted his teeth as he shoved the chair around to the front of the buggy. It was silly, but it gave him a grim satisfaction not to do as David asked.

"We're fine here, David," Mrs. Lantz said as she reached for Isaac's hand. He took most of her weight, Mary steadying her from the buggy seat. Isaac lowered her into the chair as David hovered by them. Mrs. Lantz smiled weakly, her face gaunt. The bruising on her cheek had faded to a mottled yellow, but the stitches by her temple were stark against her pale skin.

"We've got a ramp for you at the back door," Isaac said.

"How kind. Thank you."

Mother appeared. "Of course, Miriam! The deacon told us you were determined not to miss another service, so Isaac and Samuel rigged up a ramp with some old boards. How wonderful to see you. Come in where it's warm!"

"Thanks for your help, Isaac." Mary smiled softly and put the reins to the new horse, heading off to the barn.

Anna nudged David as their little sisters went inside. "We're fine. Go unhitch Kaffi."

Isaac watched from the corner of his eye as David turned on his heel. As Mother greeted more arrivals, Isaac pushed the wheelchair around the house to the makeshift ramp. Mrs. Lantz turned slightly and touched his glove, and he stopped, Anna beside him.

"Isaac, I just wanted to say thank you. The girls told me what a help you were around the place while David was with me. The first few days I was hardly awake, but it was a comfort to know that when I opened my eyes, he'd be there. And it was a comfort to know you were making sure my girls were taken care of."

"Of course. It was the least I could do."

Mrs. Lantz sighed. "We all miss seeing you. Our David is being very stubborn, and of course he's right that it wouldn't be fair to you to work without being paid. You've done more than enough already. But we'd still like to see you for lunch sometimes. You're always welcome."

Isaac swallowed hard. "Thank you. I appreciate that."

The ramp held, and he guided the wheelchair to the top, where Mrs. Lantz insisted Anna get down and clean the wheels with a rag she pulled from her cape. Mary appeared behind them.

"That was so kind of you to make another ramp, Isaac. Thank you."

He hitched a shoulder. "It was easy. I'm going to take it over to Noah Raber's tomorrow since he's hosting church next. Then he can pass it on to the Millers, and so on. But I'm sure you'll be walking again in no time." Of course he wasn't sure of that at all, remembering the white of the exposed bone.

"We're all praying for that," Mary said.

Isaac had half expected David to appear on Mary's heels, but it seemed he was playing his part and staying with the men as more families arrived. Anna knelt, wiping the wheels. They were rubber, but he supposed Bishop Yoder had made an exception. Isaac didn't imagine the English made steel-wheeled chairs.

"Oh Isaac, I meant to ask you for another favor if it's not too much." Mrs. Lantz smiled. "Would you mind terribly driving Mary and Anna home from the next singing?"

He blinked, aware of the heat of Mary's gaze on his face. "Uh…doesn't David usually take them?" Mrs. Lantz knew very well the significance of him driving Mary home, even if Anna tagged along.

There was a twinkle in Mrs. Lantz's eyes. "He does, but tonight he's taking Grace home. You know, John's Grace. Such a lovely girl, isn't she?"

Mary grinned as she brushed snow off her black cap. "*Finally*. We don't know what he's been waiting for."

Isaac was still holding one of the wheelchair handles, and he squeezed his fingers around it as his gut twisted. He tried to smile. "Uh-huh."

When he looked down, he caught Anna's steady gaze where she knelt. Lips together, she smiled at him so sadly that Isaac's breath caught. She stood and folded the wet rag into a neat square.

"Today we have to take Mother home and come back for the singing, so you'd be doing us a real favor. Although it might just be me you have to drive." Anna whispered loudly, "Pretty sure Jacob Miller has his eye on Mary."

Mary's smile vanished, and she sputtered. "He does not!"

Anna's expression was blandly innocent. "I guess we'll see."

"Isaac, I..." Mary flushed to the roots of her blonde hair. "Well, you know I'd rather get a ride from you."

He knew it all too well, and hated himself for it as he backed down the ramp. He wished he could be the man she wanted. "It's no problem either way. I'd better get back to greeting."

As he fled, he heard Mary and her mother hiss something to Anna, but he couldn't make it out over the rush in his ears. Each day he waited, the harder it would become—not only for him, but everyone who cared about him. Everyone he cared about. As he rushed to the barn, he repeated the two words he couldn't let himself forget over and over.

I'm leaving.

He didn't look for David this time as he joined one of the clusters of men, nodding to them and shaking hands. As they spoke about something, Isaac was lost in his mind. The days had marched on since it had ended with David, and he'd done his chores and repaired the fences, shivering out in the fields in snow up to his knees.

What am I waiting for?

He still had to figure out when to go. *Where* to go. His mind was blank as he thought about disappearing over the horizon with the trains, going...where? In Zebulon, the rest of the world felt like a void—even Red Hills as unreachable as the moon. He should be excited by the possibilities, but clammy sweat dampened his bangs beneath his hat.

There would never be a good time to leave, and he knew it. Isaac reached into his pocket to hold the knife. He finally understood why Aaron had slipped away in the night. The thought of telling Mother and Father he was abandoning them—abandoning the plain life—seemed impossible. They'd ask why, and what would he say? Could he say it out loud?

Even thinking it made his palms itch and his mouth dry. And if he did tell them, would they guess about David? Would he be condemning David to a life of whispers and sidelong glances? What good would the truth do any of them? As his mind spun, Isaac nodded absently at something Joseph Schrock said, wishing he could hide away and be alone.

The truth would only make it worse. Hurt his family more. If he even told them he was leaving, they'd try everything to talk him out of it. He could imagine Mother's tears, Father in the doorway, first calm and reasonable, and then his voice raising, anger seeping through the cracks.

No, it would have to be a note, and he could never tell them the truth about who he really was. They'd never understand. Neither would his neighbors. He imagined Mary's stricken face. It would be bad enough to break her heart because he didn't love her—for her to know the truth about him and her brother was unthinkable. The things they'd done, she'd never understand. No one in Zebulon could.

The things they'd done. Memories flickered—David's breath hot on the back of his neck as he stretched Isaac open and filled him. The dimple in David's cheek as they laughed about some silly joke. The sweaty stink of the barn, breathing in hay and dust and animals as he sank to his knees, David's fingers tight in his hair. The warm water in the shower, David insisting Isaac go first even though there was never enough. The wet slide of David's tongue, his lips gentle as they kissed and held each other, safe and—

"*Isaac.*"

He blinked and found himself alone by the barn. He turned to find his old friend Mark watching him, head tilted. A sea of black coats and hats retreated toward the house, David among them, although in that moment the men all looked frighteningly the same. Isaac's heart lurched as if he'd never see David again.

But what did it matter now? Even if he saw him every day, it would never be the same. He'd never touch David again. Never hear his heartbeat beneath his cheek as they lay in each other's arms. Never laugh with him or talk about the things that mattered, and the things that didn't. Never discover new things together again.

David had walked this path as far as he dared before turning back. Now Isaac would continue on alone.

"Are you coming?" Mark hitched a thumb over his shoulder.

"Sorry. I was daydreaming."

"Everything okay?"

"Uh-huh." Isaac made his feet move. The thought of the next three or four hours squeezed inside the house while the preachers droned on made him want to run now with only the clothes on his back.

Mark fell into step beside him. "Did you and Mervin have a fight? I asked him what's up with you lately, and he got all weird."

Mervin. Isaac's chest ached. Not only would he have to sit through the service, but he'd have to do it right next to someone who could barely look him in the eye now. "No, everything's fine." Once upon a time, he'd told Mervin everything. Now he was as good as a stranger.

As they trudged through the snow, Mark fortunately didn't ask any more questions. With each step closer to home, Isaac knew it was time to find his own path.

Chapter Seventeen

JUNE WAS ALREADY on her porch when Isaac reined in Silver. She pulled an open sweater around her tightly and shoved a foot into her boot, hopping in place. "Is everything okay?" she called. "Is it David? His mother?"

"No, they're fine!" Isaac jumped down and hitched Silver to the fence before hurrying over. He stamped his feet on the porch to knock off the worst of the snow from his boots. "I just wanted to..." Now that he was here, with June shivering and watching him expectantly, he faltered.

It had still taken him almost two weeks since they'd hosted church at his house to get up the nerve to make the trip to June's, each day promising himself he'd do it tomorrow. A burst of unseasonable hail had damaged the tin roof of the house, and he'd spent the week on a ladder in the cruel wind, letting himself put off the inevitable. Until today.

"Come on inside, Isaac. It's cold as a...cold thing out here." June led him into the house.

His face prickled as his wind-bitten skin warmed, and he peeled off his gloves and rubbed his hands. June had metal hooks in the shape of daisies by the door the way they had pegs at home, and Isaac hung up his hat and coat. He untied his boots, and was glad Mother had fixed the hole in the toe of one of the socks he wore. After running a hand through his hair, he made sure his galluses were straight.

June kicked off her boots and slipped her feet into sheepskin slippers. "Now make yourself comfortable."

An ornate wooden sign with delicately carved flowers hung on the wall in the entryway. Isaac traced his fingertip over the words.

God bless this home

Longing surged through him. "David made that." There was something about the curve of the flowers' petals.

"Yes, he did." June tilted her head. "Are you and he still on the outs? I asked him about it, but he hardly says a word. I hate seeing two friends on bad terms."

Bad terms. It was as good a way as any to describe the acres of hurt that lay between them. "I haven't seen him since church the Sunday before last." The image of David driving away after the singing with Grace beside him as though she belonged seared his memory. "I guess I'll see him tomorrow for the next service."

"I haven't seen him in weeks. He told me he won't be able to continue with our little business. I haven't moved anything in the workshop, though. I'm hoping he'll change his mind. He needs the money now more than ever, but he seems determined to make a go of joining the church. Following all the rules."

Isaac's chest ached dully. "He'll be baptized soon."

June sighed. "Then I suppose that will be that." She smiled sadly. "Well, do you want something to drink? Maybe some tea or cocoa?"

As much as he wanted to say yes, Isaac shook his head. He had to do this now, or he'd talk himself out of it again. "Do you think you could find my brother's telephone number?"

Her eyebrows shot up. "Your brother?"

"Aaron. He left before we moved here. Went into the world. I have no idea where he might be, and I have to find him."

June took this in. "All right. Let's go to my office upstairs and see what we can dig up."

A long piece of green and pink carpet running along the middle of the staircase muffled their steps, and framed pictures hung on the wall. Looking at June's smiling people, he was struck by bittersweet loss, as if he'd already left his own family behind. He wouldn't have a single photo to take.

The walls upstairs were pale yellow, and more pictures hung there. They passed by open doors, and Isaac peeked into the bedrooms, all neat and welcoming, with Amish quilts on the beds. The office was at the end of the hall, overlooking the front of the house. Isaac peered out at Silver waiting patiently below.

Fat flakes of snow drifted down, and he hoped the road wouldn't be too slick for the journey home. For a moment, an image of red snow filled his mind—the horrible angle of Mrs. Lantz's leg, Mary's desperate sobs, David's stillness. He shivered.

June opened the lid of a small computer on the light wood desk— another of David's creations, Isaac was willing to bet. The office was lined with bookshelves, and a red clock ticked loudly on the wall. Isaac resisted the urge to touch the brightly colored books. He could imagine what Father would say of June's worldly collection.

As the computer whirred to life, June pulled up another chair for him, and they sat side by side. Isaac was vaguely dizzy. *I'm actually doing this.*

June perched glasses on the end of her nose and tapped some buttons. A box appeared in the middle of the screen under the word *Google.* "Aaron Byler? Let's see if he's on Facebook."

"That's a website, right? Where you talk to people? My friend Mervin told me about it."

"Yep. I play Scrabble with my sisters in Rhode Island every morning. Okay, here are the Aaron Bylers. Not many, luckily enough. Now take a look at the profile pictures. They're pretty small, I know." She pointed to a button. "Just press this to go down. Unless you want me to do it?"

"No, it's okay. I can do it." He leaned forward on the edge of his chair as he scanned the faces. There were only a handful, and his heart skipped a beat as he squinted at the faces in the third picture. A blond man on the right had his head thrown back, with a grinning dark-haired woman beside him, looking at the camera. It was as though Isaac could hear the rumble of Aaron's laughter in the room. His breath came fast, his hand trembling as he pointed.

"That's my brother." He read the words under the photo.

Lives in San Francisco, CA
In a relationship
From Red Hills, Ohio

It was too hot suddenly, and Isaac tugged at his collar. June rested her hand on his shoulder.

"Do you want some water? Hold tight." She disappeared, her footsteps receding down the hall. Isaac stared at Aaron in the tiny picture until everything blurred, and he choked in a breath. Then June was back, pressing a tall glass into his hand. He gulped it and swiped his sleeve over his eyes.

"Thank you. I'm sorry, I didn't expect...I don't know what I expected. I didn't think it would be this easy."

June smiled ruefully. "That's the internet for you. A blessing and a curse if you ask me. Now we can try to find his phone number if you'd like. How are you feeling?"

"I'm scared." He breathed deeply, his pulse flying. "What if he doesn't want to talk to me?" he whispered.

"Oh, sweetheart, I'm sure he will."

"It's been a long time, and he left us behind. He left me behind." Isaac blinked at the picture of his brother. "He always loved to laugh. Especially when we weren't supposed to. Mom and Dad would— Mother and Father, I mean." He rubbed his face. "Things were so different then. We were still Amish, but it wasn't like it is here. Aaron couldn't stand it. I can't imagine what he'd think of Zebulon." Isaac touched the knife in his pocket.

"It must have been a very difficult decision for him to leave." June pushed her glasses up her nose and leaned in to the screen. "He's a handsome young man. Just like you. Isaac, I'm sure he'll want to talk to you. But there's only one way to find out. If you want, I could call him first. Or you can think it over for a day or two."

Part of him wanted to run—leave June's sunny home and carved flowers behind. But he'd only be putting off the inevitable. Isaac's knee bounced. "Do you think you can find his phone number?"

She smiled and went back to the computer. "Let's look at the White Pages for San Francisco and see what we come up with."

While she tapped and typed, Isaac drank more of his water, his fingers wet as he gripped the cool glass.

June hummed. "Well, there's only one." She plucked a small yellow piece of paper off a pad and pressed it onto the desk before writing on it with a pen.

Isaac moved closer. The bottom of the paper curled up slightly, and the top seemed to be stuck there. Aaron's name was written in neat script with ten numbers below it. June picked up the cordless phone from the corner of the desk.

"Do you want me to talk to him first? It might not be him at all—his number could be unlisted, or he might only have a cell phone. Lots of people are getting rid of their landlines these days."

The temptation to have June do this for him was strong, but Isaac shook his head. "I can do it."

"Okay, so you need to dial one first. Do you know how phone numbers work?"

Isaac shrugged. "Kind of, but I've never called anyone before. There was a phone in the schoolhouse in Red Hills, but oh would we have been in trouble if we'd touched it. It was on a wall and it had a round dial."

June smiled. "I used to have one of those. Got this cordless set quite a few years back now."

"But this isn't like the phones that are little computers?"

"Those are smartphones, we call them. No, this is just a regular old phone. I can put in the number if you'd like."

"Thank you." Somehow Isaac felt a little less guilty, even though using the telephone at all was a terrible sin. Of course it was the least of his crimes, and it wouldn't matter if he left Zebulon.

When. Not if.

June pressed a button and the telephone lit up. Isaac could hear faint beeps as she punched in the number. Nausea washed over him. What if Aaron didn't answer? What if this was a huge mistake? What if Aaron didn't want to talk to him? What if—

"It's ringing." She pressed the phone into his hand.

Shaking, he lifted it to his ear. June smiled encouragingly and raised her thumbs before closing the office door behind her. The tinny ringing continued, and Isaac thought he might be sick all over the round multi-colored rug on June's floor.

"Hello?" A woman answered.

Isaac's heart pounded so hard he was sure she'd hear it all the way in California. His throat was dry again. "Uh…"

"Hello?" A pause. "If this is that same telemarketer from two hours ago, I swear to God I'll—"

"No." He cleared his throat. "I mean, it's not." There was a faint echo of his words in his ear. "I'm trying to find Aaron Byler. I'm not a telemarketer." He wasn't totally sure what that was, but it was safe to say he wasn't one.

"Sorry. Hold on a sec." Her voice dimmed as she called out. "Babe? It's for you."

After several heartbeats, there was a click. "Hello?"

Isaac sucked in a breath, and tears sprang to his eyes. *Aaron.*

"*Hello?*" A pause. "Who is this?"

He barely got the words out. "Aaron? It's me."

Silence. "*Isaac?* Oh my God."

"Yes." A sob escaped him, and he gasped for air, gripping the telephone to his ear so hard it hurt.

"I always hoped one day you'd find me. Are you okay? What's happening?"

"I'm okay. Well, not really. I miss you so much. I can't believe I'm talking to you."

Aaron's voice was thick with emotion. "Me either. God, Isaac. You have no idea how good it is to hear your voice. You sound so different." He cleared his throat. "Okay, tell me what's going on. Did something happen? Is anyone hurt?"

"No. We're all fine. Mother and Father, and Ephraim, Nathan, Katie and Joseph. Abigail and Hannah, too, as far as I know. Wait, you don't know Joseph. He was born after you left."

Aaron exhaled. "Okay, that's good. There's no emergency?"

"No. I'm just...I needed to talk to you."

"Isaac, you can talk to me about anything, I promise. Anything you want to say, I'm here. Okay?"

He took a shuddering breath. "Okay." Yet the words shriveled on his tongue, and he listened to Aaron breathe.

"So how is it in Zebulon? I've heard how strict the Ordnung is."

"How? You left Red Hills before we came here. I wasn't even sure if you knew we'd moved."

"Abigail and I write to each other. She has to hide the letters since I was excommunicated." He huffed out a laugh. "Even without phones or electricity, somehow the Amish gossip mill manages to get all the news. She tells me what she hears from Mom."

"How is Abigail? I know she had another baby last month. Mother tells us the big news from her and Hannah, but maybe Abigail says more to you."

"She's good. She's happy. Misses all of you, but she's glad they stayed in Red Hills. She and Hannah are still close, but Hannah doesn't know she writes to me. Hannah always was a rule follower, being the oldest, and since I'm shunned... But Abigail said she heard you're working with Jeremiah Lantz's David. I'm amazed Dad let you off the farm."

"I..." Isaac wiped his eyes impatiently and concentrated on breathing. "I was."

"Did something happen?"

He wasn't sure if he could answer. "Aaron, I don't know if I can stay here."

There was a pause. "Okay. Just take a deep breath. Everything's okay. Don't be afraid."

Isaac could barely speak. "I don't know what to do."

"You can come live here."

Another sob swelled in his chest, and Isaac trembled. "Really?"

"Of course! Isaac, you can come tomorrow. Today! You're my brother. We have a spare room. It's all yours."

The relief was a warm rush through him. He sniffed loudly. "We? The lady who answered the phone?"

"My wife. Her name's Jen. We have a townhouse in Bernal Heights. I'm in San Francisco. I guess you know that if you found my number."

"When did you get married?" It was strange to think of Aaron living a whole new life. In all the years he'd been gone, Isaac had always imagined him somewhere alone.

"A few years ago. Wait, let me think—four years ago. Jen will kick my ass if I don't get our anniversary right. She's the best thing that ever happened to me."

"How did you meet her?" Isaac realized he had little idea how English people dated.

"A trip to the ER after I fell off my bike."

"You rode a bicycle? But it has rubber wheels," Isaac blurted.

"Once you leave all the rules behind, you'll find they didn't make a whole lot of sense. Cars and bikes are a lot more efficient than a horse and buggy."

It was true of course, and Isaac had ridden in June's truck himself. Still, his stomach knotted. He forced his focus back on Aaron's story. "So your wife was at the hospital too?"

"She was the doctor on call, and I never thought I'd be so glad to break my wrist. It took some doing, but I convinced her to write her number on my cast. She made me promise not to call until it came off, thinking I'd have moved on by then." He chuckled. "She didn't realize how patient someone raised plain could be."

Isaac smiled. It was like hearing a story from a book. "She sounds nice. Do you have a job?"

"I'm a high school math teacher. I got my GED and went to college."

"GED?"

"Sorry. It's a test. Instead of going back to high school, I took night classes and then I passed the GED. It means you're smart enough to have the equivalent of a high school diploma."

The thought of going to classes and learning about the world made Isaac smile. "Could I do that?"

"Absolutely. Isaac, you can do *anything*. The sky's the limit."

Aaron spoke fervently, and Isaac could close his eyes and imagine the earnest expression on his brother's face. His hazel eyes and blond hair were so like Mother's, but he'd always shined in a way Mother didn't. Of course Aaron was almost thirty now. Isaac wondered if he looked like a grownup. It was hard to tell in the tiny Facebook picture. "It's been nine years."

"I know. God, Isaac—I wanted to see you all again so badly, but after you moved to Zebulon I knew it would just make it worse for you. And I couldn't come back with hat in hand to profess my sins and ask forgiveness. I couldn't rejoin the church. I couldn't."

"I know. I don't blame you." Isaac exhaled.

Aaron's voice wavered. "If I could have taken you with me, I would have. All of you. But you have to make the choice yourself. Are Mom and Dad...are they okay?"

Isaac nodded, but of course Aaron couldn't see him. "Yes. After you left, Mother wept, and then she tried to pretend everything was normal. Father was angry, and then he went quiet, the way he does. Ephraim was furious. I didn't know what to feel. And now I'm going to do it to them all over again."

"I know how hard it is. I agonized for months before I left. *Years*. I knew the plain life wasn't for me, but I tried to make it work. It didn't do any good. Isaac, you have to be brave and live your life. You can't stay for the sake of the family. It won't work if it's not what you really want. You'll never be happy." He took a long breath. "If you decide to stay, then that's okay too. But it has to be what you truly want, deep inside."

Isaac stared at the swirled pattern of blues and greens and purples on the rug. He knew what was deep inside him. "I want to leave," he whispered.

Aaron's voice cracked. "Okay." He cleared his throat. "Okay," he repeated. "Then let's get you organized."

"But I don't have any money. How will I get there?"

"I'll pay, don't worry. I can buy your ticket online. Hold on, let me Google…"

"All right." Isaac breathed in and out, in and out. *I'm leaving.*

"Okay, you can get the Greyhound in Grand Forks, just across the border in North Dakota. Do you think you can get a ride there? It's no more than an hour from where you are. You'd get the bus at six-fifty p.m. It'll take a few days to get to California, and there are a bunch of transfers. I'd fly you out, but you don't have any ID."

"It's fine. It doesn't matter how long it takes. I can manage."

"I can't take much time off work with no notice, but I'll see if I can come pick you up partway. Maybe in Salt Lake City or—"

"You don't need to do that. I can get there on my own. I want to. Really."

"Are you sure? Just ask the drivers for help if you get confused, and call me if there's a problem—no matter what time it is."

"We took the bus here when we left Ohio. I can do it."

"I know you can. When do you want to come? I need to know which day to buy the ticket for."

Isaac wanted to say tomorrow. But the thought of packing up and sneaking away so soon paralyzed him.

"Isaac, it's okay. You don't have to decide right this second. Just let me know. It's all up to you."

He exhaled. "All right." But just as the terror started to fade, the gnawing guilt and shame rose up in him, unfurling its huge wings until Isaac thought he might suffocate. How could he take Aaron's money and stay under his roof without telling him the real truth?

"Isaac? Are you okay? I know this is scary. You'll get through this. I promise."

He realized he was panting softly into the telephone. "There's something else. I have to tell you something, even if it makes you hate me."

"I could never hate you." Aaron's voice was strong and firm. Completely confident in the way he'd always been. "Whatever it is, you can tell me."

For a minute, Isaac just breathed while Aaron waited. Then he swallowed thickly. "You remember I was working with David Lantz."

"Yes. But you're not anymore."

Words whipped around Isaac's mind in a jumble, and he struggled to find the right ones. "I'm not like you, Aaron."

"Okay. In what way?"

"I don't want a wife. David and I...we..." Isaac thought his chest might explode as the pressure suffocated him.

"Is there something between you?" Aaron asked calmly.

He pushed the words out like he was shoving against a stone in the fields. "There was. We know it was wrong, but we couldn't stop ourselves."

"Are you saying you're gay? Homosexual, I mean. That you're attracted to other men? That you love other men?"

Aaron said it all so easily, as though he were discussing nothing more than the weather. Isaac hunched over his knees, pressing the telephone against his sore ear. "Yes," he whispered.

"Then that's the way you were born, and there's nothing wrong with it. Not a *thing*. Isaac, I love you just the way you are, and so will a lot of other people. Thank you for telling me. I'm so proud of you."

Isaac could hardly believe his ears. "You don't think it's a terrible sin? The Bible says—"

"Isaac, the Bible says an awful lot of things. We can talk about it when you get here. But no, I don't believe it's a sin anymore. Most people here in San Francisco don't. Attitudes are changing every day all over the country. Around the world. Gay people can get married in some states. Isaac there's so much for you out here. Everything's going to be okay. Everything's going to be great."

For the first time, Isaac began to believe it. "Okay."

"I can't wait to see you again."

"Me either." The heaviness inside faded away. "Soon. Later this week, all right? I just need a couple of days. There's church tomorrow, so I can say goodbye to Mervin. I won't tell him I'm going, but I want to see him before I do."

"I understand. What about David?"

Although the shame and guilt had receded for the moment, now sorrow settled into Isaac in their absence. "I don't think he'll talk to me, but I'll see him at least. It's something."

"He doesn't want to leave?"

Bitterness twisted Isaac's lips. "He does, but he's too afraid." He rubbed his face. "He can't leave his mother and sisters. After what his brother did in Red Hills, it's like he has to pay penance for that."

"It's a hard thing, leaving it all behind. But if he changes his mind, I'll buy his ticket too. There's room here for you both."

"Thank you. Aaron, I...I don't know what I'd do without you." He sniffled and wiped his face with his sleeve.

"You'll never have to find out. Call me when you know the day, and we'll get it all arranged. I'll see you soon, Isaac. I love you."

"I love you too. Bye."

After a moment, there was a click, and a flat noise filled his ear. Isaac looked at the phone and took a guess, pressing one of the buttons. The lights went out, and he stared at the three letters.

END

How long he sat there, he wasn't sure. Then he was moving, and in the hall one of the doors led to a bathroom. The shadows were growing long, and inside, he took a deep breath and flicked the switch up with his finger. Warm light appeared overhead, and Isaac found himself staring into a wide oval mirror over the sink.

His face was splotchy, and his hair stood up in places. He leaned in closer, examining his red and puffy eyes, glistening still with tears. "*The color of amber—like something shiny and beautiful, but solid all the same.*" Fighting back another wave of emotion, Isaac reached for the taps. Ever so easily, water flowed out, and he splashed his face. A towel hung from a ring on the wall, and he blotted his skin dry.

Isaac rolled his shoulders and gazed at himself in the mirror. It was the first proper look he'd had since leaving Red Hills, not counting snatched moments here and there. Now he could stare at himself for hours if he wanted, with no one telling him he was too proud. But June was downstairs, probably wondering what he was up to.

He looked for another minute, his chest rising and falling as he caught his breath. He searched his reflection, although he wasn't sure what he was looking for. He wasn't sure who he was. "But I'm going to find out," he murmured. With a deep inhale, he stood up straighter and flicked off the light.

The smell of warm chocolate wafted through the air, getting stronger as Isaac reached the bottom of the stairs.

"In here!" June called.

Following the sound of her voice, Isaac found the kitchen. June stood by the stove, stirring something in a pot. Two mugs waited on the counter.

She nodded to the round table. "Have a seat, hon. It's just about ready."

He did, peering around the room. The tall refrigerator hummed in one corner, and the open pantry was stuffed with food. There was a window over the double sink, with yellow curtains that were practically see-through. On the wall by the table a pad of paper hung. It said *To do*, and the paper was in a wooden frame carved with the same flowers as the sign in the entryway. David was everywhere in this house, and for a crazy moment, Isaac wondered if he could ask David to make him something to take to San Francisco.

When June placed one of the mugs in front of him, Isaac wrapped his hands around it gratefully. "Thank you."

"Anytime. So, how did it go?"

"Good. I'm...I'm leaving. Later this week. Aaron said he can buy a bus ticket for me on the computer? That is, if you can drive me to Grand Forks."

"I'll drive you anywhere you need to go." Her smile was unmistakably sad. "We don't know each other well, but I'll miss you. And I know David will."

Isaac drank his cocoa so he wouldn't have to say anything. It burned his tongue.

June sighed. "David's torn up inside. I know you are too. He's never talked about things between you, and I've never asked. But it was plain as day to me. You boys were very close for a time. But not now."

"No." Isaac swallowed hard. "Not now." He gripped the mug. "I told Aaron. That I'm...you know." He glanced up at June. "You know what I mean, right?"

She squeezed his forearm. "Yes, I know. That was very brave of you. I'm of the firm belief that we're all just as the good Lord made us, and that love comes in all shapes and sizes. And there's nothing wrong with it."

Isaac smiled, his dry lips cracking at the corners. "That's what Aaron said."

"Well, he sounds like a smart fellow, your brother." She took a sip of cocoa. "Now, as I told you, I'm happy to drive you to Grand Forks or anywhere you want to go. But I have one condition."

"Of course." Isaac nodded.

"See David before you leave. Tell him where you're going, and see if you can't talk him into going with you." Her eyes glistened. "I know, I know—it has to be his choice. But just try, Isaac. If he stays in Zebulon, I'm afraid for what will become of him. Joining the church and getting married to a woman—it's not what he wants. I think it'll kill him bit by bit, and it breaks my heart."

Isaac blinked rapidly. He nodded, not trusting his voice.

"All right, we have a deal." She swiped at her eyes. "Let's finish our treat, and then you'd better get back home. You've got big plans to make."

As he looked to the future, there were too many conflicting feelings battling within him, so Isaac closed his eyes and concentrated on just that moment, with cocoa sweet and warm on his tongue.

Chapter Eighteen

THIS IS MY last day in Zebulon.

Isaac stared at the ceiling, listening to Nathan's racket beside him. It was still dark outside, but he could faintly hear Mother and Father stirring in their bedroom. Another Sunday begun. He'd go to church, and see all the people he'd known his entire life. He'd see Mary and Mervin. He'd see David.

Isaac squeezed his eyes shut at the thought that it could very well be the last time. He'd get David away from the others at lunch, and he'd beg him to leave. Not because June made him promise, but because he would regret it always if he didn't try again. Perhaps he was a pathetic fool. He shivered and tugged the quilt up to his chin. David had rejected him. He'd made his choice. *But maybe…*

No. Isaac couldn't let himself hope. He'd ask him, but he knew David's answer already.

He'd slept fitfully after deciding on his plan. Mother and Father would expect him to go to the singing, but he'd pretend to get sick that evening. Mary and Anna could get a ride home with someone else. Isaac couldn't stop a nasty smirk. *Or David will have to drive them and leave his courtship of Grace for the next singing.*

During the singing, Isaac would go to June's to arrange the bus ticket and ask her to pick him up at the end of the lane on Monday afternoon to get to Grand Forks with plenty of time to spare. There wasn't much he was taking with him, and he could invent an excuse if someone happened to see him with his sack. He had a little more than thirty dollars saved up, but it would be enough as long as Aaron could buy the bus ticket.

He'd leave the note on his pillow Monday afternoon, and no one would see it until it was too late. It was unforgivable, but it was better than burdening his family with the truth. He hoped they could all understand. He swallowed over the lump in his throat. Mother and Father never would, and he couldn't blame them.

But he hoped Katie and his brothers could forgive him one day. Especially Ephraim. Ephraim would probably hate Isaac for leaving him behind. But he wasn't even seventeen. Maybe once he could go to the singings and date, Ephraim would settle down. Maybe.

Tomorrow Isaac would spend one last morning at home milking and doing chores before walking away. But today he'd be with his community. The people of Zebulon weren't perfect, but they were good and kind for the most part.

Huddled in his bed with his brothers still sleeping, Isaac wondered what kind of people he would meet out in the world. When he thought of June, and Danielle the nurse, his stomach settled. There were good people in the world. And at least with Aaron to guide him, the prospect was slightly less terrifying.

Would the English like him? Would he seem strange to them? Would he fit in? He could take classes the way Aaron had. Maybe he could go to college too. To study what, he had no idea. He supposed he could study anything he wanted. The possibilities were endless—and overwhelming. Isaac's pulse raced, and he tried to focus. *Get through today first.* From the barn, he heard the rooster crow.

Here we go.

Breakfast was like any other, but he savored every bite of the scrapple mother had made, the pork, cornmeal, and flour concoction flavorful and filling. Yet by the time he arrived at Samuel Schrock's barnyard for church, his breakfast was a stone lodged in his stomach. He'd brought the rickety spare buggy as usual, and took his time unharnessing Silver, petting her neck.

It had snowed a few more inches overnight, and the sky was its familiar gray, the wind biting. The men socialized by the barn in quiet groups as usual, the women and girls already inside the house. As he scanned the men, immediately Isaac knew the slope of David's shoulders; the swell of his backside, and narrowness of his hips.

He was struck by the desire to race through the snowdrifts and throw his arms around David, to breathe in the sawdust that always lingered on him.

Instead he squared his shoulders and marched over to where Mervin, Mark and a few other young men chatted. They all greeted him with nods and understated smiles appropriate for a Sunday, although Mervin barely jerked his head. Mark glanced between them with a furrowed brow, and Isaac willed him not to ask. Fortunately it was soon time to fall into line and file inside.

When they had all removed their coats and hats and squeezed onto the benches stuffing the house, Isaac automatically looked right to catch a glimpse of David. David's hair was over the tips of his ears now, and before too long it would cover them completely. He'd grow a beard, and carefully shave the top half of his chin and above his lip. He would be a proper Amish man.

Acid in his mouth, Isaac looked away.

Beside him, Mervin was a wall of tension. Isaac didn't dare glance at him, and wondered if Mervin would even speak to him long enough for Isaac to try and make peace and say a sort of goodbye. Perhaps there would be no peace with his oldest friend.

Naturally the service was endless. While the congregation sung the dirge-like German hymns, the preachers took the applicants who were working to join the church into the Obrote—on this day the Schrock's kitchen, which had a door. Isaac watched David walk out with the others. The time was nearing when they would join the church officially. At least Isaac wouldn't have to witness that.

But I still might convince David to leave with me. He shouldn't hope, but the kernel of light in Isaac's heart still said *maybe, maybe, maybe.*

By the time one of the preachers wrapped up the long sermon, Isaac fidgeted in his seat. Whatever would come from this day, and his pleading with David, he wanted it done. He breathed a sigh as the preacher stepped back, but then Bishop Yoder stood before them. His white hair had grown wispier, and his narrow face was solemn.

"There are five here today who will become our brothers and sisters in Christ." He made a motion toward a bench Deacon Stoltzfus hefted in from the kitchen and placed at the front of the congregation.

Along with the others, David stood. Isaac's breath caught. *No, no, no. Not yet!*

As always, the benches for church were all crammed into the living room where they would fit, and people craned their necks, shifting this way and that as David and the four others made their way to the front and sat.

"If you feel as you did this morning, get on your knees." Bishop Yoder stood before them, with the deacon nearby holding a pitcher of water.

The five slid to their knees.

Bile rose in Isaac's throat. He was already too late. David was making his vow to the church and God. There would be no turning back. Aaron had run away after his baptism, but David was different. If he gave his word to the Lord, that would be the end of it. Isaac wanted to jump to his feet and scream and shout until they stopped the ritual.

He needed one more chance to convince David to choose happiness. Choose freedom. *Choose me.* His hands trembled, and Isaac clasped them together. To have to witness David's baptism was surely God's punishment for Isaac's decision to leave his family and community behind.

Utter silence descended on the room.

"Do you believe and affirm your belief that Jesus Christ is the son of God?"

Down the line, the five each answered, "Yes, I believe that Jesus Christ is the son of God."

David was last, and Isaac could barely hear his voice. It was as though only a ghost of David remained. Tears sprang to Isaac's eyes.

"Will you remain steadfast to the church, whether it leads to life or to death?"

And a death it would be. If not physical, surely in David's soul. Isaac shook as he struggled to keep from sobbing. He squeezed his eyes shut, not caring if anyone noticed. One by one, the five answered.

"Yes."

"Yes."

"Yes."

"Yes."

Silence.

Heart racing, Isaac opened his eyes and leaned into Mervin, trying to glimpse David through the crowd. David was still kneeling with his back to them.

It was barely a whisper. "No."

As a gasp whipped through the congregation, David pushed to his feet. Chest rising and falling rapidly, he faced them all. "No." His voice was stronger. "I can't." He looked to his mother and sisters. "I'm sorry. I can't."

Bishop Yoder and Deacon Stoltzfus stood motionless, staring at David in disbelief. The deacon looked as though he might shatter the pitcher with the force of his grip.

Mary and Anna sat together with almost identical, wide-eyed expressions, and a wail broke free from Mrs. Lantz in her wheelchair near the front.

"*Nooo*! Why? Why does God punish me? Please, David! Please!"

Eli Helmuth rose from his bench and crouched by Mrs. Lantz as he beseeched David. "Think this through. You can—"

"I can't." David shook his head. "Please forgive me, Mother." Then his eyes found Isaac's across the room. "I hope you can all forgive me." He strode out, almost in a run.

Isaac was halfway to standing before he knew he was moving.

Mervin shoved him back down, his arm shaking as he pressed against Isaac's thigh, pinning him to the bench. Isaac tried to yank himself free, not caring what anyone thought if he ran after David. Commotion filled the room, but when he looked up, he found the deacon's beady gaze on him.

Mervin grabbed Isaac's arm. "Are you crazy? Sit down," he hissed.

Isaac stopped struggling, and Mervin loosened his grip. Isaac looked at his friend for the last time. "It doesn't matter now. But thank you. For everything."

Then he sprang up and climbed over the others in his row before Mervin or anyone else could react. He heard Father call his name, astonished, but Isaac didn't look back as he burst out of the Schrocks' house. David's buggy was already speeding out of sight down the drive, and Isaac raced to the barn.

He untethered Silver and climbed onto her back from the fence. He'd never catch up in his old buggy, so he urged on Silver, digging in his heels and bending low over her neck, murmuring to her. After a few snorts, Silver trotted before speeding up.

"Come on, girl. That's it." Isaac squeezed with his thighs. Without a saddle, he hadn't been able to stay on Kaffi that night when the horse had galloped, but nothing was going to keep him from catching David now.

He hadn't stopped for his hat or coat, and his bare fingers were ice on the reins. The wind was so cold his forehead stung, but Isaac wouldn't stop. He caught glimpses of David's buggy ahead as the road curved and dipped, and realized David was going back to his house. Isaac prayed there were no icy patches beneath the fresh layer of snow as he kicked Silver on faster.

By the Lantz barn, David turned and watched him thunder up. Yanking on the reins, Isaac slid off Silver's back—and into David's arms. Their harsh breath clouded the January air as they held each other. Isaac clutched David to him, burying his face in David's neck.

"Isaac." David clung to him. "I'm sorry. I was such a fool. So weak.

Forgive me, please. Forgive me."

"Yes, yes, yes." Isaac lifted his head and kissed David hard.

David took Isaac's face in his hands. "I want to be with you."

"I love you so much." Isaac kissed him again. David didn't have his hat or coat either, and they both shivered, but their lips were warm.

David pulled back. "You were right—we have to go. There's nothing for us here. Not if we ever want to be happy. I can't live my life for my mother and my sisters." His lip trembled. "I hate to leave them, but I have to believe they'll get by without me."

"They will. You know Eli wants to marry your mother, and even if he doesn't, they'll be all right. They're strong. Everyone will help them."

David examined Isaac's face, running his fingers over Isaac's cheek. "You haven't changed your mind about me? About us?"

Isaac shook his head. "I have a plan—June's helping me. And Aaron. I found him, and he'll help us both."

David laughed incredulously. "You found your brother? I can't wait to hear. Oh, Isaac. Thank you for not giving up on me."

He kissed David again. "Never. We're going to be all right. We'll be together. That's all that matters."

The dimple appeared in David's cheek. "Yes, Eechel. Just you and me." He leaned their foreheads together. "I missed you so much. I wish I could tell my family—I wish I could make them understand."

Isaac brushed David's lips with his own before stepping back. "I know. But if we tell them the truth about us, we'll be shunned. Neither of us has joined the church, so at least if we leave now we can send letters. Maybe even come back and visit."

David nodded. "You're right. That would be something, at least."

"They'll be so disappointed, but as long as they don't know the whole truth, they won't cast us out. If Aaron hadn't been baptized before he ran away, he could have still written. It would've helped so much— just to know he was okay."

"You're right. We won't be shunned, and we owe our families that much. Losing us to the world will be hard enough without knowing our sin."

"I was going to wait until tomorrow to leave, but I think we should go now. Make it a clean break. After what happened in church, there will be so many questions. Questions we can't answer without breaking their hearts."

David nodded. "June can make sure Mother gets the money I've saved." He squeezed his eyes shut. "It'll hurt Mother to know that I lied all the times I went to June's. That I was violating the Ordnung for so long."

"It will." Isaac rubbed David's arms. "But maybe it'll help her see that this wasn't out of the blue. Even if they can't know the whole truth, a bit of it might help. We can write once we're settled. Let them know we're okay. That we'll take care of each other, even if they think we're only friends."

"We should go now before anyone comes looking. We'll stay off the roads and take Kaffi over the fields to June, and you can tell me your plan. I'll get us some warm clothes. Go put Silver in the barn."

Isaac led her into one of the stalls with numb hands, although his body sang with anticipation. It was really happening. "There's a good girl. Thanks for the ride here, and not throwing me off." He popped an icy sugar cube in his mouth to warm it before holding it out for her. He scratched her muzzle as she licked his palm, the warmth of her tongue and breath making his skin tingle. "I'll miss you, Silver."

His mind shifted to thoughts of home. To leave his family without saying goodbye was an ache deep in him. Would they understand one day? Would Ephraim be glad for him? Would they even read his letters? Closing his eyes, Isaac said a quick prayer that he was doing the right thing. Even if it wasn't right, he knew without a doubt it was the only thing left for him.

Outside the barn, snow drifted down. Rubbing his arms, Isaac shivered.

David trotted Kaffi over and tossed Isaac a spare coat and gloves. He reached a hand down, his eyes bright. "Ready?"

We're leaving.

For a moment Isaac's chest was unbearably tight. He thought he might fall to his knees and cry, or run back home to where he knew his way, even if he was trapped. Instead he swung onto Kaffi's back and wrapped his arms around his David, feeling warmer already.

The world was waiting.

About the Author

Keira aims for the perfect mix of character, plot, and heat in her M/M romances. She writes everything from swashbuckling pirates to heart-warming holiday escapism. Her fave tropes are enemies to lovers, age gaps, forced proximity, and passionate virgins. Although she loves delicious angst along the way, Keira guarantees happy endings!

Find out more at: www.keiraandrews.com

Made in the USA
Middletown, DE
14 August 2023

36720710R00146